LOVE
LEIYAH

SHAN LEE

G&H Publishers

Published by G&H Publishers 14/04/2021
ISBN: 978-0-620-89682-5

Dedicated To
My Mother

ONE

2020
Friday

The sunny day in May had begun just like any other. The streets outside had come alive even before the break of dawn. The hustle and bustle of a working day in London was in no way laid back as I had discovered, when I first chose to make it my home twenty five years ago and because of that, I missed South Africa. The hills and valleys, the tranquil streams, the resonant sounds of horses and cattle awakened by the crowing rooster, the fluttering wings of birds flying from their nests yonder and back again, followed by, well nothing really, for that was as busy as it got in the Natal Midlands. Well, at least that was how I remembered it to be. But that was twenty five years ago, when I had left at the age of twenty three. As the weeks passed, the slightest of longings quickly ceased; memories, buried in a matter of months.

Now, having lived more years in England than I had in South Africa, having reached the pivotal age of almost a half century, forty eight to be precise, what a contrasting view was I bestowed with, when I gazed out the window. From my bedroom window on the third floor I can see all the way down my street. A little girl in a bright orange dress skips merrily beside her mother, her blonde pigtails swinging from side to side. I doubt she is older than six. I look at the clock above my door,

7:08 a.m. right on time. I look out for her every weekday, for almost a year now. Why? I am not exactly sure.

Beatrice could be heard behind me as she brought in my morning tea, as she did every morning, but then she did something, something I would never have expected.

"Goodness Beatrice, you frightened me!" I said, lifting my shoulder so that her hand slipped off. I looked back at the little girl. Six minutes was all the time I had to gaze at her, I had even timed that. Can you believe it? It frustrated me that I had to go and waste seconds of my precious time frowning at Beatrice.

"I thought you heard me Madam Hannah, I did knock," she replied giving me a questioning look.

"Well I did but…" my tone surely seeking no need for further explanation.

If there was anyone who knew how to read me, Beatrice Zungu surely could. Unfortunately, to my extreme disgruntlement, my seventy-two year old housekeeper did not leave, lending me to once more turn away from the child in order to halt the echoes of her tribal African song. One of the many she had learnt as a child, when Underberg at the foothills of the Drakensberg mountain range had been her home.

"What did I say about you singing like that?" I scowled at her as she tightened the cloth around her head, not needing a mirror to do so.

Although the singing had instantaneously stopped, she remained hovering over my shoulder. I could hardly bring myself to believe that there had once been a time when I had actually treasured her singing but that had been so.

'*Be gone you insolent fool,*' I ought to have shouted but refusing to sacrifice a further second on her, I resorted to simply let her be, my blonde princess my priority.

"Your little girl is full of energy today," said Beatrice, resting at the edge of the window.

"She always is."

The middle aged woman, in her well attired office wear, had just begun a conversation on her cell phone, taking no heed of her daughter's attempts to communicate with her. I wondered how on earth a mother could have such an adorable child and still look so disinterested.

"I miss all those days I used to hold Zendaya's hand and walk her to school. She used to skip just like that you know," sighed Beatrice.

"Too bad her hair was stiff," I bit my upper lip at the ugliness I heard in my own words. *There you go again Hannah Gordon!*

Beatrice clicked her tongue and I could feel her stare upon me. For once, I deserved it.

I do admit that there had been days when I had wished I could have tied Zendaya's hair into two pigtails and watch them swing with every nod of the head. Unlike the little girl in the orange dress, Zendaya's father had been black and me, Hannah Gordon, well, I was white. Well at least that was what we would have been labelled in South Africa in 1995, the year I ran away.

Zendaya's father had been a native South African, isiZulu speaking, as was Beatrice. Me, well my father's family had been Dutch, my mother's family British, and my twenty seven year old daughter Zendaya, well to my greatest fortune, she was born with an unusually fair skin tone. A golden tan most liked to call it, but she was of course born with hair as black and as coarse, as was her father's.

In all honesty I never would have thought I had a reason to feel guilty for finding her hair a frustration, but damn, did Beatrice just know how to make me feel a failure, always taming and braiding it so effortlessly into the mesmerizing designs Zendaya simply adored. She must surely be the only housekeeper who could call the shots. I ought to have just taken Zendaya to a hair salon and ordered the disaster to be made pin straight and blonde, blonde like my own, pin straight and blonde like my princess in her orange dress. That would surely have given me the upper hand over Beatrice. Although I knew her gaze was still upon me I was determined not to allow Beatrice the satisfaction of forcing me to take my eyes off my princess, yet again.

Just as the little girl and her mother were approaching the pavement opposite my window, the most horrific thing happened. The doll, the child had been holding, sprung out of her hand, landing some distance away on the road itself.

"No!" I screamed before the idiotic mother, who had let go of the girl's hand, to store away her cell phone, could react. Tyres screeched, a loud bang and the sound of shattering glass! My eyes still covered, after seeing the girl jump after her treasured toy, I could feel my body trembling. "Oh God! Oh God! Beatrice is she…?"

"She is ok Madam. She is ok," she whispered soothingly, squeezing my arm.

Dropping my hands to see for myself, I could feel my heart beating rapidly in my throat. The little girl was lying on the floor, crying hysterically only centimetres from a car. The mother, who knelt beside her child, was screaming at the driver, who had already jumped out. A second car had bumped into the first. Seeing that she was unharmed, I could feel the tears welling up in my eyes. Instinctively, I rushed out the room, Beatrice, hot on my heels.

"Oh my sweetheart, thank goodness you are alright!" I exclaimed trying to hug and pacify the little girl who had been placed upon the bonnet of the red car, the very car that had only moments earlier, been seconds away from bringing an end to her very existence. To my absolute horror, she pulled away instantly, kicking me in the shin. The sea of cell phones, belonging to the highly entertained crowd, now focussed on me.

"Don't touch my daughter!" shouted the mother, aggressively turning away momentarily from the driver of the red Volvo, who continued to take details, presumably from the driver of the second car involved, a black Mercedes.

"Every little girl wants her mother!" said Beatrice ushering me away from the scene. The words she had just uttered, surely out of spite, against the ugliness I had let slip in the room, I was certain.

"Oh Beatrice I did not see it was you, can you hold Peyton for me please? Do you remember me?" asked the woman as we began walking away. "It's me, Susan's mum. She was in your daughter's class," she exclaimed, her face now painted with a jubilant smile

"Susan's mum, really? *Haibo*! I did not recognise you, you look so different," answered Beatrice, hugging the woman as if they were the best of friends.

"Old I know, our girls are big now, please, call me Alice."

"No not old, and you have another one Alice? Wow! I see her in you," said Beatrice gently running her finger along the child's chin.

"Yes, this is little Peyton, trouble as you can see."

As Beatrice took the crying child into her arms, I felt like punching her. She did not even have the decency to say Zendaya was mine, my daughter and not hers! Beatrice, always the hero! She calls me Madam but she certainly doesn't make me feel like one.

Zendaya had only been two, when we left South Africa. For an only child she was never lonely, I was quite certain of that; always busy with her theatrics. When she had first started school, the movie about the *'The Three Musketeers'*, became her greatest fascination. And so she would bestow her plastic wands upon both Beatrice and I and call us just that, *'The Three Musketeers'*. "More like the Terrible Three", I could recall saying, merely a joke, how was I to know it would end up being all too true. Getting along with each other, we were simply terrible at. Now it's just the two of us, now that Zendaya has flown the nest. How I wish that day had never come. But it did and for the last two months, it's just been Beatrice Zungu and myself, Hannah Gordon, the fabulously famous 'Terrible Two' and we are an equally terrible pair mind you.

"Goodbye Peyton," I whispered despondently before crossing the road, the distant sirens coming into earshot. Relentless in gaining her attention, I no longer was, but one last glance at her pretty face, I could not help but steal. The wicked witch of the South had defeated me once more. "Damn you Beatrice!"

Just as I thought it was safe to let my tears run free as I stepped into my hallway, I turned around to find myself being startled for a second time that morning.

"Goodness, you frightened me!" I said to the handsome young man who was smiling mischievously as he surveyed me.

It felt strangely good to finally be the recipient of a smile, after all the rejection of the morning. My watery eyes instantaneously dried. Though I knew he was probably half my age, there was something about his smile that made me want to keep being startled at the door, all day, perhaps every day.

"Quite a bit of chaos for a Friday morning, wouldn't you say?" was his response, his gaze unwavering as his blue eyes met my own.

Running my fingers down my pastel peach dress, my tears forgotten, I assured myself that the clothing I remembered putting on that morning was in fact being worn. I could not even remember how long it had been since I had spoken to a man, let alone a man so attractive. It had been too long.

"Say what?" I asked, his gaze leaving me too flustered to process his words.

The young man smiled. I smiled back savouring his sumptuous good looks. His attire was simple, a white T shirt, blue jeans and fading white sneakers, his unruly reddish hair covered by an even brighter red baseball cap. The strands of hair that had escaped looked so inviting that I felt a sudden desire to tip his hat over and perhaps I might have, had he not at that very moment spoken.

"Good thing no one got hurt!" he said.

"Yes, you cannot imagine what I would have done to myself if anything had happened to Peyton," I answered, awakened from my illusion, I was outraged at the sight of the child's mother refusing to permit an examination from the paramedics who had arrived at the scene. "Just look at that wretched woman! Can you believe she actually calls herself a mother?"

Puzzled, the man looked towards the scene of the accident.

Following his gaze, I watched, Beatrice now walking down the street with Alice, Peyton still in her arms. The African prints on Beatrice's clothing, making her easy to spot.

"Well I guess it's a good thing Beatrice has always had a knack for drying a little girl's tears, wouldn't you say so Mrs Gordon?"

"Well perhaps I would have that knack too, if only…" I clicked my tongue, "too bad she never gave me the chance to find it? That selfish witch…ooh she should just…" bringing my hand to my lips my words trailed just in time to mute my blasphemy.

"Don't stress. It's ok to be angry, though hopefully this will change the way you are feeling. I have a delivery for you," he said, gesturing towards the large brown box in his hands.

"Me?" I asked in disbelief.

"Sure as the sky is blue!"

"Looks like rain if you ask me," I answered, looking up towards the clouds.

"Rain or no rain, the sky is always blue," he said as he chuckled.

His comical response made me smile. I felt like telling the poor boy that factually speaking, at night, it just so happened to be black. Begin a debate perhaps but I halted. I for some reason, could not help feeling a tad sorry for the dim witted pretty face. *'No wonder he is a mailman,'* I thought.

"Ah, you see that line works every time. It never fails to bring a smile to a pretty face. The name is Harry."

Hearing his acknowledgement of my smile, I quickly returned a grim face.

"Well then Harry, are you one hundred percent certain it is for me? Maybe someone wrote the incorrect address or something of the sort. You can't really be certain, can you?" I asked, still refusing to take hold of the box he was trying to push into my hands. Whatever the brown box contained was actually quite heavy and as I pulled my hands out from under, it landed on the top step with a loud bang.

"Golly Mrs Gordon! It's a good thing the box isn't marked fragile."

"Wait, how do you know my name? You just called me Mrs Gordon. And Beatrice! You knew her name was Beatrice!"

Much to my disdain, the question I had just asked, received no reply, my words overshadowed by two overly hyped Cocker Spaniels, pulling at their leash as my neighbour stepped out his door.

"Why Mrs Gordon, this really is no ordinary day if I get to see you standing at your door," said Mr Goldstone, lifting his top hat. "How very lucky I am on this Friday morning. Let me introduce you to my two fine thoroughbreds. I would like you to meet Daffodil and Dandelion. Hush now girls!"

Mr Goldstone, who was an elderly man, had lived alongside me for as long as England had been my home. The first day I had met him, I had been extremely impressed by his aristocratic attire and to see him still wearing such clothing was no surprise. The names he had given to his dogs, I found to be quite bizarre. Daffodil was the cleanest white dog I had ever seen, while her companion was a complete contrast, as jet black as a chunk of coal, was Dandelion.

"Why Harry, it has been a while since I have seen you here," he continued.

"You must get this reaction from dogs all the time?" I said to Harry.

"Harry, make my little ladies bark? My Goodness! No, it's you they are not familiar with. Harry comes and visits them almost every time he visits you."

"Visits me? What are you talking about?" I asked baffled, after a moment's hesitation, I reassured myself that it was nothing but proof that the old man was now senile.

Mr Goldstone frowned at Harry, who remained silent. My eyes now on Harry, I almost believed I saw him wink at Mr Goldstone. But he surely must have, because why else did Mr Goldstone wink back. As Mr Goldstone approached the foot of my door, Harry hopped down the three steps and began gently stroking the black and white animals that had been given the names of flowers.

"Mr Goldstone, I think you are mistaken. This is the first time I have ever met Harry," the dogs finally at bay, my words at long last clearly audible. Feeling sorry for the old man, a sudden urge to rectify his memory, embraced me.

"Well, actually Mrs Gordon, I used to come and play with Zenya when I was a lad. She used to dress me up and call me Prince Harry. Beatrice used to walk us down the aisle or passage way, I guess I should be saying. Isn't that right Daffodil? Walk for Uncle Harry, Good Girl! " Harry lifted Daffodil's front paws off the ground and did a little prance with Daffodil on its hind legs, Daffodil loving the attention. "Mrs B used to have Zenya's plastic crowns laid out and she used to pretend to marry us."

"Goodness! Harry Greenwood? Is that really you? So that's how you knew our names! My word, how you have grown!" The memories of Zendaya's innocence came to mind.

"It sure is me, Madam Hannah," he replied, smiling broadly, Dandelion now in his arms, being cradled like a baby.

Harry Greenwood had been the only person other than Beatrice to ever call me Madam Hannah, and years ago I had quite enjoyed hearing him call me just that. Zendaya, he called Zenya and running through the house, he'd recite those names daily, at least until Zendaya's twelfth birthday. It was on that day, the day that I had caught him planting a kiss upon her lips, that I had banned him from my house. It may not have been their first but I had vowed, it would certainly be their last. What ambitions in life could a boy of Harry's upbringing ever strive towards after all? Nothing of distinction in my mind. That, I was certain of, his mother merely a housekeeper for a family down the street, his father spending his hours covered in blood, grinding meat at the local grocer. After all my sacrifices, I certainly was not going to have Zendaya marry a pauper's son and it certainly had been a good decision, for here he stood, the faithful mailman. As for his parents, I could hardly imagine they had progressed much further in life.

"So remind me Harry, how old are you? I mean you have changed so much. I can hardly believe it's you. You have become, well.... so, so very good looking!" I cut myself short realizing from Mr Goldstone's facial expression how strange my emphasis on his good looks must have appeared.

"Are you saying I was not when I was young?" he laughed.

"No, no of course not," I said, instantly denying such an implication.

"Aaahh shucks Mrs Gordon, don't stress now. I know I used to be ugly. I am the same age as your daughter, although I will be turning twenty eight quite soon," continued Harry, doing a good job of catching the overly excited dog that had just tried to jump out of his hands.

"Oh yes, of course. You were only a year older than my daughter.

You are about a year older than my daughter I should be saying. Time certainly does fly, to think I am already forty eight."

"Well you certainly don't look a day over thirty."

"Most definitely!" agreed Mr Goldstone.

"It's easy to see where Zendaya gets her beauty from. Don't you think so Mr Goldstone?"

"Stop it now, Harry!" I could feel my cheeks heating up with both men staring at me.

"Oh, come now Mrs Gordon! No need to blush. There will certainly be a lot more men smiling in the streets of London if you start leaving the house a bit again, that's all our dear boy Harry is trying to say."

"How old are you Mr Goldstone?" I quickly asked, trying to take the attention off myself, the flattering becoming a bit more than I could contend with.

"Ah, well that is something I vowed to stop keeping a track of, the very hour that I passed seventy. Well, I must be on my way and you thought I was going crazy Mrs Gordon," said Mr Goldstone with a merry laugh. "How is Zendaya, may I ask?"

"The big day is next month." I answered, relieved that I was no longer the focus of the conversation.

"Well done old chap! Well done!" said Mr Goldstone proudly giving Harry a pat on the back, "As I said, I best be off then. Come along girls now, come along."

Harry's eyes met mine, a look of confusion on his face.

"You must forgive him. It's the age no doubt. Congratulating you, goodness," I said pausing to laugh, "I must apologise on his behalf although I should not be having such a big mouth. We all end up in the same boat. I can imagine I will simply choose to stop keeping track of my age as he has done."

"Big day…?" he repeated still looking dumbfounded.

"It's her wedding of course! She and Mark are tying the knot next month."

"Mark!"

"Yep, he really is quite the gem. If it had not been for Mark I don't think she would have tried modelling and had the success she's had. I confess I was a tad surprised when she spoke about tying the knot with him. I hadn't seen the spark when she had first introduced me to him. It has happened awfully suddenly now that I think about it, all in the space of a few months. But I could not possibly be more pleased."

When Mark came into Zendaya's life, I could truly not have been more pleased. And the fact that he was a white man. Well I felt thrilled! My idea of what their babies would look like? Ah well, if all my life I had never really felt like a mother, I would finally be able to carry them out the door and have people congratulate me. I would at least get to feel like a real grandparent.

"Mark? She's marrying Mark? Zendaya is going to marry Mark Spencer?" The expression he wore, told a story of its own and I could not help but wonder if the poor lad who had kissed Zendaya on her twelfth birthday still had feelings towards her. "Next month…she is marrying Mark Spencer…next month. Are you sure?"

"Sure as the sky is blue!" I said, gleefully stealing his line.

"I don't know. It looks like rain," he replied, his gaze still meeting mine.

I was about to ask him how it was that he knew Mark's full name, but for some strange reason I suddenly felt pity for him. If my guess was correct, I hadn't quite succeeded in ensuring that the kiss I had seen, had in fact been their last. He turned around standing motionless against the rising sun, looking as damaged as the car being towed away. I felt a sudden urge to rest my hand upon his shoulder and pacify him, but before I could, he began to walk away.

Picking up the box, I was about to close the door, when I heard his voice right up behind me.

"I meant to ask…who is Leiyah Kleinhans? Perhaps you ought to check if that address is correct after all."

"What, what did you just say?" My heart beat racing, I suddenly felt as though there had been a rope around my neck and he had just pulled on it. Dear God! No! It couldn't be?

"The box, it's from South Africa and it's addressed to Leiyah

Kleinhans," he said.

"Get out! Get out! Get out!" I screamed, throwing the box directly at him before slamming the door shut.

TWO

usk had already fallen before Beatrice returned to find me sprawled across the couch in the darkened Living room.

"*Haibo*!" she exclaimed. "What is this, everyone going and lying in the dark? Are you ok Madam?"

"Everyone? Zendaya?" I asked searching for her across the room, as Beatrice switched on the lights. I sat up, my eyes twitching from the sudden brightness.

"Why would Zen ever be sitting alone in a dark room with you, *hmmph*, sitting and saying nothing to you? Let alone in a dark room! The two of you and your mouths! As if you wouldn't know if she were here." Beatrice clicked her tongue.

"What?" I asked, recovering from the confusion she had just brought upon me.

"Oh…Never mind!" she shook her head. "Madam what is wrong? What is the matter with you Madam?" she asked, pausing in front of me, after having drawn the curtains to a close. "You look like you have seen a ghost."

"Seen a ghost? I'm surrounded by them, but as if you honestly care!" I shouted. Leaping off the couch, I flung the cushion I had been clutching onto against the wall; refusing to meet her gaze, my disorientation having left me, I tried to calm myself by pacing the room.

"Where on earth have you been all day anyway?" I shouted furiously.

"Well, I took Peyton to school of course. Mrs James asked me to.

Oh, how cute all the little girls looked in their orange frocks, reminded me of little Zen in her blue ones. Such a pretty school dress, still only in nursery school. She is five by the way. Oh and this was on the doorstep," she said to me, placing the dented box on the coffee table.

"Yes I know." Beatrice frowned in response, "It's addressed to Leiyah Kleinhans," I continued.

"What! No! How could you say such a thing! You said you would only say that name when he was…only when he was…" Tears instantly streamed down her cheeks.

"I'm sorry Beatrice," I answered.

"No, no it can't be…" she said, snatching the box off the table and staring at it in disbelief, "is this real? *Baas* he is…" Shaking her head, unable to bring herself to say the words, I completed her sentence.

"Dead Beatrice, Yes. *Baas* is dead. Karl Johan Kleinhans is dead." As I watched the tears streaming down her cheeks I felt an unexpected release. A huge weight had been lifted off my shoulders. I was finally free. The man she had worked for in South Africa was dead.

"My KK, my KK is gone!" Her silent tears evolving into a hysterical outburst. Beatrice cursed in her mother tongue before stomping up the stairs, slamming her bedroom door behind her. We had always known the day would come, but how to face it, we were yet to discover.

"KK?" I repeated aloud after hearing her door close. *Why on earth would Beatrice call her Baas 'KK'?* It sounded simply ridiculous. I had always known she had spent more than ten years working for his family, for his parents before he himself became her boss, but goodness I was now her boss and she never called me Hannah, not even in one of her moods. *How bizarre,* I thought. Maybe she would call me 'HG' when I died. Whilst pondering over such a scenario of an even more haggard Beatrice meeting an aging Harry at the door, I was suddenly startled once more by the box. Jumping up in fright, reawakened to the reality of what had provoked such drama, I stared in disbelief at the box that lay on the coffee table.

For an entire hour I was alone with it. Like an eagle swooping over its prey, I kept my eyes on it, at times standing, sometimes sitting, even pacing angrily. Pelting it with my vexation, I damned it to the depths of hell almost expecting it to disappear. Never more relieved was I, when Beatrice re-joined me. My head pounding from all the scenarios that had played out in my mind, I did not waste a further second.

"Open it Beatrice! Please tell me if it is true. Is what I have said true? Who has written?"

After removing the tape that sealed the rectangular box, Beatrice lifted the lid and removed its contents. On the coffee table she placed a thick yellow envelop, beside it a thick leather finished green journal with a few folded letters pressed in between, some of which protruded unevenly. The cover of the journal was evidently damaged and as Beatrice flipped through it, it was easy to guess that the pages had been saved from some perilous encounter; with nature's elements, I was certain. As I watched Beatrice, both her hands now in the box that was fairly deep, I realized that she was surveying an item that had given her an emotional sting, for I last saw that expression when we had boarded our plane in Johannesburg.

"What is it?" I asked.

"Nothing, it's nothing. You don't need to see it," she answered, quickly wiping away the tear that had escaped, as she placed the box under the table.

"Open the envelope. I need to know if he is definitely dead Beatrice. At first I was shocked. I felt so angry but…but I'm also glad. If he is then…well then at least we know he can never find us!"

"Do you have no heart? Someone dying makes you feel happy?" she asked, giving me a questioning look. She shook her head and picked up the A4 envelope.

"Of course not, just…" despite my vengeful intention to re-utter the letters 'KK', something about the look in her eyes halted me, and I walked over to the window. Peeping behind the curtain Beatrice had earlier drawn closed, I tried to guess the item Beatrice had refused to reveal.

Staring out at the brightly lit street which was now quite deserted, the scene of the crash suddenly flashed before me and I could see myself on the street, the little girl kicking me before launching herself merrily into Beatrice's arms. I let go of the cloth. When I turned around, Beatrice was still meticulously peeling open the glued edge of the envelope.

As I returned to the couch she pulled out the stack of pages it contained before placing the envelope on the coffee table. After sifting through it, she looked up at me and before she could speak I knew the answer.

"You are right." The words she spoke next, I could never have predicted. "It is his Will."

"His Will? Why would they send us his Will? Why would Peterson do that?"

"Who is Peterson?"

"He had drawn up the restraining order. Has he not sent it?"

"I do not know," answered Beatrice searching for a letter.

"Well anyway, it must be from him. I had asked to be made aware of Karl's death, so that I could be certain we were safe, so of course I had given Peterson our address. He might have needed it for other reasons too. Oh but never mind any of that, all that matters is that I am free now! Oh Beatrice, finally, I can walk the streets without turning around every 2 minutes!"

Uttering no response, Beatrice stared at me with anger, the redness of her teary eyes making her look even more ferocious, but I felt such elation and relief I did not care how she felt.

"Oh wait, what if it is not from Peterson," I continued, "What if this is from Susannah, this is surely Susannah's doing, Peterson had been in communication with her when we had last spoken all those years ago, perhaps Susannah wanted to show off her inheritance. Surely that is it." I clicked my fingers as if I was a detective who had just unravelled a mystery.

"I would not know," answered Beatrice. "Well instead of all this guessing, let me just read it. Let me see now. It says here Karl Johan Kleinhans has left…"

"No Beatrice. Not now. I don't want to know. Go through it in your room. I don't need to know how much money he left for Susannah or that rotten son of hers or anyone else for that matter. I don't want to see it! Not now, not ever! I need you to do me a favour Beatrice," I said, seating myself beside her and holding her hand tightly. "Burn it! Promise me you will do that."

"I promise Madam. I promise," she replied, giving my hand a kiss.

"I trust you Beatrice. I know you will want to read it and that's fine but once you have read it I want you to destroy it."

She turned away and it almost seemed like she was again looking into the box, but what it contained, I was not certain I wanted to know.

"Are you going to read it Beatrice?" We sat in silence for the longest minute of my life and for a second, I almost imagined she was going to say, 'No' but I looked up to see her nodding.

"Yes," she whispered, her eyes meeting mine once more. "Yes," she repeated, "I will read it. It may take me some time, but once I have read it, I will destroy it."

"Promise?"

She stood up and began restoring the box with its contents. I felt as if I had been holding my breath, awaiting her answer.

"I promise Madam, I promise."

"Thank you," I sighed. "The past is in the past and there it will forever stay. At least now I can finally be certain of that." There may have been many days when I had considered Beatrice to be nothing more than a stone in my shoe, but through it all, she had proved herself to be a woman who always kept her promises.

When I had first heard the utterance of the name Leiyah Kleinhans I had felt an intense hatred and anger towards the person who had driven her life to a ruin, an intense hatred and anger towards Karl Johan Kleinhans. I felt like his ghost had come to haunt me. But while watching Beatrice, it had suddenly dawned upon me that the only other person who knew that they had ever existed was Beatrice. The answer was simply, out of sight, out of mind. Once Beatrice destroyed the box, the existence of Leiyah Kleinhans and Karl Johan Kleinhans would forever be erased.

For the first time in more than twenty years, all I could think about was South Africa. I wondered if my name had ever been spoken after I had left. I wondered whose lips it had been uttered from and for the first time since I had left, I wondered what it would be like to go back.

THREE

Sunday

It sat there like a ticking time bomb. The fear I had felt the morning it had arrived, two days earlier, reawakened. I have been sitting here staring at the box for more than an hour now. Out of sight out of mind, really now Hannah? How could I have been foolish enough to believe anything could ever be that simple? I cannot eat. I feel sick. My God, I never thought I would see the day. Am I actually going to tell Zendaya the truth? Everything I have worked so hard to conceal. She has been slipping though my fingers, for years now. If I tell her, she is gone. That I can be certain of! She will never speak to me again. I ought to have destroyed it myself when I had the chance. But maybe Beatrice is right, there is a reason she had not gotten to that stage.

But my apologies dear reader for I am afraid I have surely confused you enough. Let me take you back to Saturday and how Sunday came to be.

• • •

Saturday

"Mrs James, welcome to my home." Although Beatrice had arrived at the door first, I had hurried over to make my presence known.

Annoyingly, her only response was laughter at the commotion Beatrice was causing. After having just learnt of the death of her most '*treasured Baas*' the previous day, I was in awe of how she could still produce a smile on the chilly Saturday morning, let alone laughter.

Peyton had dived straight into Beatrice's arms the second the door had opened and after being swung around like a carousel, Beatrice was now holding her by the ankles and pushing her up the stairs as if the child where a wheelbarrow. It was the first time I had seen little Peyton on a weekend, it was the first time I saw her in clothing that was not orange. Not that I had never looked out for the pair on a Saturday or Sunday, but there clearly never seemed to be a reason for them to navigate past my window on a weekend, at least until today.

"Beatrice and Zendaya used to play that game all the time," I said, butting in. "Feel free to stop by anytime. My name is Hannah Gordon. I'm Zendaya's mum by the way and of course you have already met our over excitable housekeeper Beatrice."

"No, really, no it can't be, is it true Beatrice?"

"Yes, it is. I am her housekeeper and she really is what she says she is," answered Beatrice.

"Goodness Beatrice, I'm so sorry. I sincerely hope I have not offended you. What was that word she used to call you? Oh, how can I not remember it? Oh, I could just hear the love in her voice. It started with the letter G I think," she exclaimed.

"Ah, you mean *Gogo*!" exclaimed Beatrice.

"Yes, that's it, precisely that. I assumed it to mean mummy in some African language or the other."

"It means granny in isiZulu. It was the African language my family spoke," answered Beatrice.

"Oh how silly of me. No wonder you all look so alike. So you are her granny then?"

"Of course not!" I answered, giving Beatrice a cold stare.

Beatrice gently let go of the child's ankles before lifting her up into her arms.

How on earth did she offend Beatrice, rather than myself, I could not begin to imagine. I felt like slapping some sense into the fickle-minded woman.

"Zendaya never mentioned you. It was always B and her against the world," continued Alice.

"Why am I not surprised?" I muttered, feeling a desperate need to appear motherly, I tried to carry the five year old out of Beatrice's arms and into my own.

"Go away!" shouted the child digging her nails into the skin on my arm.

"Ouch!" my tone far too harsh, so much so that the child hid behind her mother, her instantaneous tears muffled by the clothing she held against her face.

"Peyton darling, that's naughty now," said her mother.

"Say sorry to Madam," said Beatrice, wiping away her tears.

The child hid her face behind her hands.

"Say sorry to Madam now," said Beatrice more firmly, pulling the child's hands away from her face. "If you don't say sorry, I am going to put you down and I'm never going to carry you again. Is that what you want?"

"No, no, no, I'm sorry B, I won't be naughty again. I promise. Please don't put me down," said the child, her eyes remaining solely on Beatrice.

All I could think about as I watched the sight were the moments when Zendaya would refuse to listen to me but Beatrice would succeed at disciplining her.

It became painful to watch them and so I quietly slipped away into the Living room as they continued to exchange hugs. Relieved when, finally, I heard the door close.

Hardly more than five minutes had passed before I heard the sound of the doorbell once more.

Two quick rings, a short pause, followed by two more. Anticipating the sound of Beatrice's heavy stomping as she descended the stair, I waited patiently. Whilst the ringing continued within the walls, I heard nothing more than the ticking clock. The door within sight, it suddenly occurred to me that it surely had to be Peyton and her mother, having forgotten something perhaps. Now, more than any other time was my moment to impress. If I opened the door and Beatrice was not there to steal her attention, surely the child would have to embrace me. Instantaneously bolting from the couch, I rushed to the door.

"Peyton…Oh my God! What are you doing here?" The disappointment in my voice unintentionally expressed.

"Oh, please stop it! I don't want to hear that 'Oh my God', especially not from you. You really must be the only mother who looks like she's seen a ghost when her daughter pitches up at the door."

"Zendaya! That's not what I meant."

"Of course, Mother you see me after weeks and you can't even pretend to be happy. Strange how you were smiling when you thought it was Peyton. Perhaps you should adopt that bratty little girl! You would be far happier with her than you have been with me."

"Don't say such things Zendaya, it's just that I was not expecting you back from America for another two weeks. How did you even know Peyton was a little girl?"

"Oh I know everything Mother. You can't fool me."

"Well nevermind Peyton, you have been crying. What's the matter? Is it Mark?"

"Mark? Do you see Mark crying? Because I don't! Mark, Mark, Mark. He is the only person you care about. For once in your life can you just try! Try to care about me."

"Calm down Zendaya!"

"Don't you dare tell me to calm down!"

"Why are you so angry at me Zendaya?"

"When have I ever not been?"

"Don't speak like that! If you at least gave me some sort of idea of what is going on, then I would know how to make you feel better."

"Don't you even dare! This is all your fault! I hate you! I hate you! I hate you!"

Stunned by her words, completely speechless, I knew I needed to hug her, hold her tight and tell her everything would be okay, but before I could embrace her, who should appear to save the day but my own personal 'Wonder Woman' herself.

"Zendaya, just breathe. My sweet child! Breathe in, yes that's it! You can do it," shouted Beatrice. Appearing almost out of thin air, now standing on the bottom step she hugged Zendaya tightly. Completely out of breath, it was clear that she had run more than just the pavement that was visible till the end of the street "Calm down baby girl. Your mother does not know baby girl. Let's go upstairs."

Zendaya ran upstairs, Beatrice hot on her heels.

After all these years Beatrice still knew how to deny me a hug. That was no surprise but what could I not have known that she did? *Your mother does not know?* Had my ears deceived me? What on earth was Beatrice doing out of the house. I had not even known she had left. She seemed to know what was going on. How could that be?

I could not as much as begin to comprehend the possibility of Mark calling off the wedding. I wondered whether phoning him would tell me everything I needed to know. But Zendaya would hate me for it. I knew that for certain.

A million thoughts swirling through my mind, I shut the door after dragging in her luggage and ascended the staircase, struggling to comprehend the circumstances that had brought Zendaya to the door and in such a state. After taking each step up the two flights as softly as was possible, I was relieved to find the door slightly ajar. Peeping within I once more felt a pang of jealousy as I watched Zendaya whispering to Beatrice. Her image, pure innocence despite her scanty attire, her body curled, Beatrice cradling her.

"How did he know B…How did he find out about Mark? It makes no sense. I had everything worked out. Mark will never even be in Britain, he hates the idea of travel so much, he could probably convince his own President no other land existed. Goodness B! How did this happen?" said Zendaya to Beatrice raising her voice in frustration, her tears rolling profusely, Beatrice attempting to soothe her by rubbing her back.

"He was bound to discover at some point in time, my baby,"

whispered Beatrice, words she regretted uttering, her expression clearly spoke.

"No B, how could you ever even say that to me? Surely you are spending too much time with my mother. You are sounding just like her now and you becoming evil is the last thing I need right now!"

"Calm down child, that is not fair, you know I feel your pain but," Beatrice shook her head, "I really don't know what to tell you. I love you with all my heart but you were being a very bad girl, it was all so wrong."

Zendaya's body jolted upright and she pulled at her braids in frustration.

"Beatrice Zungu, did I honestly have a choice? I wanted my mother to be happy. I would have lost her completely. You know that. For God's sake, you make me seem like a prostitute."

"I never called you a prostitute or said you behaved like one, so please do not think of such an idea again. But maybe you should start covering up a bit more."

"What! Never before did you ever voice your disapproval of my 'style of dress' as mother would call it, and now when I need you most, you agree with her."

Zendaya jumped off the bed before she began pacing the room.

"It's not about the way you dress," answered Beatrice, catching sight of me as she turned towards the door. She paused. I instinctively ducked out of sight, hardly able to breathe as I awaited the revelation of my presence. But to my astonishment, she said nothing as to my whereabouts. There was silence and I adjusted my stance to once more peer within. Beatrice's eyes met mine once more, but this time I remained where I stood. "It is just once you tell one lie," she continued, "you can only not be caught if you tell another. Believe me, I should know best." I knew her words spoken were addressed to me and not Zendaya, for she only turned away when Zendaya's howling once more echoed through the room and I was left with no other choice but to remain where I stood, waiting anxiously for it to subside.

For the first time since the start of all my confusion, my eyes fell upon what she wore. What would have left me peeved on another occasion, I had prior to this point barely bothered to register. She had arrived with her braided hair tied into a high pony tail, knee high black leather boots, mini denim shorts, of a blue stone washed shade, which made its best attempt, but alas still failed to meet a scanty white woollen top, which annoyingly resembled lingerie. Born with her African curves in all the right places, she looked simply too provocative. Basically her crocheted white top looked like enormous diamonds that someone had decided to link up because they simply did not know what else to do with them because they could not possibly have been stitched with care. Thank the Lord she had some sense, enough to wear a red boob tube instead of just her bra under the knitted mayhem.

"If you want to call me bad, then so were you!" in a broken voice Zendaya continued. "You want to know why? Well, you could have done something to stop me. Well, you didn't. You just watched. Why couldn't you have spoken to my mother so many years ago?"

"I tried to, my dear, but *he* was just everything she never wanted in a man. She thought she was doing the right thing. I love you like my own flesh and blood, but I cannot explain to you the relationship I share with your mother as well. You just would not understand. I was torn too."

Zendaya lunged herself onto the bed and burst into tears, howling her lungs out once more.

"Do not worry Zendaya, I am going to fix this today."

Unable to hear any further conversation, I threw in the towel and retreated to my bedroom. Left with no choice, other than to sit and wait for Beatrice to come and find me, for I was certain she would. '*He*' who on earth was '*he*' and '*fix what*'. Mark had been Zendaya's first and last love. That, I had always believed, but God help me, how I had been misled.

But Beatrice? How dare she! How dare she pretend that she had discussed another man with me! I had no recollection of her ever broaching such a topic. The nerve of her! And if she shared a so called '*special*' relationship with me, would I honestly be so in the dark?

Although I had not heard any mention being made of this so called '*He*' being a lover, Mark being Zendaya's only lover, was clearly a false declaration. If only I knew where Zendaya's pain stemmed from.

Well, whatever was going on, Beatrice would surely tell me. If she didn't spill freely I would make her. I always found a way to.

Selecting my favourite Jane Austen Book from the library, the shelved wall opposite my bed being my library, I sat myself upon the crook in the window, my mind unable to focus on the words on the page or the world outside. Anyway, I had read '*Sense and Sensibility*' so many times over, I could probably recite it in a crowded theatre without the book.

What could I have possibly missed all these years? Why did Zendaya say she wanted me to be happy? She only seemed to ever care about Beatrice. The idea that she even considered my feelings seemed unbelievable. I had always been the one performing acts in desperation, wishing to see a smile appear for me and not for Beatrice. Zendaya showing affection towards me? The thought of it all was preposterous. Perhaps I had heard wrong. She had been talking in between sniffles and tears, after all.

I thought back to the first time I had laid eyes on her. An absolute angel she was. I knew immediately that she was my gift from God. She loved me the moment she laid her eyes on me and I knew I would tuck her into bed every night, make her smile and dry her tears. But it just had not worked out as I had imagined. After our first year together I could just never seem to make her smile and even now, attempting to dry her tears, well it was simply not within my power. What had become of us?

The image I recollected of her, when she was young and the woman I had watched in despair, could it really be the same soul. Yes, her dressing was far too scanty and definitely too seductive for comfort but that was how models dressed. What could I honestly say? If I ever voiced my objections, she only wore less. Try to please me…really!

'*He was bound to discover at some point in time my baby*', from the manner whispered Beatrice surely knew the consequences could only be dire. '*Discover what?*' I thought. What was I still to learn?

After replacing the book to where it rightfully belonged, I lay my back against my carpeted bedroom floor and stared at the fan upon my ceiling and as my thoughts swirled in unison with its three brown blades, I drifted into a land, where, as a warrior princess, my countrymen sang out my praises. For once more, I had saved the day.

FOUR

When I awoke my back was sore and only a few hours had passed. To my surprise Beatrice had not sought me out, and I decided to venture downstairs, hopeful that she would be there waiting for me, filled with the answers to very many questions. Answers as to why Zendaya had arrived at the house in such a state that morning, answers as to who the mysterious '*he*' was. There was silence as I passed Zendaya's room and on reaching the bottom step I expected Beatrice to rush to my side, but she was nowhere to be found.

No one served me lunch and by 1:00 p. m. Saturday morning just seemed to be dragging on forever and I made myself a sandwich. I had made one for my daughter as well but not having the courage to enter the room, I knocked on the door and left it on the floor with a glass of juice. After setting it on the floor I scampered away truly fearing what I would be greeted with had the door swung open. If Beatrice was hungry she could come downstairs and fix it herself.

Whether the reason was hunger or not, I knew that Beatrice would have to come downstairs and knowing me as well as she did, she would know that I was waiting for answers and she had better provide them. Watching television had never been a pleasure of mine but I switched it on and stared at it blankly, and finally switching it off, I stared at the street.

The Indian woman living across the street had just stepped out her of house. She and her husband had made the area their home two years ago. I had never spoken with her. She had never interested me until about three months ago, when I noticed that her tummy had ballooned considerably. And, I spotted her now for the first time since then. As I watched her waddling down the steps, I imagined the baby could genuinely pop that very moment. She looked so content. I felt a palpable jealousy towards her, unconsciously playing with the silver necklace, I never removed, as I so often did, when my agitation heightened.

Just as she had begun walking down the street, Mr Goldstone appeared with his ever faithful companions, each pulling at her leash and although my window was closed, I could hear him call out to her. "Pratipal!" was the name he called, and from her gestures they were clearly talking about her unborn child.

"Well, she has eaten and now she is asleep, thank goodness. Thank you for the sandwich."

"Well it wasn't for you," I replied, still watching Mr Goldstone and Pratipal through the window.

"What's the matter with Zendaya and where did you go this morning? Wait, let me guess, you were prancing through the streets, acting like Peyton's horse? I can only imagine"

"Prancing like a horse? *Haibo*, you really can be so mean. Well if I had thought you had left the food for me, I would not have given it to Zendaya to eat, now would I?" answered Beatrice sounding quite angry, "I thought you liked Peyton anyway."

"I did…I do, of course I like Peyton but…Oh! Never mind. I don't have to explain myself to you," I shook my head. "And you want to just barge downstairs and start calling me mean? After I have had to spend the last twenty somewhat years watching you behave like Zendaya's mother," turning around to confront her about her attitude, I felt like Beatrice had just pointed a pistol in my face.

"Oh my God, Beatrice, what the hell are you doing? Get that out of my sight, Right Now!" I shouted, my body trembling, "Get it out! Get it out! Get it out!" I yelled, mortified at the sight of the package that Harry had only just delivered the previous day, being held tightly to her bosom.

"Stop shouting or you will wake Zendaya," she responded calmly, "and besides," she said raising her eyebrows, "we both know you are not ready for her to come downstairs and see it. Or are we?" she asked, giving me a sarcastic look, "but, if you are though," she continued, not seeking a response, "don't stop, please go right on ahead and shout. I do know my Madam was born to shout!" Shaking her head, Beatrice continued to place the box that Harry had delivered on the coffee table, completely ignoring my attempts to halt her, behaving as if I was not even present, she began removing its contents.

Beatrice would, of course, be right and we both knew it. The last thing I needed was to wake Zendaya and let her see the delivery. I sank into the sofa, pressing my palms against my eyes, and as I tried to calm myself I was startled to feel Beatrice's hand against my back. She had seated herself beside me and was soothingly rubbing my back.

"Why did you bring that thing down here?" I asked, still in disbelief. You promised me Beatrice. I thought I could trust you."

"I promised you I would destroy it once I had finished reading everything, but I still have the last few pages to read. But maybe God had a reason for not letting me get to that stage. You have to tell her Madam. You need to tell her about the Will," she answered.

"Why on earth would I tell Zendaya about the Will. There is no reason in the world why I possibly need to tell her anything about Karl or this wretched box!"

"Oh where do I even begin…" Beatrice looked clearly troubled.

"Beatrice, the Will has nothing to do with her. Karl is dead. We are safe."

"Safe from what? It was only you who never wanted to see him again and now you never will because your dream has finally come true. He is dead. But there was a reason his Will found us. I can promise you that much Madam."

"And my dream was to one day utter the names of Karl and Leiyah Kleinhans again. As if! Surely it was sent by Susannah. I am certain. What that miserable wife of his sent a copy here for, I don't understand.

How she could have the nerve to want to show her fortune off to me, it really is a disgrace. I always knew she only married him for his money," I answered furiously.

"It's not a copy of the Will, at least I don't think it is. Actually, I'm quite sure. It is the original, Madam, and he did not leave the money to Susannah. He left it to YOU, to you and to Zendaya. Every last cent of it!"

"What! Stop it, Beatrice! How dare you joke about such a thing," I shouted, my body trembling.

"It's not a joke. Do I ever joke? You know what, I am so fed up of you always playing the sympathy card with me. For once in your life, will you just open your eyes and think about someone other than yourself," shouted Beatrice, her fingers clenched.

Beatrice picked up the green journal and began flipping through it frantically as if her life depended on it, pressing the pages firmly apart she handed to me what appeared to be her desired content.

"It's *Baas* Karl's diary. Read it!" she said.

I got the impression that if I refused she would slap me. She looked that angry. Her build-up of emotions, nearing its climax. I silently took the book from her and looked at the page her fingers had pressed against.

January

Today my precious eighteen year old leaves.

'Insufferable man, Beatrice, a malignant, incomparable, insufferable man, that's what he is. Oh, but I will never be free!' My daughter's words do not surprise me. She has never voiced them. Her feelings, not to me directly, but I am certain Leiyah would feel no guilt, had she only known I was walking past the kitchen the minute she spoke. Her words just keep ringing through my head. Even after walking up the three flights of steps. Finally, in my study, even as I watch her now, her words still haunt me. I went straight to the window. I cannot sit at the table. No, not as I usually do. I had to

watch her. It could be the last time. I wish I did not have to spend so much time in the Transvaal, always leaving her behind here at the Estate. I could be walking down to the pond with her right now, perhaps. I have failed to include myself in her routine, these morning walks. It could have been 'our' walk. If only I had tried. If only I could be here more.

Oh my childish Mary Anne, you loved the sight of the distant mountains didn't you. Oh, you knew exactly how to make me tag along to the edge of the forest before luring me into the water. Oh my sweetheart, every time I look at the pond, I think of you. You could swim across it all day. You never could resist jumping into that water on a Summer's day, especially one like today. Why did you leave us? My Leiyah needed a mother. I needed a wife.

I knew I was on watch early but I could not help myself. I waited. I could close my eyes and picture Leiyah's every move. They never changed. Out the door at the crack of dawn as always. But her actions were not the same today. I wonder. Why were they so different? Why did she fetch a spade from the shed? Did my girl even know how to use it? What had she been holding so tightly? I will find out.

Beatrice had not stirred while I read the entry from the journal. My absorption of its contents prevented me from venturing past the page, and so I succumbed to reading it aloud, though reading it only once, his words had almost been memorized.

My father had been watching me, it seemed beyond comprehension.

"He was a father who loved his daughter. He just didn't know how to show it," said Beatrice resting her hand on my back and seating herself beside me. "You need to read the rest of it today. I will leave it here. That way it won't fall into Zendaya's hands," she continued slipping the green diary into my handbag.

I said nothing. The words I had just read still ringing in my head.

"This was also in the box." Beatrice picked up a wooden case which replicated a miniature treasure box and placed it on the table. I was stunned!

"How is this possible B? It belongs with her. I buried it myself, at her gravesite. You remember, don't you?" I looked towards her, pleading an answer. "You don't think that monster moved my mother's coffin, do you B?"

"I think he only wanted to find what you had buried. He was watching you, remember? I think your father just felt it belonged with you."

Fetching the jewellery case from her, I could see that the box did not contain anything else. So this was the item she had refused to reveal to me the day the delivery had arrived and I didn't need to ask her why. It was that very item that I had been showing her in the kitchen so many years ago on the morning I had decided to bury it on the 15 of January 1990, the very morning I had described my father to be a malignant, insufferable man. Its emotional significance, she understood all too well. What it had contained, she had not known at the time.

I ran my fingers over the letters that had been delicately carved on its lid. 'Leiyah Catherine Kleinhans.'

I knew what I would find within, but I opened it nevertheless.

Opening the little treasure chest as if it was a fragile piece of glass, I first removed the silver necklace and pendant before carefully pulling out a now discoloured sheet of A4 white paper that had been neatly folded several times over to enable it to fit perfectly into its rectangular base. Taking the tightly packaged paper momentarily between my fingers, I felt tears rolling down my cheeks. On the top were visible the words 'Love Leiyah'

I knew too well what was written inside but I opened it nevertheless and read it out to Beatrice before placing it in her view.

"Blood is thicker than water."

I cringed at the red trickle across the words knowing exactly what it was. I was aware that it had caught Beatrice's attention from the movement of her brows. I immediately expected her to question me about it. Strangely her lips did not move. She said nothing. I wished to explain but while I pondered over how to do so, I realized that from her silence she had already guessed it to be the remnants of my blood.

"Ever since that God damn box arrived, everything seems to be far too complicated," I shouted. After Zendaya's early arrival and the little knowledge I had managed to acquire of her scandalous secret, how else was I to feel after all?

Beatrice simply nodded.

"Damn this very box! Damn it to hell!" I shouted, restoring the treasure box within.

With both of us deep in thought, it was several minutes before I broke the silence.

"Why did Zendaya fly back early Beatrice? Why was Zendaya crying?"

Oh my poor baby Zen!" sighed Beatrice, "I never should have said yes when you begged me to come here. She is right. This is all my fault too. I kept quiet too much, for too long. She would have been happy in South Africa. She would have been free."

Digesting her words of regret, I suddenly didn't feel like I had a right to scold her anymore. Beatrice agreeing to leave South Africa, had been the biggest gift I could ever have asked for and although raising a child had not turned out to be quite what I had hoped for, it would never have been possible without her.

"But she has been happy here too, Beatrice. Gosh, maybe happier than she would have been in South Africa. How could you make such a statement?" I asked, shaking my head.

"Because…well because my poor child has lived her life trapped. As trapped as you were in South Africa. I should have stopped all this lying years ago," she shouted out but after several seconds of breathing in deeply, she whispered, "…but my love for you is as great as my love for her. I wanted to protect you too."

I didn't know what to say. I could hardly believe what I was hearing. I had never heard Beatrice speak in such a manner before, not since my arrival in England.

"I know you don't want his money, fine, don't take it, but who will it go to next? You have the power to change Zendaya's life," she said taking a grip of my shoulders and shaking me violently.

"You are hurting me! Let go of me!" I shouted.

"I'm sorry Madam. This is just becoming all too much for my old heart to handle." She seated herself once more. "You may not need the money but Zendaya does. Please Madam. I beg you. Show her this Will."

"You sound simply ridiculous, Beatrice. Why on earth would Zendaya need money? She has Mark."

"Exactly the reason why Mark is so bad. She is only marrying him because of his money." answered Beatrice.

"Zendaya loves Mark. His money is just a bonus."

"Tell me, if he did not have money, would you have her marry him then?"

I shook my head. I could not for the life of me understand what Beatrice was trying to say.

After a while she continued, "I don't know where to begin explaining, Madam. If she had her own money she would never have needed Mark. She chose Mark because of you."

"That is ridiculous Beatrice. I had nothing to do with it. I did not go out into the world and find her a 'Mark'. She met him on her own. "

"Maybe so, but it was still done for you. All she was trying to do was try to please you."

I shook my head in dismay.

"You may not have meant to do it but you put the idea into Zendaya's head that she had to marry for money. Someone rich!"

"No I didn't! I have no idea what you are going on about and you are starting to frustrate me. I set goals! That is all I did, besides Zendaya has never behaved the way I hoped she would. Did I send her to one of the most prestigious schools in England to become a model? God No!" I shouted back.

"Well, since you never got what you wanted, then perhaps it is time to throw in the towel and tell her the truth. Because right now Zendaya needs the money from the Will if she is to have any chance of being happy."

"What money?" I yelled, clenching my fists, desperate to avert swinging at her a mighty punch. "Just let me read that." I snarled snatching the WILL out of Beatrice's hands. Of course, English not being her first language, Beatrice misconstruing what she had read was highly possible. That, I did not dismiss. But in my heart, I knew that Karl, naming me an heir was very possible. Myself, as well as Zendaya, his sole heirs, sounded far-fetched but from what I had seen on the first few pages, Beatrice's claims seemed to be more than probable. After flipping through the first few pages, I flung it onto the couch, whilst a furious Beatrice scampered to retrieve it. "Oh, who am I kidding Beatrice!" I felt like pulling at my own hair.

Ensuring the pages were still intact, Beatrice restored the document to the box.

"This is all because of Harry, if he had not delivered this…" I finally responded, placing the folded paper back into the chest, feeling an absolute vengeance towards him.

"Harry Greenwood…*Eish*! Of course! Poor Boy!"

"Why on earth do you say '*Poor Boy*? Beatrice, what is going on? If he had never pitched up at my doorstep with this box, I would never have to remember all of this. How did you know his surname was Greenwood?"

"How could I not? I should have guessed it was you who told him about the wedding. But I could never have thought of a reason for the two of you ever speaking, even if I had tried for a whole year. Oh, Poor Harry…"

"Just forget about Harry. Tell me about Zendaya. Was there a fight?"

"Yes and No."

"What? How can the answer be both yes and no?"

"Yes, it is about the wedding, but No, not in the way you think. And yes, there was a fight. But it was not Mark and Zendaya that fought. It was Harry and Zendaya."

"Do you hear yourself Beatrice? Does Zendaya even remember him? What does Harry Greenwood have to do with Zendaya's wedding?'

"More than you could ever imagine Madam. If only you knew."

"Then help me understand Beatrice."

"You see, when I opened the door yesterday to find you sulking in the dark, it was not the first time in a matter of hours that I had been left frightened and ready to run…" she began before hesitating.

"Go on Beatrice. Tell me everything."

And so she did. She told me her tale and as I sat baffled, I learnt from Beatrice that the remorseful expression worn on Harry's countenance, when he bid me farewell, had not altered when he had reached his humble abode. That evening he had sat crouching at the foot of his bed, so deep in thought that his blank stare took no notice of the darkness that had engulfed him. For that very morning, the light that flickered in his heart had been blown out by a storm. He was heartbroken. And the woman who had betrayed him, was none other than Zendaya.

There he had sat, until the knocking on the door, led to the eventual opening of it by Beatrice herself. They sat together for hours as Harry poured his heart out to her. For the life of her she could not imagine how Harry had learnt of the truth, but Beatrice just listened. It was now up to Zendaya to answer his questions.

Feeling an equal pain after learning of her *Baas's* death, Beatrice decided to again visit Harry that Saturday morning. But to the astonishment of both Harry and Beatrice, who should arrive, but the heartbreaker herself and Harry wasted no time in confronting her. While Beatrice had been a witness to the first part of the exchange between Harry and Zendaya, she had quietly exited the apartment, waiting patiently for Zendaya to emerge. She had stood anxiously on the pavement. However, when Zendaya did at last emerge she had rushed off so quickly into a taxi that she had failed to catch sight of Beatrice who had been pacing to keep warm and who had unfortunately, at that very moment, been too far away for her cries to be heard.

"And so I ran all the way home. I knew my Zenya would be desperate to speak to me. Thank goodness when I arrived, she was still standing at the door," said Beatrice.

"I refuse to believe you Beatrice. You are lying. I know you are. How could you even try to pull off such a scheme? What on earth would you even be doing at Harry's Apartment?" I was shocked.

"Believe it or not I have always visited him, quite often to be honest. Even more so since Zendaya moved in with him two months ago."

"What! She has been living with him? No, Beatrice it cannot possibly be true." I could not believe what I was hearing. I must surely have been losing my mind.

"I'm afraid it is very true Madam. You cannot let your daughter marry a man she does not love. She is marrying Mark because all her life, she has felt rejected by you. She wanted a mother who didn't stare at every other child as if she didn't have one of her own. She wanted your approval."

"Nonsense Beatrice! The nerve of you! I do no such thing."

"And you refuse to admit that you do not stand at your window and stare at Peyton like a crazy woman, wishing she was your child."

I could do nothing more than shake my head in frustration. I almost allowed myself to say that Peyton at least resembled me more than Zendaya, but that would have only proved Beatrice's words all too true.

"Please Madam. You simply have to tell her that she has a life waiting for her in South Africa," continued Beatrice.

"She would have said something and what life is waiting for her in South Africa, honestly Beatrice. I am ordering you to stop this. Stop this nonsense at once! Anyway, if you say she loves Harry, well he lives in England not South Africa. I mean the closest the poor bloke has possibly been to an aircraft, is handling the mail in the cargo hold no doubt."

"Would you ever have acknowledged Harry, Madam?"

"No, I would not, but Zendaya loving Harry, simply isn't possible."

"Then why did she cry herself to sleep? Think Madam, I am begging you. My poor child, *ubaba*…oh, her heart is torn, broken, crushed. Oh, and it's all my fault! I tried to tell you earlier. But those were just hints. I should have told you the whole story earlier. It's not too late Madam. If you tell her about the money she will be able to marry him."

"Well, even if Zendaya did have feelings for Harry, Mark will be able to take care of her in a way that Harry never could. Mark has an education, security, pedigree. New found cash is never going to give

Harry all of that. Sometimes it is better to act with one's head rather than one's heart."

"Please Madam, I beg of you. I did not want to have to tell you this just yet but I have no other choice. Zendaya is pregnant! I never dreamt I would be going through this, but Madam you just have to. That's the reason she moved out. She was terrified you would notice a change in her body weight. Give her the family life you always dreamt of. You can show her a way to make all her dreams comes true. She and Harry, they were just meant to be. They deserve to be together. She feels she has not lived up to your expectations and all she wants to do is give her baby the rich lifestyle you had in South Africa. The rich lifestyle you have brainwashed her into thinking she needs. You don't want the money, fine, but give it to her. With *Baas's* money she can marry Harry and have a happy family, if anyone should understand, you should."

I could not comprehend what I was hearing. Pregnancy before marriage? My own daughter. I took my time to digest what I had heard and Beatrice made no attempt to force a response. Rather than feeling shocked, I instead felt puzzled.

"Even Harry learnt about the pregnancy only now. Zendaya had told him that if there was one thing her mother had taught her, was that money mattered and she would not allow her child to be raised in a tiny one room apartment. The poor boy must have been broken. But he vowed that whomever she chose to marry, he would love the child with all his heart and soul, even if it meant him having to watch from a distance. But if she knows about the inheritance…"

"But what do I tell her? What Beatrice? That a man named Karl has left her an inheritance. Don't you think she would have questions, like well I don't quite know, but perhaps one of them would be why? Do you expect me to tell Zendaya the entire life story of Karl and his shenanigans?" I asked standing up in dismay.

"No I don't."

"At last, you speak some sense," I answered, sighing in relief.

"I expect you to tell Zendaya the entire life story of Leiyah Kleinhans."

I felt as if I was being sucked into the earth, for the ground I stood on felt like quick sand. I tried to convince myself that I was asleep, for this had to be a nightmare.

"Just start by telling her about Karl. That Karl was your father, or who exactly Karl is, she does not have to know. We will take it one step at a time and I am here for you. When you do, she will make the right decision. She does not need to marry Mark. You can finally give her everything you have ever wanted Madam, and I know you will this time."

"Oh Beatrice, how is it that my past has come to haunt me?"

"She will understand Madam. She will understand."

"No, I wish I could have made her a different daughter, but the Zendaya I know will never understand!"

"How do I know you are not lying to me? What if she isn't even pregnant? You have no real proof that she is," I said.

"And you have no proof that she is not. Anyway, my word is all the proof you need."

If she wasn't emotional enough, Beatrice suddenly burst into tears. Sitting in confusion I waited for her isiZulu condemnation to come to a halt, before attempting to once more seek the root of the problem.

"I saved her when she was just a child." I could see the anger in Beatrice's face, realizing I was perhaps pushing it too far, I halted before continuing, "Why could Zendaya not use her head rather than her heart. How could she choose to love a poor uneducated boy like Harry Greenwood? How can you be happy when you are poor?"

"But you can have money and still be unhappy. If anything you should know that," said Beatrice.

Tears began streaming from my eyes, the tone in Beatrice's voice catching me completely off guard, as she uttered the words '*you should know*'. I sat down and she slid towards me, allowing me time to dry my eyes, she said no more.

"How could Zendaya possibly have lied about so many things," I shook my head in disbelief.

"As if my innocent Madam has never told a lie herself!"

"Shut up!" I shouted, instinctively slapping her across the face, stung by her words.

I swallowed hard, my action leaving me aghast.

"Oh God, I didn't mean to. I'm sorry. I'm so sorry. I have to go." I said, rushing into the hallway, having grabbed my bag and coat. Almost breaking my front door key as I pulled it out, I slammed the door behind me, before running out into the cloudy street.

FIVE

If I had felt like Friday had been one of the longest days of my life, today was beginning to feel so much longer. After walking aimlessly for almost an hour, I found myself seeking comfort on a wooden bench overlooking the pond in the park.

"Mrs Gordon, it is you. I thought I had recognized you."

"Mr Goldstone…" I answered, recognizing the voice behind me before I had even turned around.

"Heavens, what on earth are you doing sitting here with your coat off!" he exclaimed, helping me slip my blue coat over my sleeveless pink dress without waiting for permission to do so.

"I…I…I…" my voice shaking as I spoke, the tears slipping down my cheeks like water from a spout. Gazing into the eyes of the familiar face, I suddenly felt a million times more malicious for having just struck Beatrice.

"Oh dear me, you look like you need some coffee. Can I get you some?"

I nodded, feverishly trying to wipe away my tears, fighting back the urge to utter a response, for if I did, I knew I would only sob harder.

"What can I get you, cappuccino, a latte, plain coffee, expresso, decaf…" his list went on until he had completed tying his dogs to the bench.

I nodded, biting my lips. He smiled.

"You just relax dear. If my memory is as good as I believe it to be, I know exactly what to get you.

As he marched away, one of his dogs began to nibble at my shoe and I pulled my feet up onto the bench, crossing my legs under my dress. For the strangest reason, I felt as though they knew I had done something ghastly, that I had slapped their beloved Beatrice. Mr Goldstone really seemed to be appearing everywhere I looked recently, but I couldn't have felt happier.

Zendaya love Harry? The idea seemed preposterous. Could it really be true?

"Of course!" I shouted out, one of the dogs barking in response, as it stared at me. For the life of me, I couldn't remember which flower belonged to which dog. "I will ask him when he gets back. If anyone will be able to tell me what has been going on between Zendaya and Harry, your daddy surely will. Ask Mr Goldstone. Of course!"

The flock of pigeons that had been pecking nearby, were suddenly sent fluttering into the air by Goldstone's second loyal servant, who, finding me a bore, sought a better means of playing tag. I laughed at his canine daughter, who now wandered back, but my smile quickly faded as I remembered why it was that I sat here.

I didn't have to wait much longer before Mr Goldstone returned with two hot take-away drinks in his hand and by then my tears had completely dried. If anything, I was rather excited by the idea of proving Beatrice wrong. Once I got the information I wanted from Mr Goldstone, I would be able to enter my home, fulfilled, my new found knowledge proof that Beatrice had been more than deserving of my slap.

"Cappuccino with cream, three sugars, did I get it right?"

"Goodness you remembered!" I exclaimed, in awe of how he could accurately recall what I would have purchased. Perhaps he was not so senile after all.

"It was in the very month of my meeting all of you that we went down to Miss Muffin's, the new Starbucks, you must have seen it?"

I shook my head.

"Well never mind," he continued "but how could I ever forget the image of the little three year old, excitedly rattling off her mother's order. And when I asked her how she knew what mummy wanted, she smiled and told me *that's what mummy always wants silly* before she kissed you on the cheek."

I smiled. It felt so surreal. How had I allowed such happiness to disappear?

"You used to come here often and play with your daughter. You played for hours in this very park, for a good few years after you moved here. You looked like such a happy mum, but then you just stopped. Why my dear? I could see the sadness in the child. She looked so confused."

"She would have been confused, but I couldn't lose her."

"You are not making very much sense dear. How could you have lost her?"

"Someone from South Africa followed me here. At least I think they did and if they found me, then I would not have been able to be her mother."

"I see," was all he replied and though he sought no expansion of my reasoning, I could tell from his frown that he clearly 'did not see'. For a while, we just sat in silence sipping on our drinks.

"So when did you first meet Zendaya's father?" asked Mr Goldstone, finally breaking the silence.

"I didn't," I answered. My mind having wondered so far away I hadn't realised what I had said.

"Insemination was it?"

"Oh my, God no, not that at all. That's not at all what I meant. I, it's just, her father and I were never married, that's all."

"And she looked black. I guess with the Apartheid government you really didn't have a choice. You did the right thing dear."

"Why did you say insemination?"

"It would make sense."

"There was always a sort of distance between you. You always seemed unhappy about something, you know. Zen sensed that about you. Her only dream in life has been to satisfy you. Poor dear, she was simply petrified to tell you about Harry. I am so glad she finally plucked up the courage. I always told her you would give her your blessings. You really had me going there for a minute, pretending as if it was your very first encounter with Harry. I was almost fooled until he winked. A mighty fine actress you are though, mighty fine I must admit."

I didn't know what to say in response. So Beatrice hadn't lied after all.

"Ducking and diving for all those years," he continued. "There was a stage when I almost came over to tell you about them. I always knew you would understand you see. Any parent would of course, all a part of the mystery of loving one's child, but then it struck me that all the secrecy, gave them a sort of added *je ne sais quoi.*"

"A what?"

"French dear, added spark I only meant to say, I'm not certain that word was quite appropriate, but anyway. I mean their love was just so fierce and passionate. But well now just look at it, everything has just worked out perfectly. I was expecting a modern Romeo and Juliet, if it hadn't."

"Yes, I'm sure." I didn't know what else to say. After everything I had just heard, I didn't have the guts to tell him that her groom was not Harry.

"Shall I take that cup from you dear?"

I could not for the life of me remember handing it to him, but after several minutes in silence, I realized the seat beside me was now empty and as I looked around for Goldstone, I noticed that the park was becoming very much alive in the setting sun. What surprised me more than anything, was the sight of young fathers laughing with their children, whilst mothers rested lazily on benches. One lay upon a blanket, deeply absorbed in her book and another mum was holding out her mobile device, excitedly capturing the play between father and child.

"What are you looking at dear?" asked Mr Goldstone, his sudden re-appearance startling me.

"The spoilt women," I felt jealous. "I mean, when did fathers ever start becoming so active in entertaining their kids? Nothing of the sort ever happened when I was young. I barely saw my father. And even when he was home, he never cared to play with me. It all looks so wrong."

"Times certainly have changed dear," he laughed. "You know with my kids, it was pretty much the same as when you were a child. Changing nappies, doing the cooking, playing with the kids, it was all just a mother's job, so many years ago. That's just the way things were, but it didn't mean I didn't love them."

"I'm sorry Mr Goldstone. I wasn't trying to say you didn't. To be honest, I didn't even know you had children." In all the years I had known Mr Goldstone, it had never occurred to me that he could care for anything other than a four legged mongrel, for William and Arthur were the only names I had heard him singing along to, so many years ago. From '*Kings*' to '*Flowers*', I could not help but smile.

"Oh, indeed I do, my daughter is in France, happily married, given me three grandchildren to date. My son…well he is in India, living like a tramp in some ashram in Calcutta, after I had worked to the bone to provide him with the finest education money could buy. I was mortified with him. One of the finest advocates in London, he was. I visited him once, in India. I was going to bring him back home, mind you, even if I had to drag him by the hair. But I saw this serenity, a sort of aura in him and I realized that all the money in the world could never have given him such happiness. I always told Zendaya your anger would subside as mine did."

"Money cannot buy happiness. It's not the first time someone has tried to make me understand that today." I could not help but wonder if my meeting with Goldstone had not been a co-incidence after all. Instead, arranged by the masterful Beatrice. However, he said nothing further on the topic.

"It's a pity Zendaya's father never visited. She always yearned to be reunited with him, but what about your father dear, is he still alive."

Just when I was starting to feel normal I felt like I had run straight into a brick wall.

"No…my father…my father is gone. He is dead. He is dead and I never got to say goodbye," I said, emotionally breaking down as I heard my own words and as the tears streamed down my cheeks, I pressed my face against Goldstone's chest in an attempt to drown the sound that bellowed from my lungs.

"There, there dear. It will be alright."

As I attempted to speak in-between my tears, Goldstone nodded in acknowledgement of my confessions and if he didn't understand what I spoke of, or even if he could not hear what I said, I could not have been more grateful for the relief I felt from just resting my head against his chest. I felt safe.

"My father…dear God, my father…he…" as I wiped my nose against his tie, Mr Goldstone instantaneously offering me his handkerchief, "he was the man who followed me here. I saw him here…in the park…I know it was him…why couldn't he have left me alone. He still can't. He has haunted me all my life but now he really can. He stole my mother from me and now he is going to steal Zendaya too."

"Hush now dear, a man who is no longer alive can do nothing in the world to harm Zendaya."

"Oh, if only you knew!"

I lifted my head off Goldstone's chest and blew my nose into his handkerchief, returning it into his top pocket before he could advise otherwise. As I stood, I could feel my body trembling, and as I looked at all the happy families, I only cried more. I felt scared.

It had to have been a long time before Goldstone stood up to join me, for when his voice next interrupted my thoughts, my eyes were completely dry, not because I had calmed, but because I could produce no more tears to shed.

"Shall we take a walk then, dear?" asked Mr Goldstone. "I think a change of environment will do Mrs Gordon some good. Don't you think so now Daffodil?" he added childishly, touching the white dog's chin as he spoke. She barked responsively. Although his question had been more of an instruction, for his eyes had never met mine and neither had I answered, I was glad it had come, and I followed. After remembering the day I saw my father, every other memory was suddenly flooding back.

As we walked together silently, his dogs in the lead, I waited for him to ask his next question. However, my patience quickly ran dry. I was yearning to know what he thought of me. I had somehow miraculously managed to conceal my being unaware of Harry and Zendaya, but my success did not please me. Perhaps a response from him about Leiyah would prepare me for what would be in store, if I submitted to Beatrice's pleas and told Zendaya the tale she ought to have already been told.

"Do you not wish to know why it is I hated my father Mr Goldstone?" I asked as we exited the park, pausing at the crossroad.

"I only wish to be of service."

"I learnt of his death only yesterday, from the parcel Harry had delivered, you had just been stepping out for your morning walk."

"Oh, I'm so sorry dear. So that was what brought you to the park," I nodded, "I did not realize his death had only just occurred, be strong dear. We all have to go through it. It's the cycle of life. I suppose the wedding will have to be postponed. Zendaya must surely want to accompany you to South Africa for the funeral."

"No, she could not possibly. Zendaya did not even know my father was still alive. I had told her that my father's death was the reason I had left. That is how much I hated him." Even though my father had not been the only reason I had lied, I felt a sense of relief.

"We tend to do the strangest things out of love, Mrs Gordon."

"Mrs Gordon? Who is Mrs Gordon?" I yelled, grabbing my hair in anger. "That's the question Harry should have been asking Mr Goldstone. Not who is Leiyah Kleinhans?" From my sudden tantrum I expected Mr Goldstone's expression to alter to a look of disgust, but I failed to read his expression and so I continued. "You see I changed my name to Hannah Gordon when I moved here, Mr Goldstone. Leiyah Catherine Kleinhans, that's my real name, the real me, and Zendaya knows nothing about the life I lived in South Africa. It's not that I lied to her Mr Goldstone, it's just, I never had the guts to tell her. How can I expect Zendaya to listen to my tale now after all these years? The moment she learns that I was born under a different name, she will be repulsed. That alone will rob me of my daughter forever."

"Changing your name is really quite understandable, you felt threatened. And you are who you are, Mrs Gordon or Mrs Kleinhans…"

"Miss Kleinhans," I cut in far too cheekily.

"Well, even if I called you Daffodil or Dandelion you are the same woman you were in South Africa and nothing and no one could ever change that. If you intend on telling Zendaya the story of your life in South Africa, why don't you leave the names till the end. Just tell her Leiyah's story. Everything will be just fine." He smiled and unexpectedly gave me a tight hug. "I guess I have to say goodbye."

But I wasn't. I was not the same woman I had been in South Africa. Not in any way.

"Goodbye? Why?" I asked, puzzled as to why he would want to abruptly end such an intense conversation.

"Do you have your key or shall I knock?"

I could not believe we had already reached my door. I wanted to continue walking. I wanted to tell him everything. I wanted to know what he would think of me before I told Zendaya. I wanted to be completely prepared for what was still to come. I could hear the words in my head, but nothing came out of my mouth. Before I could respond to his question, the door had opened and Beatrice stood before me, staring at me like an angry mother who had been awaiting her defiant child.

"Well, let me leave you ladies to it then. Go rest now dear. Zendaya will understand. Remember you are the very same woman you were in South Africa." I felt a shiver, his departing words being the last thing I wanted to hear him repeat.

"I'm not," I whispered softly, "I'm not." As I stood under the street lamp watching Goldstone disappear into his house, I reassured myself that Goldstone was wrong.

Just before completely shutting the door, Mr Goldstone popped his head back out and called out, "Oh, Mrs Gordon…Mrs Kleinhans…oh forget the names…"

"Yes," I answered as one of the dogs attempted to escape.

"You are going to be an amazing Grandmother," he smiled before shutting the door.

My heart sank. So it was true. Even Goldstone knew Zendaya was pregnant.

I turned to see Beatrice mortified by the proof that had been delivered.

"Hannah Gordon and Leiyah Kleinhans are not the same!" I said to Beatrice.

"If you say so," she answered before retreating within.

I silently followed, closing the door behind me.

• • •

Curling up on the couch, after a sparse supper, I felt what I could only imagine to have been the very same doom any poor discriminated Jewish soul must have felt in the minutes prior to being gassed in the Holocaust. Well, except for one obvious key difference of course. I was praying for a faster annihilation. Instead, no toxic fumes engulfed me.

Could it really have been possible that neither Susannah nor her son had inherited the money? Well, there was only one way to find out. And so despite my reluctance I opened the yellow envelope and read it for myself.

On my first attempt, I could barely comprehend what I had read. And it took me several attempts before I could. Beatrice had been right. It was all mine! Everything I had run away from, was now legally mine.

I finally resorted to reading my father's journal and it was a little after 3:00 a.m. in the early hours of Sunday morning that I was finally able to close it.

Tip toeing past Zendaya's door, I quietly crept into Beatrice's room.

"B...B...wake up," I whispered, bending down onto my knees and rubbing her shoulder.

"What is it child?" her eyes still closed.

"Look at me B!" I said shaking her body more roughly.

"Oh child, not now," she moaned, shooing me away. "I'm sleeping. I know why you slapped me. Just go and put the light off!"

"I know what I need to do B. I'm going to give Zendaya the money. That way she will be able to marry Harry. I am right, aren't I?" I squeezed her hand. "I'm going to tell her in the morning. I'm going to tell her everything. My father threw in the towel. It is time I did too."

Her eyes shot open and Beatrice lovingly reached out to hold my hand.

"You were right B…I am going to tell Zendaya everything, everything about Karl and everything about Leiyah. Help me, will you B, please? I'm just not strong enough."

She took my hand and put it around the necklace. "She is with you always, and so am I. Get some rest now," she said, running her hand through my hair exactly the way I remembered, once upon a time.

"Can I…" I hesitated. It had been so long, "…beside you?"

She moved over and I crawled in under her sheet, her tribal singing finally taking me to the land of fairies and pixies, for a few hours at least.

SIX

Sunday

When I awoke Beatrice had gone. My head hurt and I had to remind myself of how I found myself to be there. I felt ashamed, so stupid. My mind was abuzz, trying to conjure an excuse plausible enough that my stature as Madam would be retained, when I re-joined Beatrice. Opening the door more discreetly than I had done when I entered, I peeped out. I could not possibly allow Zendaya to see such a sight. Scuttling into my bedroom, I dashed into the bathroom and tried to calm my nerves.

"IDIOT, IDIOT, IDIOT…" I muttered, staring at my tired face, teeth clenched.

There was a knock at the door.

"Zendaya…is that you?" I asked, praying she had not caught me in the act.

"No Madam, it's me."

"Oh, what do you want?" I deliberately snapped.

"I brought you something to eat."

"Well I did not ask you to!" I shouted, opening the bathroom door and frowning at her angrily.

"Well Madam, just try, it's going to be a long day. We will meet you downstairs."

Before I could think of something to say, she was gone. She still knew her place. Thank God for that!

• • •

It sat there like a ticking time bomb. The fear I had felt the morning it had arrived, two days earlier, reawakened. I have been sitting here, staring at the box for more than an hour now. Out of sight, out of mind, really now Hannah? How could I have been foolish enough to believe anything could ever be that simple? I cannot eat. I feel sick. My God! I never thought I would see the day. Am I actually going to tell Zendaya the truth? Everything I have worked so hard to conceal. She has been slipping though my fingers, for years now. If I tell her, she is gone. That I can be certain of! She will never speak to me again. I ought to have destroyed it myself when I had the chance. But maybe Beatrice is right, there is a reason she had not gotten to that stage.

As they joined me in the Living room, they had both been engrossed in a hushed exchange which I had no doubt, revolved around Harry. They became silent upon the sight of me.

"So B says you have something to tell me," said Zendaya, being quick to break the silence.

"Yes I do," I answered.

"Well out with it then! I have a hell of a lot on my mind right now and frankly you don't deserve a bloody second of my time. You are so damn lucky, Beatrice here convinced me to stay, so Spill!"

"Zendaya child, don't speak so rudely to your mother. You need to hear this," scolded Beatrice.

The scene, such a replica of what had occurred the previous morning with Peyton, I felt hopeless. How was I going to get Zendaya to listen to my tale if there was already such malice? I had not even mentioned the delivery yet, let alone shown her what it contained, and that was only just the beginning.

"I'm sorry B. Go on then."

'*Goodbye child,*' I thought, as I watched Zendaya cosy up under a blanket on the couch across from me, her head resting on Beatrice's lap.

The moment had arrived.

"Well this arrived from South Africa on Friday," I said, not wasting any time at all, I lifted the box off the coffee table and set it on my knee, "I guess you could consider it to be a wedding present for you, now that I think about it," I said, removing both the diary and the yellow envelope. The little treasure box, I had decided to let remain in the box. After all, it ought to have been at my mother's gravesite.

"Oh! I'm so excited Mother. Finally! You always refuse to talk about South Africa," with an unexpected jovial tone of voice she sprung up with childish ecstasy. "Oh, it looks so exotically ancient. This must be genuine leather, surely, and green. I love green, mesmerizing!"

"Yes, well you will never find another like it, that is for certain," I said, looking towards Beatrice and wondering whether she would add commentary for she fully understood the meaning behind what I said. At that moment however, she had eyes for only Zendaya, or so it seemed.

"Mother, what is the meaning of this? It has already been used." The extremities of the cover finally surpassing the desires of her satisfaction she opened it to disdain. "Is this some sort of joke? You really can be vile Mother. How could it possibly be a wedding present if it has been used? What are in these envelopes?" she said, the few envelopes hidden within, falling out as she continued flipping the pages to find that even the very last page had been sealed with writing upon it.

"It's the writing on the pages that is the present child," added Beatrice, looking towards me with a nod of encouragement as I set the box down.

Zendaya, however, still appeared disgruntled. "What is this?" she asked, pointing to the A4 sized yellow envelope.

"It is someone's Will," I answered.

"A Will? What on Earth! Yikes Mother! How could you possibly end up with someone's Will?" she asked in disbelief. "Who's Will?"

"*Bass, Baas* is dead! He is dead! I promised him I would come back and now he is gone," intervened Beatrice, her tears raining forth once more.

"Oh God, B, don't cry. Hush now, he must have been old Beatrice, if he was your *Baas,* surely," said Zendaya, planting a kiss upon her cheek and wrapping her arms tightly around her. "And all this time, I have been talking about no one but myself. How could I have been so selfish not to see your pain B?"

Forgotten once more, I watched, but to be ignored at that moment, I could not have felt happier.

"But I thought you always worked for Mother? Who is this *Baas?* You never mentioned anyone being your *Baas*, B."

"Before I called your mother Madam, before she could even be born, Karl Kleinhans was my *Baas* and his father, Johan, was before him."

"You don't have to talk about it, B, if you don't want to," offered Zendaya, soothingly rubbing her shoulder.

"No, I must child. I want to tell you his story, I need to tell you her story," she said firmly, wiping away her tears before blowing her nose with the same cloth.

"Who is he? It's ok, never mind, just take your time Beatrice."

"There is so much I wish to tell you about *Baas*. Karl Kleinhans, my KK. Oh Zendaya, if you had only met him! He was no everyday man. He was a rich man, a headstrong man, a handsome man, I could never forget. But I will and have always believed that he was a good man. But it is not just Karl's story. It is Leiyah's story. And who was Leiyah, I know you are going to ask me, child. Well, Leiyah was his daughter. She wasn't perfect, Leiyah was not, but if anything, she was just a child. There are things she did that you may think so wrong but she did them out of love. Hear her story and then tell me if you still want me to see to the RSVP's. But I think I shall start at the very beginning, of everything I remember." Zendaya nodded and at that moment, I knew that Beatrice had kept her promise from the previous night.

Beatrice was actually about to relay my story. It felt surreal. If I had ever slapped her, it must surely have been in a parallel universe. Would she speak of things I would rather her not, I wondered.

Her lips parted and my heart skipped a beat as I felt a sudden sense of panic, but then they met again and Beatrice turned towards me. She smiled. The smile I knew spoke only of her motherly love. She would not let me down, her eyes promised, and at that moment I instantly calmed and waited to hear what words she would speak next.

. . .

SEVEN

Lungisiwe had been the name the Induna of our village had thought best matched me and so my mother agreed, but the day I arrived at Kleinhans Estate, my name would change to Beatrice.

In all of South Africa, Kwa-Zulu Natal was the most uphill and downhill of lands you would ever get to walk on. But dry and barren it never was. Bushes growing dense and forests that grew tall. Springs became streams and streams became rivers, all flowing to the coast like the veins across my hand.

When my mother used to visit once a year, if I was lucky, maybe twice, she always brought a present. On my fourth birthday she brought me a pram without a doll. It was a very special birthday, but not because of the pram. The pram, I didn't quite understand what it was supposed to do, but it proved useful when carrying the food to the animals. I once used it to bring home the eggs and my grandfather gave me an awful hiding since most of them broke. But it was on that birthday that she told me the story of the Kleinhans Estate, all its money, all its beauty and how they owned a gold mine, a magic place where yellow rocks came from, and after hearing it, I made a promise to my mother that one day, I too would live at Kleinhans Estate. She had overheard a story that her Madam had been telling their young son, Karl, and so she told it to me. I was fascinated. When my mother visited, she spoke only isiZulu but I shall tell you her words in English.

"Guess what Lungi, I have a secret to tell you," she said as I sat on her lap, outside the *rondavel*. "Do you want to know why the land looks so up and down," I had nodded excitedly and she kissed my forehead, "The land, where we live was once all flat, but not now child. Many years ago, so long ago that the people, not even animals had come to make South Africa their home, when the stars fell!"

"*Haibo*! No! Really *uMama*?" I asked pointing up at the stars in disbelief.

"Really my child. They crashed on the earth and some of those same stars left holes in the ground that the white people call a gorge. Some of those stars, had hit the ground at the very same moment," and she banged her feet against the ground, hard and close, "so hard and so close together that they had pushed the land between them up towards the sky, leaving behind the mountains that still stood before us." I hugged her, feeling so proud.

Kleinhans Estate had made my mother clever and it would make me clever too.

I asked my mother if I could go back with her to the house where she worked and learn stories about the world just like the ones she told, but it was only when I had turned eight that she finally took me, old enough to look after myself and help her out too.

If my mother's stories alone had made me excited about Kleinhans Estate, I was still to learn how I would feel about meeting the people that lived there. They were the first white people I would ever set eyes on. Mrs Kleinhans was as white as the clouds on a sunny day, while Mr Kleinhans's skin reminded me of the underneath of a cow; pale, but he had more colour than his wife. They scared me and I stayed away, but if ever I went too close, they made me think I smelled. They were forever shouting at me, my mother too, and I began to wonder why my mother spoke of Kleinhans Estate with such excitement. It took me more than a year before I understood the words they spoke and I would find out in time that being chosen to work for such a rich family, my mother believed to be a blessing. The house was after all a palace compared to our village and our *kraal* and after seeing such a sight, well I guess…well who would ever want to leave.

If learning to speak a new language is difficult for everyone, I was quite shocked to discover that the Kleinhans spoke two and I was trying to learn two in the belief that they were one. English was the one I started to get right. It was the language the black workers spoke to each other, even after work. It was so much easier than the Afrikaans. I always thought it funny when my mother and I would mix up the English, isiZulu and Afrikaans.

Mr and Mrs Kleinhans might have been scary, but their son... Oh their son Karl! He was so different, he was someone else, even though he was only ten and still a child, always full of laughter and smiles. His skin had much more colour. A little yellow I called it. My mother used to tell me it was because he used to love to run around outside and that if he stayed inside long enough, he would start looking like his mother. I wanted my skin colour to change too and so I scrubbed my face so hard I was left with scratches on my skin and my mother gave me a solid spanking with a stick. A worse hiding than grandfather had given me, when he had punished me with his belt, for the eggs that had broken on my pram.

To Mr and Mrs Kleinhans, Lungisiwe was too Zulu a name and as they had done with all their black workers, they gave me an English name that they could more easily pronounce and so Beatrice is what everyone started to call me when the Estate became my home. The name felt like such an honour at my young age but only as an adult, did I realise that it had been nothing more than an insult. Even my mother started calling me Beatrice, everyone except for Karl. Lungisiwe, he continued to call me and my Zulu name felt even more special.

I remember the first day I met Karl as if it was yesterday. He gave me a piece of chocolate and kept saying "Karl". I thought that 'Karl' was what I needed to say if I wanted more of the sweet thing in my mouth and the game of understanding each other kept us full of laughter. He pointed at me and said "Lungi". He pointed at himself and said "Karl". Then he took a stick and wrote the name Karl Kleinhans in the wet sand. I took the stick from him and pointing to the words as he had, I repeated what I could not read. What I had recognized were some of the letters. I pointed at the first letter and said "K". Taking the stick out of my hand, he pointed to the beginning of the second word "K" he said. I bent down and ran my finger over both the large K's. "KK" I said. He laughed and from that moment Karl Kleinhans became 'My KK'.

The Kleinhans house stood on a hill overlooking the land they owned, the back of the house facing the most majestic scenery, something I had heard many people speak of as being strange, since that was the job of the front of any house. Well how was I supposed to understand them as a child if my *rondavel* village house had been built in the shape of a circle. But after coming here to England, believe me, when I say I never travelled to very many places in South Africa besides my village and the Estate. Well, here in England I got a chance to learn of so many things, I would never have known of, if only South Africa had been my home, and from what I learnt, the front of the house should have been the prettier side. But I guess in those years of apartheid, all that really mattered was that it was the side of the house that the whites entered from.

Anyway, where was I…oh yes, well, I guess you could say Kleinhans Estate was like Buckingham Palace, built to be beautiful from every angle. When people came to visit, they would stand at the back of the house and I would laugh from the look on their faces and their complete silence. They would stand still and stare as if they were under a spell, for far longer than I could balance on one foot, and believe me, I was very good at balancing when I was young.

Although only a little stream flowed through the valley at the back, someone had built a very clever dam. In the distance, on the right, the Drakensberg could be seen, and a forest stood to the left, the trees crawling down all the way to the water's edge. Pine trees stood tall across the water's edge. It was not very far from town, but it wasn't very close either, but in those first few weeks, everyday was a new adventure and little Karl became my friend and although he was two years older than me, I started looking after him the way I used to look after the chickens upon grandfather's farm, but he soon quickly meant more than any newly hatched chick.

We were two children who just wanted to have fun.

Things about Karl started to change after the summer he was packed off to some sort of fancy boarding school near Pietermaritzburg, the prestigious Hilton College. My mother told me that it was where all the richest of the rich boys were sent to be groomed. I had asked my mum, why he could not just be groomed in the stable. She laughed uncontrollably and told all the other servants, who mocked me for a week. I had never had a chance to attend school and well I guess Kleinhans Estate had not made me as clever as I thought it would. About the outside world, I had in fact really learnt very little and most of what I had learnt, I would, in time, discover to be nothing more than a story.

Hilton College was a school his mother could not stop telling everyone about. He stopped coming back to visit me in the servant houses at the Estate. My mother told me that it wasn't me and she scolded me when I used to cry. She had heard his parents talk about keeping him away for a while but they regularly visited him, instead of bringing him to see me, taking him all across the country, on ship cruises and planes. How I dreamt he would ask if I could join.

When Karl finally did return, he had already turned eighteen. With his schooling finally over, the day I had been longing for, did not take place, the way I had expected. I had been walking up the hill towards the house, balancing a bucket of freshly squeezed milk on my head, when he came speeding up the driveway, driving an open-top car, filled with young men who looked a lot like him. All of them, I had never seen before. He looked so very different but I recognized him immediately. As he jumped off the car, immediately starting to offload it, he stopped to gaze at the view he loved and I waved at him excitedly, but he only turned away as if he had not seen me. The other young men laughed when they saw my foolish wave. I was stunned and quickly stopped when I realized no one would wave back. Was that really my KK? But then I quickly reminded myself that I probably looked very different too and he must not have recognized me.

"Hey Karl, this one here seems to like you," said the young man with the broadest shoulders. "Hey but I can never understand them, why must they always go and put things on their head. You would think they were practising for the circus or something. Hey Pieter, do you want to ask her to teach you some tricks."

"*Voetsek!*" shouted the young man, who must have been Pieter, pushing him roughly against the car.

"Would you mind if I give it a test run," said the third more muscular man who had been tossing a rugby ball up in the air, "Oh don't look at me that way Karl, as if the thought never crossed your mind, mighty fine for one of them black ones. Anyway, what difference would it make if I scored a touchdown? She would just pack the kid off to the farm, no fuss." He did a slow motion action of aiming the ball at me and just before it looked like he was about to throw it straight at me, he tossed the ball up into the air instead. I quickly put the bucket down with fright. I knew I was different but not even Mr or Mrs Kleinhans had so openly called me black.

Karl said nothing and only continued to walk away and I could not have felt more relieved than when Mr Johan Kleinhans's hoarse voice echoed his welcomes through the valley, the boys finally walking away.

I stayed as much away from the main house as I could while the men stayed there, and it was only on the second Sunday since he had arrived, that Karl remembered I lived there.

"I knew I would find you here," Karl spoke so sweetly.

I had been sitting along the banks of the dam gazing up at the stars, my feet in the water in between the trees in the little clearing, we had so often met.

"Where are your friends?" I asked.

"I'm sorry about my friends Beatrice. It's just the way it is. I just I wanted to tell you for myself that I will be leaving for England tomorrow" he answered, ignoring my question.

"And you tell me this today because..? What do you expect me to say?" I looked towards him, horrified.

"I just wanted to tell you sorry and goodbye, that's all. Goodbye

Beatrice!"

He turned and walked away without even a handshake. It was a quick 'goodbye' before he had even uttered his 'hello'. It was the first time he had ever called me Beatrice but I knew he would never call me Lungisiwe again. I had wanted to ask him why he needed to say sorry now, ask him why he had not said anything then, for his friends to hear on the day he had first returned, but I knew he just wasn't my KK anymore. He was now a white man and I was his black maid. The man whom I had thought of every morning, upon waking, was gone and if it was not difficult enough for me, feeling I had been living my entire teenage life without seeing him, it would be several years before I ever saw Karl again. However Karl chose to think of me, nothing could ever remove him from my heart.

My mother sent me to marry and I had a child of my own. But my mother's stories were just stories and I promised myself that the Estate would not become their home. That they would go to school, unlike me, even if it was just a rural school.

After spending three years in my rural village, I left my child behind and returned to the Kleinhans Estate after being begged to do this by my mother. Mrs Kleinhans suddenly took ill, all the servants knew it was Tuberculosis but none of the whites would dare say that was what killed her. Well even if they did deny it, the workers knew what it was, because my mother became ill in the same way too, just months later. Not going to see a doctor until it was far too late to be saved. But Tuberculosis, was what he called it, TB he had said, when I could not pronounce it. The white doctors seldom even cared to give us their full attention anyway, but my mother died only a few weeks after Mrs Kleinhans was buried.

Karl's mother was buried across from the forest, on the flat land not far from the water's edge, her tombstone faced the house, although I found this new found burial ground to be sticking out like burnt grass, many called it peaceful. Well, it was surrounded by such beauty after all, I could not argue, but I wished they had buried her somewhere else.

On the day of Mrs Kleinhans's funeral, Karl finally remembered where it was that he had been born, at least, that is how I thought of it, but who will ever know the real reason he returned, because when he did, he behaved as if he was just another visitor and to someone who did not know the family, they would have never guessed that he was the son of the woman being buried. It was half way through the priest's speech that Karl decided to make his appearance with a young lady, I did not recognise, at his side. I had never seen a woman with lighter hair before. She was definitely younger than him but she did not look very much older than me, whatever her age, she was behaving like a child. She giggled constantly and I kicked a stone towards her in the hope that she would stop. It hit her quite hard on her ankle and she only fussed more. I was pleased she had felt some pain. It was clear that they were lovers but what Karl saw in her, I could not understand. I was jealous.

I was glued to the sight of the coffin being lowered into the ground, awaiting the moment when Karl's muscular arms would once more heave a shovel, but he did not join his father in picking up a spade of soft red sand from the earth. The old Mr Kleinhans summoned Karl but the young woman immediately whispered into his ear and he turned away in silence.

"Karl, I am so happy to see you," I said giving him a tight squeeze after the funeral. "Please tell me you will be staying. We have been struggling to keep order without you. Your father has not been himself and my mother is ill and…"

"John, this is how the King of Russia got killed baby," snapped the annoying woman.

I frowned. Karl had always hated the name Johan being his middle name, that being the first name of his father. But to John he did not object. Had this woman completely changed him?

"Beatrice I want you to meet my wife, Mary Anne," he said, a look of guilt on his face as his eyes met my own.

Wife! I pinched my fingers. It had to be a nightmare. Marriage was a must. I knew he would marry someday but why now. He was only twenty-three and that young witch. I closed my eyes wishing she would disappear once they re-opened, but there she still stood.

I wanted to slap him and if his mother could rise from the dead I could picture her marching up the hill and doing just that. Slapping him the way she had once slapped my mother when her favourite dress had been burnt with the iron. Had she learnt of this news before her death? Perhaps the servants had been wrong and the words priest had spoken at the sermon were true. Perhaps she had died of a heart attack? How could he have made such an idiotic decision?

"Why on earth are you explaining yourself to her?" asked Mary Ann.

"Well she runs the house you see, my dear," he answered.

"What on earth are you saying John? Can you hear yourself, this creature run our palace? Your mother did that and now I will. You cannot trust these sort of people John, you are still jet-lagged, my poor darling," Mary Anne continued, "These sort are diseased, diseased I tell you. Use my soaps, it's on my bed and go have a quick hot soak in the tub before any of her disease seeps in." said the miserable woman with colourless hair.

Karl's expression was unreadable. I could not believe what I had just heard. After gazing at his wife for several seconds, he glanced at me looking almost helpless.

"Go now then! Unless you wish to force me to spend the night in a different room," YELLED Mary Anne, as if scolding a child.

Karl turned and marched up the stairs.

"And you, you little wretch," she shouted at me, shaking her finger at me, her eyes looking as terrifying as the bats I saw at night, "don't you ever think you can just go and call my husband Karl ever again. Call him Sir. Do you understand what I am saying? Does this creature speak English?" she asked old Mr Kleinhans.

"Yes, but they can't help being dumb," he answered, sounding the least bit interested.

"I'm just trying to get this imbecile here to comprehend that if she dare utter the word Karl again, I will send her to *Prison*. Sir and Madam is what she will be calling us, her new Masters." Mary Anne's back towards me, the whole time she spoke, her hands on her hips, her gaze following old Mr Kleinhans who had been lumbering up the stairs.

"*Baas* and Madam, she ought to understand that well enough," said old Mr Kleinhans, not bothering to turn around.

"Well then wretch, *Baas* and Madam it will still be because I am the new Madam around here."

"Mr Johan Kleinhans is my *Baas*," I answered, as I walked away, uninterested in her childish tantrum.

Well perhaps I should not have had such a quick mouth for Mrs Kleinhans grave would not be left to stand all on its own for very long, not even for six months for Mr Kleinhans shot himself only a few months later.

And so from that moment onwards, Karl did become *Baas*. From what I have already said, I know you have already guessed that I did not like Mary Anne at first, but Karl worshipped her and so I warmed to her in time, but only just for him.

Mary Anne was a selfish woman who cared for no one but herself. When old Mr Kleinhans died, he was buried alongside his wife as anyone would expect and Mary Anne Kleinhans promoted herself to be the Grand Madam of the Kleinhans Estate. That was what she demanded to be called, not just Madam but Grand Madam. So grand a Madam she was, she did not even bother to attend the funeral of her father-in-law. I was pleased with her decision. At least Karl was not denied the opportunity to respect his father at the funeral. If Karl instructed the other workers to call her Grand Madam, I refused, of course, but he did not scold me. The look on his face often showing irritation, each time she demanded the title. But still he loved her, even if he was embarrassed.

After she became the head of the house she was very much in her own world, though speaking of nothing but England. She never seemed to like the Estate or South Africa for that matter, and kept saying England had died. At first I thought England was a person until I remembered it was the place where Karl had gone to live, the place where he had fallen under her spell. After all I could see no other explanation as to how he could love such a woman.

After the death of old Mr and Mrs Kleinhans I was surprised at how little work I seemed to have and I managed to make an unplanned trip to see my son but instead of feeling unexplained joy, I felt scared. My child looked so different I would not have recognised him had he not been playing in my grandmother's arms.

Despite the joys of being re-united with my son, I yearned to once more walk upon the grounds of Kleinhans Estate. I realized it had become a part of me and it needed me as much as I needed it. I had even started to miss all the work old Mrs Kleinhans used to create out of nothing at all and I returned to the Estate hoping to find that Mary Anne had gotten over her obsession with England and I would find myself once more occupied by never-ending instructions. But that did not happen.

When I returned to Kleinhans Estate, the so called Grand Madam was furious with me, throwing everything that could be moved in my direction, she claimed that she had never given me permission to leave in the first place and so she dismissed me. To make matters worse, she refused to even give me my month's pay, claiming that it was my duty to replace what she had destroyed. The nerve of the woman!

I was heartbroken when Karl did not object. After all, it had been him, who had permitted me to leave.

So much for the Estate needing me!

• • •

EIGHT

Rather than the village of her birth, I had always known that Beatrice had regarded the Estate in Dargle as her real home, but her friendship with my father I knew nothing of. She was clearly distraught and as I studied her face, the pain she had managed to keep hidden from me for so many years was clearly visible. What she felt for my father was true love in its greatest form. To love someone and watch them marry once was heart-breaking but Beatrice had been a spectator to him marrying not once but twice. Not only had he married my mother but Susannah too. However had she survived it? I began to wonder which great love story I ought to compare their love to, was it *Romeo and Juliet*? No, they did not die for each other so it could not be that, perhaps *Pride and Prejudice*? No, how silly, Elizabeth Bennet, did after all her drama, get the hand of the esteemed Mr Darcy. Oh, of course, why had it not immediately crossed my mind? It just had to be the epic *Wuthering Heights*. The upper class Catherine Earnshaw and Heathcliff, the poor unaccepted gypsy sort, yes transfixed in a love that was doomed to fail, except in this case, poor Beatrice was more of a Gypsy Cathy castaway and my father the upper class Heathcliff.

Dargle, which fell into an area almost in the heart of Kwa-Zulu Natal commonly called the Midlands Meander of the province, had indeed become a home to Beatrice when she was but a child, but after listening to her tale, I wished that she had never walked upon the grounds of the Estate. It almost seemed a punishment that she had, it was a punishment she had been born black. Had it not been the case, had she been born white, the daughter of Karl's Tutor perhaps, might not she herself, become the next Mrs Kleinhans? The bitter words she always spoke towards my mother, for the very first time, made sense. 'My KK' made sense.

"Gosh Beatrice what a story, how I wish you had shared it with me before," said Zendaya to Beatrice as she wipes away the tear that had just rolled down Beatrice's cheek. Beatrice held her head in her hands, her mind clearly swirling with thoughts. "Oh, that awful Mary Anne, what a wicked dreadful woman that spoilt Mary Anne was. Oh my B! You should have just walked out the moment he brought her there. I mean the way she spoke to you at the funeral, the nerve! How strange for her to be such a racist when Britain had no such laws," continued Zendaya.

I could feel Zendaya's wrath as she spoke. To listen to Beatrice speak of my mother was one thing, but to listen to Zendaya voice her agreement, I felt like a block of ice being melted over a fierce fire. What was to become of my life, how would I ever survive? The secret itself I had not even come close to disclosing.

I felt an intense sense of anger at Beatrice for painting my father as being such a saint, whilst she painted my mother as the complete opposite. Just because Beatrice thought of my mother as being a heartless villain, did not mean she was one. Why had I not intervened in the telling of her tale when she had first spoken of kicking a stone against my mother's shoe? I had after all been aware that it was at my grandmother's funeral that Beatrice had had her first encounter with my mother. I needed to tell Zendaya that Mary Anne was a good wife and the best mother I could have ever asked for. I knew I should say something but why could I not muster up the courage to do so? A part of me wanted to shout out and thank the heavens for ridding the world of a Monster, tell Zendaya that Karl had been the devil himself and had it not been for him we, all three of us, wouldn't be in such a mess. But I couldn't. I couldn't because that meant I would have to say I was Leiyah. Was I ready to?

Zendaya was now seated upon the floor, her head resting against Beatrice's lap. The entire time Beatrice spoke she had sat, listening in silence, lovingly massaging Beatrice's fingers. But now that Beatrice had stopped talking, she lifted her head and looked up towards her with concern.

"You loved him, didn't you Beatrice? Your *Baas?*" she said to Beatrice, the tone with which she spoke, answering her own question.

"Yes, I did. I loved him then and I still love him now. There are times I almost believed he loved me too. He will always be mine. 'My KK', no one else's."

Beatrice shook her head and clicked her tongue, her emotions clearly getting the better of her. While she sounded frustrated from the events she had just recalled, the tears had already welled up in my eyes, not out of sympathy but out of malice. My body trembled. Could it ever be possible that Beatrice had played a role in provoking my mother to her death? Goodness, no, I quickly dismissed such a notion. That had completely been my father's doing. Had it not been for Beatrice, my father might have driven me to my death too and a great many years ago at that.

"So I guess that is when you started working for my mother," said Zendaya.

"Not exactly," answered Beatrice. "I did not return to the Estate for a full three years and in that time, I gave birth to a second son. I relearnt how to smile and even laugh. Things that Grand Madam made sure I never did and had she not fired me, I'm sure she would have erased it from my memory completely. You know, Zendaya, I was so glad that wicked woman did fire me. Had she not ordered me to leave the Estate, I never would have gotten a second chance to experience what it felt like to be a *real* mother."

"Whatever do you mean?" asked Zendaya, a look of confusion on her face.

"I mean the joys of motherhood. The first time around I had surely been too young to understand what a blessing it was to be pregnant. Feel those first kicks of new life inside your very own tummy. The feeling when the baby grips your nipples and sucks the milk you have produced in your very own breasts." Suddenly awakened to reality, Beatrice looked at us both regretfully. She knew she had broached a topic which neither Zendaya nor I wished to contribute to. "Well anyway it must not have been that important," she continued quickly, trying to undo any damage, "because I never had another child and I left my sons in the care of my mother."

"Oh the idea of balancing a baby in my arms for an hour, while it hurts my nipples, well I could never see myself doing that," said Zendaya, "I will leave mine in a crèche or just hire a nanny. Not that I have had the time to think about that," she added quickly, throwing me a quick glance.

"Of course," I replied, finally finding the courage to muster up two words. I watched Zendaya's facial expression with the utmost curiosity wondering if she had just revealed the truth of her pregnancy.

"But B," said Zendaya, "you speak of such a love with your children, well I mean even to have a child you need a man. You did say you got married. What happened to your husband? You must have had feelings for him too."

"He died while I was still in South Africa, but our marriage had been arranged, as all Zulu marriages in my custom were. I did not love him and neither did he love me. We were like animals who had to just, at some point mate, I guess. As a husband it was his job to take care of me but he never even did that and when he died, his family acted as if they did not even know who I was. I did not care, but I did feel sorry for my sons though. But at least I knew my own family could be trusted to see to them."

"Oh how I wish you had spoken of your sons more. So what next B? What exactly made you leave the Estate and work for my Mother and come with her to live here in England," asked Zendaya, quickly changing the topic.

I could suddenly feel my heartbeat in my throat once more.

"*uJesu*! How I came to England?" Beatrice looked towards me and nodded reassuringly before turning back towards Zendaya. "Well that my sweet child is still a very long story. I truly do not know how to carry on telling you about it but excuses have been made long enough. I have to warn you though child, it is a very long story indeed. Maybe you might like a snack first."

"No, no, no, not at all! I am far too excited to eat right now," answered Zendaya.

"You Madam?"

Shaking my head was all I could manage, for I felt far too sick to even swallow my own spit.

"Shall I go on then?"

I nodded with mixed emotions relieved that she would still be speaking, but at the same time anxious and scared as to what she would say.

"Zendaya are you ready to listen again my child?" asked Beatrice turning her attention now completely to her.

"Oh yes B, to every word, I'm all ears," she answered.

"Well, there are a few more things that were sent with the box. But wait, before I show it to you, I think there is a little more I need to share with you. Let's see, now where was I…"

· · ·

NINE

The hole that had been left at Kleinhans Estate was as deep as the gold mines they blasted. Nothing could fill the damage to make it what it once was.

Thembi, the only other servant I had trusted with my friendship, had sent me word of her endless troubles. It would have become her task to keep order after I had left and as I read her letter, it was clear that it was all far too much for her to handle, she was still only a teen after all.

But God it seems could see that that the deaths at Kleinhans Estate had left too great a pain for anyone to bear and I would soon learn that the Almighty had decided on another addition to my old home, apart from that of the Grand Madam, one that I prayed would this time heal it. But who should share with me that news but Karl himself.

My baby tied to my back, my older son running around me as I made my way back to the *kraal*, the firewood we had collected stacked high in my hands, my body suddenly froze, my boy tripping over my legs as my feet stopped moving. Was it really Karl, or was I imagining that the man I had thought I would never see again, was pacing the land in front of my house.

Spotting me, he waved excitedly before putting his hands together as if saying thank you to God.

I placed down the wood and waved back, wanting to walk quickly and slowly at the same time.

"Is this your baby?" he asked.

I nodded.

"Both of them?"

"Yes," I could just about force myself to speak and so I gave him the shortest answers necessary.

"Do they have the same father?"

I was stunned and it took me a while before I responded. He sounded like a Kleinhans. I never thought the day would come and it made me think about when his mother had demanded proof of who my father was? I had never known who my father was but not knowing him or what his job in my life was, is I guess, what made me not miss him. I suppose it would have been different if I had gone to school where all the children I played with had a father, but the only child I knew who spoke of a father was Karl, and Old Mr Kleinhans was a horrible man so what was there to miss in a father, I would never understand.

I was born out of wedlock, you see, and my mother had cried herself sick that night and she finally told me once she had stopped crying that Mrs Kleinhans had demanded I be kept away from Karl until she could produce the proof on paper that both my mother and I did not have 'it', the 'it' being HIV/AIDS. My English still improving, I was very confused as to why my mother cried. Was being an AID not being a good worker. I thought my mother should feel proud. I could not understand why she was crying if Mrs Kleinhans had called her an AID, for once saying something kind but it was Karl who would eventually explain that AIDS was actually an illness that made you die a painful death and it was not unusual with black people because the men who went to the cities often had children with woman who were not their wives, and very few white people ever got it because the whites would never do such horrible things. It only gave me another reason to wish I had been born white.

I couldn't believe he had asked such a question. Whilst my thoughts had drifted to the past, I wondered if I had heard correctly. I mean the idea of me having children from different men having crossed his mind, made me completely disappointed in him. But from the look on his face, as he waited awkwardly, I could tell that that question had been asked and he knew it was more stupid than inappropriate and growing up with me as he had, he should have known better.

"You are actually asking me if they have the same father! Well, of course they do," I answered, "and he is not just their father, he is my husband." I wanted to add that my children did not have HIV/AIDS either just like my mother and I had tested negative so many years ago but I didn't, knowing I would only upset myself further.

"What! Your husband! You…you married? Why didn't you tell me?" Karl looked away clearly upset.

"You did not tell me when you decided to marry that Grand Madam of yours, did you?" The number of years I had been a wife being more than the number of years he had been a husband, I did not bring to his attention, but from the age of my older son he should have surely figured that out.

"Yes but I did not think you would ever have a relationship with any one. I mean do you love this man…your husband?"

For the first time in all the years I had ever known him, I realized he could be selfish. I had, of course, been a married woman when Karl had returned for his father's funeral but chosen not to say anything, but if I had ever known it would make him show any emotions that he even slightly cared about me, I would have reminded him of it every time his childish wife treated me like cattle.

"Why should you be allowed to find love and not me? Was I supposed to spend my life all alone just because you could not find a way to marry me?"

Karl looked stunned and so was I. I could not believe what I had just said. Had I finally found the courage to say aloud what he could never say? Maybe or maybe not, perhaps it wasn't really a moment of showing my true strength but my turn to be stupid instead and I could not be more grateful to my first born, who, clearly bored of listening to the conversation he could not understand, rescued me by kicking one of the chickens.

I scolded him in isiZulu for far longer than he needed a scolding and then ordered him to carry the wood indoors acting as if my supervising him was needed. He knew exactly what needed to be done, but it gave Karl and I enough time to forget what I had just said.

If it had not been forgotten, at least Karl managed to act as if I had never practically said that I should have been his wife when he next spoke.

"The house is so beautiful. It's a *rondavel* isn't it? Such a perfectly circular shape, I mean it's built without machines and its geometry is so perfect. Like the perfect triangles of the pyramids," he smiled looking towards the mountains.

I smiled at how he could possibly call my *rondavel* such a beauty as compared to his house which was big enough to keep my entire village, but I was just happy he had changed the topic.

"Yes, it is called a *rondavel*. My father and grandfather built it themselves," I answered.

"I love the way your son helped with the wood. The running of your house is so perfectly seen to. Well you see that is why I need you to come back. I need you to run the house for me Beatrice."

"What! Your wife was enjoying that job just fine when I left. I thought she never wanted to see me again."

"She is no longer herself. She wants to go back to England but she can't."

"Why not? She would make so many people happy if she were gone," I knew I sounded far too bitter but I didn't care.

He looked into my eyes and we stood in awkward silence until my older son reappeared and I shooed him away.

"She can't go because…" he hesitated, rubbing the back of his head he turned towards the setting sun, staring at it for so long that I began to wonder whether I should say something about its beauty but before I could he turned to me and continued, "she is expecting a child and well some strange things have been happening. Thembi just cannot seem to manage and you are the only person I trust."

Not only was he married but he was about to become a father too. There really was no going back in time.

"But I have children now," I said.

"I will double even triple your salary and you can bring your boys as soon as everything is more settled."

I thought about my children's future and what the money would mean for them. Their entire lives would be changed for the better with that amount of money but to be bossed by Mary Anne again. I had promised myself long ago that I would never take my children there, so it would mean I would have to sacrifice being a mother. Would it all be worth it?

"What about my husband?"

Karl took out his box of cigarettes, lit one and took a few long puffs before he replied, "Well the Estate is the only place you have ever worked, so I really don't think he will say 'No'."

"I don't think he will."

"But if I need to offer him a job at the Estate to make you come back to Dargle, then I will.

"No, he is happy where he is," I quickly replied. The last thing I wanted was to have to wash his clothes and cook his food every evening in addition to everything else. What else did woman in loveless marriages do after all?

"That's good."

"Yes it is. But if I do return I will only be returning on one condition."

"What's that?"

"Don't ever expect me to call her Grand Madam again."

"Agreed," Karl instantaneously said, "you need not call her any name other than the one she had been born with."

I was stunned. Karl so quickly agreeing that I never had to address his wife by her self-given title of Grand Madam was not what I had expected. From the look on his face I realised he really was desperate, desperate not just for a housekeeper but desperate for someone he could trust, desperate for me.

"Well I will have to think about it."

He threw his cigarette to the ground, barely a quarter of it smoked, stamped out the light and pulled my body towards him, hugging me so tight I thought he had suffocated my sleeping baby. Untying the shawl and quickly swinging him around from his station on my back, I checked that he was well and placed him on the floor, the shawl cushioning him so well that he still slept soundly.

"Thank you! Thank you! Thank you!" said Karl, his voice trembling with emotion.

"Why are you saying Thank you? I said I will think about it. I did not say I will come."

"I know you better than anyone does and 'I will think about it' means 'Yes'," he answered.

Just when I thought he was about to leave, he surprised me once more with a kiss upon my forehead. I felt all giddy inside me for the first time in years. I smiled and returned the kiss on his cheek and before I could understand what had happened he planted a quick kiss upon my lips. A kiss I closed my eyes and returned and a long kiss it became. Every part of my body felt strange. It was a feeling I had never felt before, not even with my husband. I no longer felt stupid for the words I had spoken, before my son kicked the chicken.

It really must have been a very long kiss because when my mind returned to earth I could see my family crowded around the window peering from inside my home. Thank God my husband had returned to his job in the city. I knew I ought to have felt ashamed but I didn't. Karl on the other hand was already walking off, disappearing with the setting sun.

I returned to Kleinhans Estate the following week. Everyone spoke of nothing else but the Grand Madam expecting the Master's child. There was a buzz of excitement but I instead felt angry. I couldn't understand how Karl showed no memory of the kiss we had shared and neither of us would ever speak of it.

The idea of me being able to address that racist, heartless monster as simply Mary Anne, well it was simply amazing but as advantageous as that would have been, I knew the others would talk and so wilfully decided to call her Madam Mary Anne.

It turned out that Mary Anne actually quite hated children. It did not take me long to discover Mary Anne to be dumber than she believed any black person to be, because when she fell pregnant she clearly never expected her body to change. Growing up, I had always believed England to be a clever country, but I must have been wrong if living in such a country had taught Mary-Anne not to expect her body to get fat. She complained about it constantly. As she put on weight, she cried worse than a new born baby and she well, well you could say she just became a little crazy.

But Karl still loved her, I could never understand why, soothing her tantrums in the months of her pregnancy, forever at her beck and call. Each time I watched him I was furious. It always made me touch my lips and remember our kiss.

• • •

When Mary Anne gave birth, everyone who even knew there was a place called Kleinhans Estate celebrated, everyone except the woman who had just become a mother. The baby was born at the Estate and when the nurses, two of them as well as the Doctor arrived, Karl fetched me from the kitchen and asked me to be present. I was astounded. It felt an honour. For the first time, I understood why my mother had always put up with Kleinhans Snr.

"I don't think she should be here," said the Doctor pointing at me. "We have brought along everything we need."

"I need her," answered Karl sternly.

The Doctor frowned and the two nurses glanced at each other.

Mary Anne was in labour all night. A full 12 hours it felt like, but finally the moment arrived.

"Congratulations Mr Kleinhans, it's a girl," said the doctor, as he gently placed the baby into the arms of the nurse beside him.

The white nurse, in turn, hastily made her way to what had been stationed in the corner of the bedroom, quick to begin cleaning up the infant. I wished to help her but the moment I approached her, she gave me a look so evil, it was very clear that she was having trouble understanding why I was even present in the room to begin with. Reminded of my place, I retreated to the doorway, where I continued to watch in silence. I could just as well have been watching it all on a TV box for that matter. The second nurse, it seemed had been brought with her sole purpose being to tend to Mary Anne and she did during the labour and almost the entire day even after the birth, but to me she was not very good at her job. Mary-Anne refused to even set eyes on the child, let alone carry her.

"Take that thing away from me," cried Mary Anne, "Please John, get rid of it."

Karl signalled to the nurse and she removed the howling child, making her way as instructed to the nursery.

"Just give her a little time Mr Kleinhans, she will come around. It happens to some woman. I shall be on my way now Sir. The nurse will tend to her. I think perhaps it best you leave the room now." said the Doctor.

"No, I can't. This is my fault. She was not ready to become a mother. Thank you for coming here," answered Karl.

"Well if your wife knew, this one here, saw her in this state," pointing at me, the Doctor continued, "well we can't allow her to go downstairs and lie about what she saw, if you understand what I mean…"

"She won't say anything Doctor. Trust me!" snapped Karl.

The doctor looked at me and shook his head.

"Well, just call me if your wife needs anything Sir. I'm a phone call away."

"Yes, of course I will, Beatrice please will you see Doctor to the door," instructed Karl.

At that very moment, I did not want to leave. I wanted to watch Mary-Anne make a greater fool of herself, I wanted to tell Karl to slap some sense into her, but I had no choice. I exited the room as slowly as was possible, the Doctor following.

In the days to come, as was the desire of her mother, the newborn child may very easily have met with death, had it not been for me, or at least I like to think of it that way.

It was the day after her birth that life took a drastic turn for both me and the child. Whilst the rest of the household may have been immune to the ear piecing wailing of the unwanted baby, I certainly was not.

The commotion of the previous day almost forgotten, I started my day continuing to carry out my daily duties as did every other servant on the estate. Under the same circumstances as so many of the other ladies, walking past the Nursery room door could not be avoided. But unlike the others, I did not just walk past the noise echoing from within. I stopped! Peeping inside, a feeling of guilt suddenly took hold of me and despite knowing what I should have been doing, I crept inside. Having just become a mother myself, I instinctively lifted the crying infant from her crib, rocking her to silence, before deliberating over what I should do next. She smelt horrid and finding the nappies not very far away, I changed her quite easily.

But yet again she cried. 'Oh what is wrong child?' I wondered. Of course! The baby needed to be fed and if my guess was right, the child had not been fed since the hour of her birth. It seemed a simple task but after searching the room thoroughly, in every nook and cranny, much to my disbelief, there was not a single bottle to be found. 'Had the poor child not been assigned a Nanny?' As I thought about it, I realized that a new white face had failed to arrive at the estate that morning and if the child's mother was still the woman I knew her to be, feeding the baby was something she would not even have thought of doing.

"What a beauty you are sweet baby. Well if no one else will love you, do not cry, I will!" I said giving her a kiss upon her forehead and then both cheeks.

Much to my own indiscretion, I slid my hand down the front of my V-necked dress and pulled out my left breast which was still swollen from the unrequired milk I still produced, my own infant being cared for in my rural village.

The baby latched onto my nipples tightly and instantly pulled. The feeling was amazing and for just a little while I almost believed she was my own, mine and KK's, she was ours.

I rocked her around the room until she finally drifted to sleep. I smiled and as I redid my dress, I looked up to see Karl standing in the doorway. How long he had been standing there, I was terrified to ask. I held my breath wondering whether he would now chase me from the house but the response I received was in actual fact quite unexpected.

"Thank you! I don't know how to properly thank you," he said, tears rolling down his cheeks.

Karl and I starred at each other a long while, both clearly very embarrassed.

"I should put her down Sir."

"You can call me Karl of course," he answered hesitatingly.

"Sir will be just fine, maybe *Baas* as I called your father. I will see which one I like." I answered.

We once more stood in awkward silence, the baby now in the cot. It seemed to be becoming a habit between us.

"Well I will leave the bottles and milk powder, the formula…I mean I did buy everything. I mean I cannot believe I did not see to it…I have just been such a failure," he covered his face with both hands, clearly frustrated with himself, "I'm really sorry. Tomorrow you won't have to, oh you know," he pointed to my breast. "I think you will know what time to feed her."

"Me? What about her Nanny?"

"I trust you Beatrice. Will you manage?"

"Yes of course. I will love her like my own," I answered.

"Yes! Good! I know you will love her like your own Lungi," he said hugging me tightly before walking quickly out the room.

I never thought I would hear him call me Lungi once more. I wondered if he would ever call me Lungi again. My body tingled all over and I touched my lips.

TEN

But I am afraid I have been talking about myself for far too long because this is not a story about me and Karl but a story about the baby I had watched being born. The baby Karl would name, Leiyah.

Oh goodness, the new Kleinhans family! Where to begin? Well to everyone who did not live at the Estate, to perhaps even some of the servants that did, they seemed like a perfectly happy family, but I knew better. Leiyah was a happy child, that, I cannot lie to you about. The poor girl really could not have known any better. She believed that every child had someone like me to shower her with love and attention and do the things that I know no other white Nanny would ever come close to doing, and worse still, she believed her mother's actions to be exactly what mothers did. To throw daily tea parties and glamourous weekly dinners, sending for her only when she wanted to speak of her dramatic child birth, at which point I would then bring Leiyah in to be gazed at by the guests. It made me angry. I found it hard to believe how they would look at the child and speak of her as if she was a horse being sold. What I found even harder to believe, was how happy it made the child. I guess any form of attention from her mother made her happy and how could I possibly tell the sweet girl how her mother really felt about children.

As Leiyah grew older, Karl started putting his heart into running the gold mine and his visits to Johannesburg grew more frequent.

The amount of time he spent there on each trip grew longer. Each time he left, Mary Anne would fuss about being left alone, but I could never understand her. How could she ever be alone when she had her daughter? To make up for all her fussing every time he returned, Karl would bring with him a gift, for his darling daughter as well as for Mary Anne, and, well something that I guess has been a secret until now, a gift for me too, a small something just to say thank you to me for caring for Leiyah, he made clear was all it was. I knew that was not true.

Leiyah loved the gifts and the attention but her feelings towards her father started to change. I cannot really say when but I started to see it when he returned for her seventh birthday, from feelings of confusion to sadness and before I could prevent it, into the deepest form of hatred. Karl had returned bringing with him a large pram and a plastic doll. The pram, goodness, was almost life size, so unlike the one my mother had brought to my village home. But from the day the pram arrived, it seemed to bring with it a strange evil. Mary Anne who had never really healed from her craziness after childbirth, started becoming even crazier. She refused to allow Leiyah to play with it in the house. She seemed to be afraid of it and she threw even more childish tantrums but much to my own shock, Karl started to argue back, which would only send Mary Anne into a fit of tears where she would sometimes dramatically cry for days on end. I could not care less about Mary Anne but what started to trouble me was that the child started to watch.

"He isn't happy with me, B. He wants a son. He wanted a boy baby and I am a girl. He only brought me that stupid pram because he wants mother to have another child. I heard mother on the telephone," said Leiyah tearfully in the kitchen.

"Don't be silly child. It is only a toy. Your father bought it to make you happy and you have been happy, very happy. You have been pushing that pram up and down the garden every single day for months now. Well, at least on every day it did not rain, and if you did not have me to go and fuss about the rain, you might just have gone and done so then too," I replied.

"And now my mother won't even speak about me anymore. She

doesn't invite her friends over anymore. She doesn't show me off. Oh B, I hate my father!"

"Don't say you hate him child. He is a good man and he loves you."

"I don't care what you say about him or how he feels about me. Because of him my mother does not love me anymore."

"Stop this right now!" I shouted, "I won't listen to another word. Just go to your room this minute."

The poor child burst into tears and disappeared. What else was I to do? Even if I did believe it to be true, how could I possibly agree with her about her mother not loving her?

The very next day, Leiyah ordered that the toy pram and its matching doll be thrown into the shed. Her father was heartbroken. The tradition of gifts stopped.

• • •

The next two years were rough, but it was on Leiyah's ninth birthday that the storm really hit and it hit hard. It would be the last birthday Leiyah would ever celebrate because it was to be on that very day, the day that her mother had faced a most painful childbirth nine years earlier that her life would be brought to a painful end.

Filling the poor girl with even more sorrow, was that her mother had died on a trip she had asked to take. A trip she had chosen to be her birthday present. As their arguing got worse all Leiyah had wanted was for the three of them to be together, nothing extravagant for her birthday, not a new pony or a fancy party, not even a trip to see the castles of England her mother showed off to her friends. No, just a mere road trip, with the people she loved, within the country she loved. It had not seemed like too much to ask for at the time.

Leiyah chose a historic guest farm in Hilton, called The Knoll. Hilton was a very beautiful and popular destination in Natal, well-known for its hiking trails and Leiyah had often heard her father say that Mary Anne had loved The Knoll Historic Guest Farm when they had visited not long after she had arrived in South Africa. I knew she wanted to bring back memories, which was a clever idea from a child so young. It seemed more than a perfect idea. Even I agreed. But how could any of us ever have guessed what we would have to face. Mary Anne disappeared from the guest farm that night and poor Leiyah would never see her again.

Thank goodness Karl had insisted I go along with them. Of course who would have looked after Leiyah, if I hadn't? The poor child, she called herself a murderer! Had I not been there who knows what she might have done?

And so with Mary Anne's death the graveyard at the edge of the pond only grew larger and the chosen ground it stood on, no longer seemed like the ugly burnt grass that I once thought of it to be. Only a few months later, Karl made the craziest of decisions. He would marry again and of course the bride would not be me. I don't know who was more horrified, Leiyah or I? But apart from my pain, for the first time, I felt pity for Mary Anne, the sand upon her grave was still heaped and fresh.

At least Leiyah stopped calling herself a murderer. Her father now was, and I guess she had every reason to think he was.

I had accompanied Leiyah to breakfast that morning and ensuring she was seated, I was about to leave, when Karl unexpectedly stopped me.

"Please don't leave Beatrice. I have something to say to both of you. You see Leiyah, I know that you are missing your mother very much but be that as it may, you must understand that as the wheel of time does not stand still. As life begins, so too must it end. When you are done with one bottle of milk…" he said pouring out the last bit of milk into his cereal, "…well you simply open another." He smiled and opened the bottle of milk which stood within his reach.

"I do not understand what you are trying to say, Father," said Leiyah, looking quite confused.

"You need not worry Leiyah, I have found you another mother."

"What!" I screamed. I was horrified.

Had he really just compared his daughter's mother to a bottle of milk? Poor Leiyah was too shocked to speak. I wanted to slap him. How could he even talk about a stepmother at a time of mourning? How often had I heard Karl reading Snow White to Leiyah? Had he never listened to his own words? Was her step mother not an evil monster? Leiyah would be happy with just me and Karl knew that. I just could not understand him. Had I not raised her and done everything a mother should be doing after all.

That night, at the edge of the pond, hidden from sight by the trees, Karl and I had our fight. I had been so angry at his announcement that I had changed out of my uniform hours earlier than I should have.

As I sat on a tree stump I spoke my frustrations to the stars, before I was made to jump up in fright from the sound of Karl's voice behind me. The stars had heard me and given me a chance to get my answers from Karl himself. I said everything I wanted to, more like shouted. We had spoken for almost an hour before I just started crying.

"Please don't cry Beatrice. At least her school will have someone they can call her mother," pleaded Karl.

"Her mother is dead and everyone from her school should know that!" I shouted, pulling at my braids, the missing cloth upon my head had now allowed my braids to fall free, hanging down almost all the way to my waist.

"You look so beautiful in the moonlight. Do you know that? The way the light shines upon your skin," Karl replied.

"Why? Is it because it makes me fairer? Don't you even dare start with any of that…"

"It has nothing to do with colour to me but you know that I cannot marry you," answered Karl.

"If colour means nothing to you then what is stopping you? We could leave the country," I replied in despair.

"And if I had to marry you, do you think Leiyah would just understand? Besides, how could I when you are already married." There was nothing I could say. I had almost forgotten that to be true. "To me and to Leiyah, even if she will not say it, you have been a mother to her. She has you and that's all that matters to me, and I know she will continue to have everything a mother ought to provide with you in her life, whatever I decide," answered Karl.

"Then decide not to marry." I folded my arms and looked towards the sky.

"I have to. She needs a family feel, someone who everyone will look at as being the *Mother figure* of the Estate, someone to run it."

"Have I not run it from the day your mother died."

"Yes, you have, but you cannot be all those things. You are not white."

I felt like he had just shoved a knife through my heart and I turned around in shock. He held up both his hands as I marched towards him. If anyone was watching from a distance they would surely have believed me to be holding a gun in my hand.

"I'm so, so sorry Beatrice! You know I did not mean it like that…it just came out and…"

Karl's hands now together in prayer as I got closer, the look on his face begging me to forgive him, but I could not care. I knew what I wanted to do and I did it, slapping him far harder than I had intended to, before marching straight up to the house.

I was completely broken because despite the things I said, he was still determined to marry again. At least this time he got his slap, one that must have really hurt because my hand sure did, it stung all night. I was glad my hand stung, but I spent all night crying, wishing I could go in search of a *Sangoma* who would change me into a white woman.

The wedding took place exactly six months after Mary Anne's death. As much as I knew Leiyah needed my support I could not bear to watch and so I took a trip into town, returning in the evening with enough time to dry the poor child's tears.

"He killed her, B. It was not me, it was him. He didn't love her, so he killed her so that he could marry again. Now he has a son too. He has everything he wanted. Do you think he wanted to kill me too? I wish he had," said Leiyah, in between her tears.

"He didn't kill anyone." I answered. I too had to stop and think about whether Leiyah could be right. But if anyone knew the real Karl,

I did, and as much as he had done many stupid things in his life I knew he could never have killed anyone and through it all, he did after all, love Mary Anne. That, I had accepted years ago.

"You were with me that night. How would you really know if he did or didn't."

"Because he couldn't even kill a frog when he was a little boy," I answered.

"Well, people change. My father changed. He murdered my mother. I know it!"

"But, he was with the owner of the Guest Farm all night, with the owner and the owner's friends. It simply is not possible."

"Well, he must have made her cry, that's why she took a walk into town. That still makes him a murderer."

"You are nine years old. These are things you will not understand. It was an accident. Things will get better child," I said, trying my best to calm her,

"How can they? My mother is gone!"

There was nothing I could say to bring her mother back and so I massaged her back and sang her favourite tribal song until I fell asleep in her bed, slipping out quietly in the morning before she could wake up.

Leiyah vowed never to forgive Karl. She hated Susannah even before laying eyes on her. Susannah van Wyk was an Afrikaner as was her father and she had been working in his company. The boss marrying his secretary, Leiyah believed to be all too cliché and as she grew older, it made her more and more convinced that her mother's death had not been an accident?

Susannah was a woman with far too much extra baggage because she brought with her, a son, a baby only nine months old. After his marriage to Susannah, Leiyah felt as if her father had forgotten she had ever existed. From the day of the wedding, all he ever did was cuddle and cradle the baby in his arms as if the child was his own flesh and blood, and by the time she had turned thirteen, Leiyah was convinced that little Willem van Wyk was of his blood.

With Susannah in her father's life, Afrikaans became a language spoken in the Kleinhans household, by the new Kleinhans family, the family Leiyah refused to recognize as her own. It infuriated Leiyah. Whilst her mother had been alive, Karl had never spoken Afrikaans when at home. His English, so British an accent, no one would ever have guessed he was an Afrikaaner. And as Susannah settled herself into the life of being the new Mrs Kleinhans, Leiyah found only additional reasons to despise her.

The more love and affection Susannah showered upon her, the more Leiyah's hatred for her grew. Leiyah believed herself to be an orphan, when her mother had died, in her heart and mind, so too had her father.

But I agreed with Leiyah on one point. Susannah's love was all just act. She remembered Leiyah existed when Karl was at the Estate and forgot about her when Karl was in Johannesburg. I was quick to talk about this to Karl but it hurt when he said nothing. The tree stump I had sat on when I had begged him not to marry had unexpectedly become a meeting spot for the two of us and we met each evening before he was able to sleep beside his new wife. He would smoke as he stood along the water's edge while I gave him a full report on Leiyah and after I had answered all his questions, he would quietly slip away but just the opportunity to speak freely to him was satisfying enough for me. I had years ago stopped touching my lips. Karl knew that marrying again had been a bad decision but neither of us would ever say anything about it or Susannah.

Unfortunately, for Karl, the one thing Leiyah needed was to hear him talk about her mother and that was the one thing he could not bring himself to do, for he too longed for her as she did. And, although his silence about her death helped him deal with his pain, it only made Leiyah believe he had never loved her at all. She believed that his feelings towards her in public had all been just an act and that he really did still grudge her for not having produced a son. A son he now had.

The more Leiyah shut herself away from him, the more Karl would shower her with more money than she could ever have dreamed of, but he should have known then, that money could not buy her happiness.

• • •

The months and years passed by as time must, and Leiyah grew in age, each birthday bringing with it fresh memories of the past and no reason to celebrate. As her teenage years passed, Leiyah started to show more affection and appreciation towards me, shunning her white step mother more and more.

Passing her matric exams with brilliant results, her high school years finally behind her, eighteen year old Leiyah was able to gain acceptance into a university in England, finally able to provide her father with a reason to go and live with her mother's sister, Viola. Finally she would be free of her father and the land that had robbed her of a mother. A cunning scheme, so she believed it to be.

"Oh, you simply have to let me go and stay with Aunt Viola! This is an opportunity of a lifetime!" were Leiyah's words to her father.

"I could not possibly think of anything better. Of course you shall!" was her father's quick response, as he tossed the rugby ball to ten year old Willem, out in the garden. Karl was proud of her achievements and oblivious of any hidden agenda, he was keen to let his daughter go off and succeed.

Leiyah had dealt the cards and won the game. She was now finally in control, except, triumphant was not in any way how she felt. She had expected him to resist. She wanted him to, she needed him to. She was stunned! He had responded so quickly she almost believed he had been waiting for such a question. He simply seemed too keen to let her go. As if an enormous burden was being lifted off his shoulders. It pained her.

"B, he really never loved me or my mother. I don't care what you say. If he had loved me, how on earth would he just let me go like that? He is always in Johannesburg and whenever he does find the time to be here, all he can do is find the time to play with that brat."

There was nothing I could say. How was I supposed to defend Karl? He cared for the boy. That, I could not deny, but while he loved Mary Anne, he did not love Susannah at all. But how on earth could I prove that to Leiyah? Was I to tell her that he met me each night next to the pine that had fallen from the lightning storm?

Leiyah wanted Karl to hurt. She wanted him to feel the same lack of affection he had made her endure. But she did not get what she wanted. She never seemed to.

If only Leiyah had known then, that as he watched her walk away, her father had gripped the cross around his neck, praying that the dying flames within her would once again be ignited and that the fiery passion that had last burned before her mother's death, would burn once more in England.

"I have lost her, haven't I, Beatrice? But it's ok. I am willing to make the sacrifice if it means she will be happy. She is going to be happy again, Beatrice, wont she?"

"Yes *Baas,* she is," I answered. I wanted to remind him that I was losing a daughter too, but looking at the pain on his face, I decided to keep my heartache silent.

It was strange how I still called him *Baas* under the roof of the house and KK under a starry night sky.

• • •

ELEVEN

"So you raised the baby as your own?" asked Zendaya.

"I did," answered Beatrice.

"And you actually breast fed a child that was not your own flesh and blood. Wow! The feeling must have made you really miss your own sons."

"Yes, it did. But, you know, I never got to really bond with my sons or watch them grow up. They had spent months in my very own tummy, yet I was closer to Leiyah than I ever was to my sons. I realised very soon that I loved Leiyah more than my real children and I always would. I felt guilty for it."

"B! How could you? Don't you dare try to tell me you didn't love your own children! You made such a huge sacrifice for them, choosing to go back to the Estate. If you hadn't, you would not have been able to give them an education. The love you felt for Leiyah and your sons were equal, it just felt different. But Love is still Love."

"Oh child!" Beatrice smiled and hugged her. "Thank you for that. And you know what, I love you just as much," she continued, giving Zendaya a kiss on her forehead. "But sometimes, I just wondered; did I make the right decision? I was never educated and I had a job. I could have watched them grow up if I had brought them to the Estate. Karl had, after all, given me the option of having them stay there. They could have been labourers like me, without an education. Even with an education, there was not much progress a black man could make in

South Africa, during those years when skin colour mattered."

"B, you had your reasons. Can you imagine how Mary Anne would have treated them?"

"Thank you for reminding me child. You have always been so very clever." answered Beatrice, squeezing her hand tightly.

Zendaya's words barely registered with me. I had once drank milk from Beatrice's breasts. Could it really be true? Maybe, but even if it was true, Beatrice was wrong about one thing, my mother had loved me, she had to. How could she not? There must have been another reason she had been unable to breast feed me. And that kiss. Had my father really once kissed Beatrice the way lovers do? The memories Beatrice had just revealed, made me want to throw up and that was just from listening to her version of the story, her secret. How would I feel, when the moment came for me to reveal my version of the story, my secret?

Zendaya paced the room, digesting the information and while she did so, I grabbed the opportunity of whispering 'Thank you' to Beatrice. Why I did so, I was not quite sure.

"To be honest though, B, I don't know who had it worse, you or Leiyah," Zendaya continued.

Finally Zendaya was showing some sympathy towards me. Did I still have a chance to make her understand, I wondered.

"Definitely, Leiyah," was Beatrice's quick response.

"Gosh, that poor girl! What a sad life. I would have felt like a murderer too. So what exactly happened when all of you went to the Knoll? How did Mary Anne die? You just said she disappeared. What happened?"

• • •

I awoke with a fright on the morning of Leiyah's ninth birthday. Karl and Mary Anne were sadly having one of their worst arguments. I looked at my clock. It was still only a little after 5:00 a.m. Quickly putting on my gown, I opened my door. Karl's room was at the end of the passage, while mine was across from Leiyah's and if I could hear the pair, I was terrified Leiyah could too and this was really the last thing she needed to wake up to, on her birthday, but after opening her door and peeping within, I was relieved to find her still asleep.

Without even realizing it, I suddenly found myself standing outside their door. "You are going to get out of bed, put a smile on your face and wish your daughter a happy birthday." I managed to hear Karl shout, as I listened from the passage way. "Where is the necklace I had engraved?" Her response was such a whisper, I could not hear.

The door was flung open and I ducked, the passage still in darkness, I managed to stay hidden. Marry Anne looked like she was about to storm down the passage and God knows where, after that, when Karl grabbed her arm and yanked her back. She let out a small scream and I almost jumped myself. I had never seen Karl being so rough with her before. He dragged her all the way to Leiyah's door and from the light at the stairway I could see him place something in her hand.

"Wipe your tears and go!" said Karl sternly.

She opened the door and went in, while he waited outside, the light from the room now reflecting on his grim face. To my absolute shock, Mary Anne began singing 'Happy Birthday' and Leiyah awoke with the happiest of screams. I had never heard Mary Anne sing anything for her child before. It was so crazy, that for a moment, it all seemed like a dream. Finally Karl's angry face calmed and he walked downstairs. Returning to my room, I looked into Leiyah's to see Mary Anne putting a necklace around the child's neck. I had never seen the child so happy before. I returned to my room and dressed for the day ahead. I knew we would be leaving early. All the other workers thought it strange that I was going along on the birthday holiday, even I did, but deep down I was really very excited.

The Knoll was not far from Hilton college, the fancy school old Mrs Kleinhans could never stop talking about, and whilst Karl drove us there, he told Leiyah of the many times he had visited the Knoll during his college holidays. Karl spoke non-stop. Mary Anne never said a word.

I really didn't know what to expect from this place, they called a *Guest Farm*. It couldn't possibly look like the village farm where I had grown up. Rich white people couldn't possibly go for a holiday in huts that looked like my own. After leaving the main road, we drove through a town and before I knew it, we were there. Wooden fences, the greenest grass, beautiful flowers, all types of trees, horses and cute white buildings, I would soon find out, were called cottages, each cottage standing a good distance from the next. I loved the sight. I could not believe there could be places smaller than Kleinhans Estate that looked just as beautiful.

As we drove up the dirt driveway, a woman could be seen playing with her children outside a large white building.

"That's Cathy and her kids, my sweet Leiyah. Their children are around your age. I cannot wait for all of you to become friends. Don't you think so, Mary Anne dear," said Karl, knocking her shoulder with his elbow. Mary Anne nodded, although it looked to me as though she was not listening to him, "They own the Knoll and guess what, they even live here. That building behind them, is their house."

Cathy and her children immediately stopped playing and I could hear her calling out to someone. A man rushed out the house and he was at the car before it had been switched off.

"Happy Birthday!" they all shouted out, showering Leiyah with hugs and kisses.

Karl quickly did the introductions. The owners, he introduced as Cathy and George Evans. George Evans, being the man who had, of course, rushed out the house. Their twelve year old son was Tom and their eight year old daughter was Charlotte. It turned out that George had schooled with Karl at Hilton College, although I thought he looked a good few years older. Maybe, it was just the beard. As I looked at him, I wondered whether he had been one of the young men who had made fun of me at Kleinhans Estate, calling me a circus act, but when he reached out his hand to shake my own, I knew at once it could not be possible.

"Would you like to go to your cottage first, Mary Anne, or can I take you and Leiyah for a walk around?" asked Cathy.

"Oh mum, please let's take a tour. I want to see everything, the horses, the animals, the vegetables. Oh! Everything! What do you have on the farm Aunt Cathy?" asked Leiyah.

Mary Anne did not even look at Leiyah and continued staring around.

"Oh it's not that kind of farm anymore sweetie." Cathy continued, "We only have horses here now, although many, many years ago, it used to be a dairy farm, but now it's just a special place with very special cottages you will never find anywhere else. Each one is special in its own way. One even looks like a library.

"Really, can we go see it," said Leiyah jumping up and down.

"Of course, you will see it. Beatrice will be staying there," replied Cathy.

"Oh B, you are so, so lucky."

"Because of you, I am lucky child," I replied. I wasn't quite sure what to do on a holiday and I had been standing rather awkwardly and quietly in all the excitement.

"So what do you say, Mary Ann? We have a birthday girl waiting," asked Cathy again.

"Can you fetch someone to drive me into town?" was Mary Anne's answer, not addressing anyone.

"Vuyani can take you there in a bit?" answered George.

"What!" shouted Mary Anne, looking horrified.

I almost laughed in amusement.

"Well he is our driver for the kids, mainly for school, but when Cathy and I are too busy with the guests, he takes them around."

"But he is…"

"You can always walk if you want to, it's not too far," replied George, smiling in a strange way.

"George," scolded Cathy, "You know she is entitled to her opinion. Don't tease her."

"Let me catch up with George just a little bit and then I will take you, my darling," answered Karl, quickly coming to her defense, "why don't you go freshen up first?"

"It's the same cottage Karl used to book when you just got married," said George, pointing to a double story white building not very far away.

Mary Anne grabbed one of her bags from the car and walked off towards the cottage.

"She probably just wants to buy Leiyah a cake and some gifts," said Karl, not sounding very convincing.

"Oh thank God you mentioned it. I have already bought all the ingredients. Charlotte and I wanted to bake one with our special Leiyah, dear. I was hoping Mary Anne would join," she looked at George and I might not have been very educated, but something told me that the friendly owners knew exactly who the real Mary Anne was.

"Wow! I didn't know mum could bake," said Leiyah innocently.

"Well your mother has a lot to do in town for your birthday, my dear. Cathy, if we are not back in two hours, please do not wait for us."

"Not a problem, John," answered Cathy.

"Would it be ok if Beatrice joined you on your walk and with the baking if Mary Anne and I are not back by then? Leiyah is comfortable as long as Beatrice is nearby, you see, if that's ok?"

Leiyah was already having a world of fun playing with the kids.

"Oh dear John, it would be no problem at all," answered Cathy.

"You don't have to worry about a thing Karl, my boy, Cathy will see to everything," answered George, giving him a pat on the shoulder.

"What would I ever do without you? Let me go and fetch Mary Anne. Have fun, Leiyah," shouted out Karl, trying his best to look happier than he was. He waved before jumping into the car and driving it down towards the cottage.

"Right kids, lead the way. Let's climb up the hill first and show Leiyah and Beatrice the view," said Cathy to her kids.

The kids led the way and I started following them along the path. Mrs Evans put her arms around me, much to my shock. "It's not a steep walk, but just let me know if you need any help balancing," she said.

I nodded. I could not believe that a Madam could speak so kindly.

"Wow B, is that your village?' asked Leiyah.

As we got higher, a forest of gum trees could be seen to one side, greener than green. Opposite, was a dry hill with traditional Zulu houses built on it, a village far bigger than my own, stretching on and on.

"No, no my child, it's not," I answered.

"Bee, like the insect?" asked Tom.

"Tom! How can you ask such a question? You have already been told her name is Beatrice. Other than that, mind your own business," scolded his mother.

"Sorry," he responded without being asked to. I was quite impressed.

"We are here. Isn't it stunning," said Cathy. "I would walk up every day if I had the time."

Leiyah was thrilled. "Oh wow! Look at that. Aunty Cathy, what's that water there? And over there, what is that?" she couldn't stop with her questions.

"Calm down child," I said, but I myself could not believe the view and listened carefully as Cathy explained what each beauty was.

On the one side, tribal lands met the forests and in the distance, the beginning of the majestic Drakensberg mountain range could be seen, as well as a sea of sparkling blue, which was the dam that had been named Midmar. When I turned around, I could see the town which met another town and then another and another, stretching on towards the city.

As I stood on the top of the hill, I felt I never had to travel anywhere else in South Africa. Every beauty I had ever heard people speak about, could all be seen from one spot. It was simply magical. All the stories about the places in South Africa, all seemed to meet at that one point, all under the same blue sky.

"Right, let's go back down to do some baking, kids. I'm not forgetting you of course, Beatrice" she said, giving me a smile.

"Do you think mummy will be back?" asked Leiyah.

"I'm sure she will be," I gave Leiyah the best smile I could. In my heart I knew she wouldn't.

The children ran on ahead and I was about to hurry after them, when Mrs Evans touched my hand.

"How are Mr and Mrs Kleinhans managing, really? Do you think there is hope? I am surprised their marriage still survives. Poor Leiyah."

"Well Ma'am, Mr Kleinhans does not want to give up. He loves her very much. He always will. She likes to swim. There is a little dam or pond, I don't know what to call it, there is some water at the bottom of the hill, where they stay."

"Yes we did visit, before Leiyah had been born. Karl was unhappy about Mary Anne firing you."

"Was he?" I felt I sounded too happy to hear this, but quickly reminding myself about the question I had been asked, I continued, "Oh you know it then. He always swims with her, relaxes on the lawn with her, he tries everything to make her happy."

"Poor dears, I hope this trip will make the difference."

When we reached the main house, Mary Anne had not returned, but the baking went ahead and Leiyah was still as delighted as ever, even though she had not yet been spending any of her special birthday with her real family.

Whilst Leiyah remained at the main house, with the children, Mrs Evans took me to my cottage. When we got there, I felt as though I was a child and it was my birthday! The room looked simply magical. One entire wall was made up of glass, something I have never seen before and it made my view from the room feel even better than a dream. The bed looked too pretty to sleep on and across from it, was a wall with shelves, reaching all the way to the ceiling, with the most beautiful looking books, that looked even better than the books at Kleinhans Estate. I even had my own bathroom.

"Do you like it?" asked Cathy Evans.

"Goodness, I love it," I answered.

"Let me show you the way to Karl's cottage. I am sorry, it's a bit of a walk, but it is safe. Anyway, the path is well lit and it can actually be quite fun, walking under the night sky. Here we are." We had reached the front of the cottage, I had earlier seen from the back, "and that is our famous barn," she said pointing to the large white building just across from the cottage.

"Lovely," I replied. I didn't know what else to say. I was more interested in the horses that were grazing in a fenced area just across from where we were standing and the beauty of how the green of the forest met the dry grass of the rural land.

"We have a sort of music festival once a week. Tonight just happens to be one of those nights, so guess what, Karl does not even know it yet, but I have planned a little party for Leiyah there tonight."

"Oh wow! That's fantastic," I was so excited. Mary Anne had to be at the party and it was exactly what the child needed.

"Let's go and see what the kids are up to. I must tell you, if anyone asks you, you are not staying at the cottage, you are Leiyah's babysitter and when she goes to bed, you will be joining the other workers in their rooms," she smiled. I was confused but said nothing. "Well it is the 1980's," she continued, "Apartheid won't be around for much longer but that's the way it has to be, even if I don't like it."

I didn't know what she meant or what *Apartheid* was, but I would learn in time.

By 4:00 p.m. that afternoon, the Guest Farm was filled with people, music and activity. Fortunately, Mary Anne and Karl were back. But despite this and the 'family holiday', Leiyah was once more in my care.

As we made our way down to the barn that evening, I noticed small tin drums, cut in half, being balanced on a table like metal frames. Leiyah told me it was called a braai stand and the white men stood around it, drinking beer and cooking meat over a fire. I had not seen anything like it at Kleinhans Estate, but apparently it was the common thing done in the city.

Inside the barn, children ran around freely and adults sang and danced. No one paid any attention to me and I realized I was enjoying myself. It was a little after 6:00 p.m. when Mrs. Evans called both me and Leiyah and walked with us towards the mike. The festivities in the barn stopped.

"If I can have everyone's attention, tonight we have a very special birthday girl, so can we all sing 'Happy Birthday' to Leiyah." The crowd immediately began singing. Leiyah was searching the room for her mother and so was I, when I saw her arguing with Karl at the entrance.

Thank goodness, everyone was singing Happy Birthday, because she looked like she was screaming.

Karl must have won the argument because she walked over to the front and cut the cake with her daughter, looking very red in the face. In a flash, she disappeared. Leiyah was so excited by the gifts the Evans children were giving her, that she fortunately did not notice that her mother was gone. It was only when Mrs Evans told her children to go to bed, that Leiyah remembered her own mother.

Karl, who was still outside the barn with George and a few other men told us that Mary Anne was not feeling well, so she had gone to bed early. I was not surprised and offered to take Leiyah to my room. Both were more than glad. Leiyah had been eagerly waiting to see the library room and she was now even more excited that she would get to sleep there. I gave her the bed and slept on the couch, a little disappointed that the pretty bed could not be mine, but I knew tomorrow was another day.

At around 3:00 a.m. I awoke with a shock, to a knock on the door. It was Karl.

"Is Mary Anne here?" he asked, his voice sounding different.

"No, why would she be?" I answered. We both knew she would never want to enjoy my company.

"I thought she went to bed, but she didn't. The sheets are untouched. The police are on their way."

"Can I help?"

"Yes, stay with Leiyah. Don't leave her alone for a moment. Keep her here as long as you can." He ran off.

They searched everywhere for an entire day and night. The police spoke to everyone in town, they went door to door, but no one knew what had happened. Karl even offered a reward.

I managed to keep Leiyah in my cottage for the morning, but Cathy came to fetch her just before lunch and only once inside the main house, did she answer Leiyah's questions about the police cars. Leiyah was of course hysterical and she immediately tried to run away in search of her mother, but Cathy and I managed to stop her. Little Tom locked the front gate for his mother, and until her mother was found, the main house became a prison for Leiyah.

At last, the next morning, Mary Anne was found, but not in a way even I would have wanted to hear! Her body was found floating in the Quarry, in the town she had seemed obsessed over. Mary Anne had died from a fall. Whether she had jumped or been pushed, no one would ever know.

Leiyah clung to my waist and cried hysterically. Even I, who knew her best, did not know what to say. When her father arrived, she hit him fiercely. He grabbed a hold of her and hugged her tightly, crying hysterically too.

Before we returned to Kleinhans Estate the police questioned all of us.

"The poor woman had gone crazy," I told the police. 'At least she will no longer be so unhappy', I was about to add, but looking at Leiyah's face, I didn't. Thinking about it now, I am certain God had stopped me from saying anything cruel. Being black, I'm sure they would have named me, the murderer. After all, the only person who could speak for where I had been, was a nine year old child.

* * *

TWELVE

"So Mary Anne killed herself on her only child's birthday. How cruel!" exclaimed Zendaya.

"She always was cruel to me, although I have to tell you, my poor KK, he was a murder suspect for many years. But to Leiyah, from the very moment, she found out he was going to marry Susannah, he was a murderer, and not even I could make her change her mind," answered Beatrice.

"Oh yes, Susannah, that woman, I had almost forgotten about her. If I were in Leiyah's shoes, I would have spent the rest of my life proving Karl was indeed the murderer, I don't care if he was or he wasn't. To go and marry another woman so soon! To make matters worse, she had a son. Wasn't that the reason Leiyah got rid of her toy pram? She suspected Karl was disappointed that his only child was a girl," Zendaya looked towards Beatrice, but didn't wait for a response. "How could he even think he was doing it for Leiyah's own good? No, I would never have believed my mother had killed herself either. I feel for Leiyah. I really do."

"I'm glad you do," answered Beatrice, smiling at me. For the first time I could breathe a sigh of relief. Was Leiyah about to actually understand why I had changed my name and run away? Why I had hidden so much from her?

"So Mary Anne died, Karl married Susannah and Leiyah left South Africa. You still have not told me how you met my mother," asked Zendaya. It was a question that was beginning to clearly irritate her. "Would you prefer to tell me instead mother?" she asked, now turning to me, "You have been awfully quiet. What do you think of Beatrice's story? Who do you think had it worse, Beatrice or Leiyah?"

The question stunned me and I grabbed the glass of water that had been sitting on the coffee table for several days now, almost choking as I drank. Having only finally calmed down, my heart-beat once more escalated. Thank the heavens, Beatrice quickly responded to her question.

"Oh Zendaya! Everyone has troubles. Why do you want to compare who's was worse? Anyway, about the box that arrived, you see, there is something else very important still inside that your mother did not take out to show you." Beatrice reached into the box to remove it, "and once you see it, I promise you, everything will make sense, but actually...." Beatrice let go of the treasure box before it was visible to Zendaya and it landed at the bottom of the box with a thud. "Wait before I do, I need to tell you about something that happened, the morning my eighteen year old Leiyah left for England."

"Oh B, stop keeping me in such suspense."

"Patience child, patience, you will be happy once you learn everything."

* * *

That December felt like the shortest month I had ever lived through and before I knew, it was time for Leiyah to fly off to the land of her *Mother's* people. Like all my mother's visits to our village to see us, the summer holiday was gone before it had really come. After eighteen years of mothering her, I was about to let her go too. To me it was impossible for Karl's pain to be greater than my own, even if he did speak of it daily to me.

The night before Leiyah left for London, Karl threw Leiyah a fancy dinner. Much to my surprise, Karl invited me to join. As I entered the room with Leiyah by my side, I felt as out of place as the night I had watched Mary Anne give birth. I was given the chair in-between Karl and Leiyah, and I could not have been happier to have them on either side.

Leiyah looked exhausted. She had spent the last week pacing the grounds of the Estate from dawn to dusk so much so, that a part of me wondered if she was having second thoughts about leaving the land in which her mother's body would forever lie sleeping.

"Oh, I can't believe OUR little girl is eighteen," said Susannah.

"OUR little girl is a woman now, isn't she," Karl replied.

They continued to express their excitement, whilst Leiyah merely ignored them, staring blankly out the window.

"Well done, Susannah. You did such a fantastic job taking over and raising her," said one of the guests.

"Taking over?" Leiyah repeated softly. I could immediately see the anger on her face.

"Oh Leiyah, how I will miss you," said Susannah.

"Why should you?" Leiyah gave Susannah a horrible stare before turning to the guest, "and who said she raised me. That woman did not raise me and neither did Karl. Beatrice did," snapped Leiyah.

"LEIYAH!" shouted Karl in disapproval.

"I love you Leiyah, as if you were my own daughter, my own flesh and blood!" exclaimed Susannah

'*What a liar?*' I thought.

"Well I'm not! "I'm not her daughter and I never will be! Blood is thicker than water and your blood does not flow through me," Leiyah shouted.

"I love your father and his blood does not run through my veins Leiyah," laughed Susannah.

Tears immediately began streaming down Leiyah's cheeks.

"Stop this nonsense at once! We have guests!" shouted Karl, loud enough to turn many of the heads that had been staring at their plates.

The pain of listening to her father stand up for Susannah, was probably more than she could bear. Saying nothing further, Leiyah merely got up and walked away. I got up and followed her.

The next morning, Leiyah refused to eat with her father or Susannah and instead she joined me in the kitchen, shouting out her feelings about everything that had happened the previous night. Even though I had been there, I didn't try to stop her. Her hatred for her father was the worst I had ever heard.

"What's that you have there on your lap?" I asked.

"After all Susannah's lies last night, it's my promise to my mother."

"What do you mean?" I asked, confused.

She revealed her treasure to me. It was a little treasure box with her name carved on it and so she explained what she intended to do. I thought it strange, but seeing the happiness on her face I encouraged her, telling her that her mother's spirit would be very happy.

After barely eating anything, she quietly slipped out the back door as she did every morning around sunrise, heading down towards her mother's grave.

Leiyah had made it almost a ritual, something everybody knew about, but no one spoke of. Knowing that she was already packed for her flight that night, she could afford to spend a few extra hours on her morning walk, which usually took her just under an hour. Unlike other mornings, however, she also knew that on this particular morning the extra hours would be needed. Though what she did not know, was that unlike other mornings, on this particular morning, her father was watching her closely from the centre window on the third floor of the three story building. Something I found out, after being sent to his study to hand him an urgent letter.

Karl, was however, not interested in the letter and so I left it on his desk before I joined Karl at the window in wonder of what had captured his attention.

"What on earth is she doing with a spade in one hand Beatrice?"

"I have no idea," I answered. I knew exactly what her plan was, but I stayed silent about it.

As we stood watching, Karl described to me how Leiyah had come to be in procession of the spade. Leiyah had apparently seemed in no rush as she walked slowly down the bank, but instead of heading straight towards her mother's grave at the water's edge, she suddenly turned towards the shed. After spending some time there, she exited in haste and then walked briskly towards the water with a spade over her shoulder. Karl was clearly puzzled but I was certainly not about to betray Leiyah.

Karl continued to watch Leiyah until she had disappeared from his sight. I watched too. And when finally she could no longer be seen he turned to me, "you know Beatrice, I own almost all the land you can see, but I would trade it all in an instant, just to see my daughter happy again. Now…" he pointed out the window, "…she was not happy!"

"I know…" I answered.

"Well whatever she has buried, I will find out."

"Please don't! Don't dig it out," I pleaded.

"Why not?"

"Just trust me," I said, squeezing his hand.

"OK then, not today. Not anytime soon but someday," Karl replied.

"No, not ever, please, promise me," our eyes locked for what felt like forever.

"Ok then, as you wish," he answered, smiling as if he had made a promise to do exactly as I asked. But he hadn't.

I turned and walked away.

• • •

THIRTEEN

It was not just my story. It was not just my secret. For the very first time I realized that it was '*our*' story. Beatrice really did have as much to hide as I did but what she had hidden was of a life intertwined with my own. After listening to her tale, the impact of this dawned upon me for the very first time. The bond I had once held so dear felt strong once more. She was my B too. She always had been and I promised myself, I would never turn a blind eye to that again. For the very first time since we had left South Africa, I understood her. The silent appreciation I would feel for Beatrice every time Susannah frustrated me at the Estate, was suddenly rekindled in my heart. I tried to think of how best to express it, but before I could control my lips, it just spilt out.

"I love you," I said, before my sense of reason could kick in. The words I had just uttered earning a response of three bewildered expressions.

"That was bizarre of you Mother. Have you been feeling left out? Relax, I know you do," she raised her eyebrows before turning her attention back to Beatrice.

Beatrice smiled and tapped her nose, the way she often would before tucking me into bed at the Estate. I couldn't believe it. She knew I had been speaking to her. I smiled back and sighed in temporary relief. The worst was yet to come but whatever resulted from the truth, I could be assured that she would forever be by my side.

Knowledge of Beatrice's past had, if anything, only invigorated Zendaya's sense of curiosity and she had already begun with her next question. "Did you ever for even one moment believe that Susannah's son was Karl's, that Karl was really the biological father of her baby?"

I immediately sprung forth on the coach. This had been a question I had often asked Beatrice, but alas, it was a question that had only been met with her most reprimanding stare before being followed by a command that I never venture to make such an accusation again.

"That's a strange question for you to ask child," answered Beatrice.

"Well, it's just from the way you have described their relationship it makes me think about a father's love. What it's based upon? I wonder…"

"Wonder what child?" answered Beatrice looking puzzled.

Zendaya's question certainly came as a surprise to me too. Was she suddenly yearning to learn more about her own father, especially after all this talk about South Africa? A truth I was about to disclose fair enough, but I certainly had no intention of telling her every detail that was not necessary to promise a brighter future for her and the details of her father, she really did not need to know.

"Oh, never mind," answered Zendaya, playfully tickling Beatrice's chin.

"Well you know what Zendaya, Karl may not have been able to marry me but he could have very easily found his way into my bed. But he never did. Not even in the six months he mourned Mary Anne's death, where, if I was to be entirely honest, I had very much wished he had. He was a loyal husband. And even if he married Susannah for all the wrong reasons he was a loyal husband to her too. I am one hundred percent convinced that she had been widowed, as she claimed, and her being chosen as the new wife was, if not mere convenience, an act of kindness too."

Zendaya bit her lips and it almost appeared as though she was suddenly ridden with a sense of guilt.

Hiding her face momentarily behind her hand, she quickly continued, "Well I guess you are right. If Karl had fathered Susannah's child, the Will surely would not have ended up with you. If you never got to make love to him well, at least you can be comforted by the knowledge that he left you something in his Will. At least you can always think of that as a way in which he wanted you to know he always loved you. What does his Will say anyway?"

"Well, actually Zen, before we get to the Will, there was something I had been wanting to show you," Beatrice glanced towards me as she once more reached into the box.

We were getting to that moment. Oh God! Oh God! Oh God! I took another sip of what was left of the stale water I had earlier almost choked on.

"You know what B? I guess it all makes sense now," said Zendaya as she stood up to stretch her stiff back. If my body was stiff I was simply too anxious to notice.

"What does, child?" asked Beatrice.

"Why you came to England. Why you left your sons," continued Zendaya, strangely forgetting she had even made mention of the Will, "I would have thought Leiyah leaving the Estate would have been a perfect opportunity for you and Karl to kindle a real romance but when you came here you were hoping you would see Leiyah again. Aren't I right? You really chose to work for Mother because of Leiyah. Sorry to hurt you Mother."

Although Zendaya only glanced my way, I dismissed her apology with a wave of my hand but she did not seem to care.

Beatrice simply smiled. "I am seated her right now, only because of my sweet child Leiyah. Everything I have ever done in my life was done out of my love for Leiyah, yes, you would be right to think that."

"You must have thought England was this really small place, not much larger than your village perhaps and you would find her in a matter of days. Oh my poor B! Did you ever come close to finding her? Did you ever see her again?"

"See her, yes. Find her, No."

"What! That sounds ridiculous Beatrice," responded Zendaya.

This was the moment. My heart beat was racing. What was Beatrice about to say next?

"I did see Leiyah again but I don't think it would be right to say I found her, because when we finally did meet, she just wasn't my Leiyah anymore."

"What do you mean she just wasn't '*your*' Leiyah anymore? Oh why are you being so difficult B?"

"Well you see, I thought I would never see her again, but Leiyah did return some years after she left South Africa, when she had set off to go and live with her aunt. You know, Zendaya, I had been absolutely thrilled at the time, you can only imagine, but *Eish*, if only she had not set her feet upon African soil again. Oh child, even my life would be so different right now."

"How would your life be different, B? Oh, now you are deliberately making me so confused!" shouted Zendaya.

Why Beatrice was allowing Zendaya to lose her temper again, I could not fathom.

"You see, if Leiyah having to face Mary Anne's death had been a storm, she was still to face a hurricane or a tornado. Well I guess whichever of them is worse and my precious Leiyah would never be '*my*' Leiyah again. That is the truth, I'm afraid, my darling Zendaya. I know I really have confused you. You know what? Maybe it will be best, if I let your Mother explain the rest. I think she would definitely be able to better explain what happened to Leiyah and why instead of writing my next Madam's name to be Leiyah Kleinhans, I instead write it to be Hannah Gordon. I have definitely spoken a bit too much today. After all, I did ask you to come downstairs because your Mother had something to say. Madam, I think it's your turn, why don't you go ahead," said Beatrice as both women now looked towards me.

With bated breath, I waited for Zendaya's response. To me, Beatrice had practically just confessed that I was both Hannah and Leiyah. What else could Zendaya possibly have understood, when Beatrice had declared that she now writes her Madam's name to be Hannah Gordon, I could not imagine, but as I studied Zendaya's expression, I quickly realized that she had clearly not caught on.

"Oh, alright then, if you insist, go ahead Mother," was Zendaya's response, her tone of voice suggesting no suspicions after the hint that Beatrice had just dropped.

But the time had indeed come and I was ever so glad that Beatrice had the sense to allow me to reveal it in my own way. Beatrice did love me. I smiled, but as my eyes met Zendaya's, I was suddenly reminded of what I was about to say.

'*Please God, please, please let her understand,*' I thought, but I was done with wasting time and so I continued, trying my very best to get straight to the point, "Yes, yes I do have something to say. Well you have already seen the diary and you know that we have received Karl's Will. And well, thank you Beatrice, thank you so much for explaining to Zendaya who Karl was and telling her about your life in South Africa. Thank you for getting the ball rolling, I guess. But there is something else that I need to show you. Zendaya, this is not just about Beatrice, please don't think that, because if you feel that way, you have really misunderstood."

"Gosh Mother, what about the story that Beatrice has just told us, has to do with anyone else?"

'*If only you knew,*' I wanted to say, but there really was no point. The time had come for her to learn the truth. "Well you see…" I abruptly stopped and stood up. I felt I was about to faint and Beatrice must have been able to read me because she rushed to my aid and helped me seat myself once more. Zendaya however did not sympathise.

"Oh God! Will one of you just show me whatever it is I need to see? I am fed up now. Your story has been fascinating, B. I mean, I have always wanted you to tell me about life in South Africa, you and Mother both, but why now? I mean, you said I needed to listen to something that would help with…you know…" Zendaya looked at me and bit her lips, I knew she was implying Harry, "you said it just might be a solution to my pain but you have been doing nothing but talk about you and Karl and Leiyah and how is me hearing about your pain going to be the solution to my own? Just how, is you being torn apart from the love of your life supposed to make me feel any better, and what on earth, does any of this have to do with Mother? You eventually started working for her. That's an obvious fact, but that too, you have not once answered me, as to how? Well!" Venting her frustration, she kicked the box.

Listening to Zendaya's interpretation, I could not possibly have agreed more. I could not have been more grateful to Beatrice for speaking when I had no tongue, but had I been a total stranger with an estranged lover, I would also have been dumbfounded as to exactly how the tale I had just heard would be the answer to uniting us. The tale of a maid who loved her boss and now that he was dead, they, Beatrice and her KK would never be reunited. She had revealed too much, and learning of this love, they had managed to hide from me, I really didn't know what to make of it. I had to agree with Zendaya, we really were not getting to the point.

"Well Zen this is how. It was…" began Beatrice.

"No it's quite alright Beatrice," I said, my quick response, halting any further explanation. "Zendaya, I do have something I need to say to you. It is I who should have actually been telling you about South Africa and not Beatrice." Where I plucked up the courage to speak from, I had not the faintest idea. "I should have shared it many years ago, but I had made myself believe that all of it had been in another lifetime, just a nightmare. But it's time that it isn't a secret anymore."

"What isn't a secret?" Zendaya looked flabbergasted and from the fear in her eyes, she clearly had her own in mind.

"You have heard what Beatrice has had to say and now it is my turn and from what I am about to say, you will understand why B's story is my story."

"How can it possibly be your story Mother if you have not said a thing?"

"Well this will help you understand," I said, picking up the treasure box, "This was also sent." Placing the treasure box into Zendaya's hand, I turned the cardboard box over to make sure she knew it contained nothing else.

"B, is this not the box Leiyah buried before she left to stay with her aunt?" asked Zendaya, the intrigue bringing on a sense of calm.

"Yes it is," Beatrice answered.

"How Cruel! Oh B, Karl broke his promise to you. He betrayed you B."

Beatrice nodded.

"Oh B, I don't know how you could ever have loved a man who was constantly letting you down. Gosh but anyway, just look at this Mother, how very strange that it was sent?" Zendaya ran her fingers over the letters that had been delicately carved on its lid before saying them aloud, "Leiyah Catherine Kleinhans."

I could feel a sudden pulsation in her throat. I watched gravely, wondering what was going through Zendaya's mind.

"It looks so antique, almost like a real treasure chest. How unusual. It is so very beautiful. Oh I absolutely love it."

"Open it," said Beatrice

I felt like Beatrice had just shot me. Unable to remain still, I sprung to my feet, intent on removing the treasure chest from Zendaya's possession and I would have succeeded in my quest had Beatrice not intervened.

"No, No Madam. Sit!" she said firmly, shaking her head and signaling that I not act otherwise. "You can do this," she whispered

I obeyed.

Zendaya enthusiastically opened the jewelry box, her face glowing for the first time since she had made her dramatic entrance the previous morning. Her anticipation in finding something extraordinary, clearly evident. Opening the box, she however looked clearly despondent as she removed from it nothing further than the off white sheet of paper that had been folded over several times. Zendaya, looked deep in thought as she read out the words, "***Love Leiyah***," She frowned. Unfolding the stained page, she ironed it out flat on her lap before reading out the words that had been concealed within, "Blood is thicker than water."

"It was Leiyah's way of telling her mother she would never accept Susannah as her mother, I guess," said Beatrice.

"I guess so. This handwriting looks so much like yours, Mother," having returned the paper into the box, she now picked up the necklace,

"Mother don't you have one just like this?" she asked. Fortunately, Zendaya's eyes were not upon me, because I completely ignored her question.

"You know sometimes we get so caught up in our lies that we tend to forget the truth or perhaps we just choose not to face it," I said. "Sounds strange, but it's true. I am so glad you have now had an opportunity to have a good look at the treasure chest. Trust me when I say that I know exactly how you feel right now. Why your heart cries?"

"What? How could you possibly know what I am feeling? You do not even know what my dilemma is, and how on earth is this treasure box supposed to help me understand that what Beatrice has been telling me, has anything to do with you?" responded Zendaya with a vicious glare. "Can you just tell me straight out? What is the connection between you and Leiyah?"

"Oh damn Karl! Damn him to the depths of the sea! Damn him to Hell! Why did he have to dig it up? He has ruined everything!"

"Leiyah! Stop blaming your father. He has saved us! It is only because of his Will, that it is still in your power to fix things for Zen." yelled Beatrice.

"Leiyah? Why did you just call my mother, Leiyah?" Zendaya jumped off the couch and yanked the necklace off my neck. "Could it really be?" Zendaya looked mortified.

Matching it to the necklace in the treasure case, she opened the pendants to reveal the same photos of my mother and I, her body started trembling and I no longer needed to say it, but I did.

"Yes, I am. I am Leiyah Catherine Kleinhans. We are one and the same."

"Oh my God! Why Mother?" Beatrice helped her onto the couch. "You mean to say I have spent my entire life calling my own mother by a name that is not even her own. And now what, do you suddenly expect me to so easily start calling you Leiyah. Is that it? Why couldn't you tell me your real name earlier? Has my entire life been based on a lie?" shouted Zendaya, shaking her head.

I clenched my teeth, the guilt hitting me, well aware that the last sentence uttered by Zendaya could not have been more valid. If this was Zendaya's reaction after only hearing about her name, I could not begin to imagine how she would react to the complete revelation of my secret past. Thank goodness I had no intention of revealing everything there was to reveal.

"No I did not lie to you I legally changed my name to Hannah as soon as I left South Africa, in my heart and in my mind, right now my name is Hannah. But a name is only a name. It does not change who you really are," I said, remembering Mr Goldstone's words.

"No, it does not, because whatever your name may be, it does not change the fact that you are a liar."

"Zendaya, do not be so harsh," scolded Beatrice

"Wait a moment, B, even you knew. How could you have kept this from me?"

"I made a promise to your mother when you were still a baby. I do not break my promises, you know that."

"Let me rephrase that Mother, ok not a liar, just a person who decided not to tell me a whole lot of essential facts I should have known, a person who hid the truth. Is that better, B?"

"I had no choice! You see I did not flee South Africa because you had an abusive father. I left because of my father," I began, breathing in deeply before speaking. "I changed my name to protect you. I was terrified that he would come after us, or he would hire God knows how many spies, investigators, or whatever. What if you accidentally said my real name on the streets and someone heard. Zendaya, it was a chance that I just could not take. I was terrified that he would take you away from me. I refused to let him find us. I couldn't lose you"

"Why would he have taken me away from you?"

"If I could explain everything to you about what happened in South Africa, when I returned just before my twenty first birthday, well then you would understand why my father was such a threat. But right now none of that is important. I know you are shocked, but just trust me when I say I have only kept my name a secret because, my darling, I just wanted us to be happy. But still I failed. You are not happy Zendaya.

When this parcel arrived from South Africa, I was horrified. Do you know Zendaya, I even asked Beatrice to burn it. But she didn't and I know now that Beatrice was right when she said it arrived here for a reason. I know why you arrived here in such a state Zendaya. Beatrice has told me everything."

"What? Beatrice, how could you!" she yelled.

"Beatrice told me about Harry," I continued. "I'm sorry I made you feel he wasn't good enough. I thought I was doing what was best for you. But God has given me an opportunity to make it all up to you. With the money from Karl's Will, you can marry Harry. Karl didn't leave his fortune to Beatrice. He left it to me. The Gold Mine, the Estate in Dargle, the money, everything now belongs to me and now I'm giving it to you. You can finally be happy. Zendaya, I can finally make up for all my mistakes. Zendaya, I know about the baby. You can have the life I never had. I want your baby to be able to have both a mother and a father. I want your baby to have what I could not give you."

"Money! All my life you were so obsessed with money. Dear God now I understand why. You made me believe, that me becoming rich, was the only thing that would ever make you happy but if you hadn't been running away from your father you could have had access to his money all along. I could have been with Harry all this time. No ducking! No diving! I could be marrying Harry next month."

"You still can marry Harry. Are you not listening to me Zendaya? Call off the wedding with Mark and marry Harry. You'll love each other. You and Harry now have a chance to finally be happy and raise your child together."

"Our child! Our child! You think it's that simple" shouted Zendaya, her lips trembling.

"Yes, I know about Harry and I know that you are pregnant with his child too. Falling pregnant out of marriage is never simple, I understand."

"Understand! You don't understand anything! You have never understood me at all! Well guess what? I am pregnant. How clever you were to discover that! But you know what, Mother? You really are not as clever as you think you are, because Harry is not the father. Mark is!"

"What!!!" shouted both Beatrice and I in unison.

Within seconds, she had fled the room, and we were left in disbelief with the sound of the front door, that had just been slammed shut, echoing through the house.

"Don't just stand there Beatrice, go after her," I shouted.

"You always expect me to do something. Have I not done enough! For once in your life, GO fix it yourself!"

I couldn't believe what she had just said. Beatrice just sat there, her face in her hands. Could it ever be possible? My ever faithful Beatrice, faithful no more! I was completely bewildered, but I had not the time to contemplate her loyalty, and so instead I dashed out the door knowing I had not a second to spare.

FOURTEEN

Only when I opened the door, did the time of day register. Night had fallen and under a dark sky, a steady rain fell. A shiver ran through my body. I scanned the street, desperate to find her. I just had to. But which way she had run and where to, I had no idea.

Whilst a woman on the run might otherwise have been easy to depict, typical of my luck, it simply was not so. If the visibility was not already a challenge, the strengthening shower only aided in making every figure appear to be fleeing the jaws of a carnivorous beast.

As the thunder rumbled, a bolt of lightning lit up the sky, and I was certain I had caught sight of her. Desperate to halt her, my eyes remained locked on the figure I knew to be hers, I ran down the steps, slipping and almost falling to the ground in the process. Any pain caused was worth it, as long as I could reach her.

"Zendaya! Zendaya! Stop!" I yelled. Yanking the arm of the figure I had been trailing. To my absolute horror I was met with the face of a man.

He pushed me away and with the rain now pelting the ground, he did not waste his breath on me. Already having reached the end of the street, I turned around and rushed up the nearest staircase. Lightning flashed once more and I wondered whether a figure on the other end of the street could be Zendaya's. I rushed in pursuit, however, this time I was not so certain.

As I got closer, I suddenly saw no one, the storm that had begun within my house, was now raging fiercely outside; I had somehow lost sight of her. I could only guess she had crossed the road and so I began to do so too. Just having stepped off the pavement, I turned around to see what I believed to be an extremely large owl flying towards me, its two very large bright yellow eyes, soaring forth rapidly.

A loud sound started to echo in my ears and the bird's eyes began to waver, suddenly steering away from me. Wondering why it was flying away, I stepped towards it and reached out my hand to touch it but just as its eyes began to cover me with light; my body was thrown against the pavement with a hard thud.

"Dear God! Mrs Gordon, were you trying to kill yourself? You almost let that bus run right over you!" screamed Mr Goldstone. Lifting his body off my own he pulled me off the ground before ushering me into his house, which was fortunately only a short distance away.

Entering his home, his 'flowers' rushed towards me, licking my wet legs. And, leaving me in their care, he dashed up the staircase.

A fire burned strongly at the hearth and it was relaxing to stare at. Although a fireplace stood in my own home, it had been almost twenty years since I had allowed Beatrice to light it. I had told Zendaya it had been because she had almost burnt her hand as a child. A believable story she had never questioned. Beatrice however, knew it was because of him, my one true love.

Now, as I watched the flames dance, I could almost feel him kiss me, his deep voice whispering in my ear, the words he had last uttered, repeating themselves as he gripped my body tighter, my body suddenly felt hot and my wet clothes, for the first time, could be felt.

Mr Goldstone returned, carrying with him a pile of towels and blankets and with his return, so too did my presence of mind. Dropping them down in haste, he grabbed one of the blankets and after wrapping it tightly around me, he seated me on a chair beside the fire.

"You cannot afford to catch a cold my dear. Wrap this towel around your hair and dry yourself with this one," he said, tossing me two towels.

I did as he had asked and as he stood and dried off too, his black and white dogs settled themselves beside me. At first I smiled at the idea of them enjoying my company but I quickly realized that it was the fire and not me that they enjoyed. How foolish of me?

"You could really have killed yourself! Are you hurt dear?" he asked, seating himself at his table.

I shook my head, physical pain, now a thing of the past.

"Thank goodness I got to you in time dear."

"How did you manage to see me in that storm Mr Goldstone? I could barely see anything."

"Well clearly! If you ended up standing in front of a bus! I heard the door slam and as I looked out the window, I saw Zendaya run out, followed almost immediately by you. It looked like you may have injured yourself at your staircase, so I had grabbed my coat to assist but when I came outside you were running up and down the street in an absolute frenzy, as if you had lost your marbles. Why did Zendaya run off like that? Oh please tell me Harry is alright and was not in an accident or anything of the sort."

"You mean he actually owns a car?" I asked.

Mr Goldstone frowned at my response, "Not that I know of dear, but after your near death experience, I would not be surprised if accidents were the order of the day. What happened dear, where did Zendaya rush of to?"

"That's just it Mr Goldstone. I have no idea. You see, she learnt the truth about my name. That it is in fact Leiyah and as I expected, she was horrified and that is why I was so desperate not to lose sight of her. But I am afraid, I did, and that is why I was running about so frantically."

"Aaah that explains it!" he nodded. "Well at least I know you haven't lost your marbles. But rather than dashing up and down the street like that why didn't you just make your way straight to her apartment."

I felt a horrid sense of embarrassment and hesitated before I replied, unsure whether I needed to, but eventually I did, "The thing is Mr Goldstone, well, I don't actually know where she lives?"

"But you are her mother dear. How can you not know where she stays? Have you never visited Harry before?"

"She moved in with Harry? Did she tell you that herself?"

Mr Goldstone looked simply flabbergasted but instead of answering my question directly, he continued, "Finding out you changed your name, would surely have come as a shock to Zendaya. Why didn't you just allow her the time to drown her sorrows with Harry before she was ready to return?"

"To be honest, I don't think she is with Harry right now. You see Mr Goldstone, I have already told you that Zendaya is getting married next month, and she is. But the man she is getting married to isn't Harry Greenwood."

"What! God in heaven! Have the stars begun to fall?" Mr Goldstone jumped off his chair, knocking over his tea in the process, the least bit interested that he had, he rushed towards me, falling down onto one knee as if he were about to propose. Dandelion barked. "I beg you dear, please tell me, you do not speak the truth," he pleaded, squeezing both my hands.

"Please Mr Goldstone, return to your seat." He did, but not where he had been stationed. "I wish it were not the case, but I'm afraid it is the truth."

"But, I do not understand, how can this be? Zendaya and Harry have been madly in love for years, for as long as I have known them, almost."

I could not bring myself to admit that I had been blind to this, so I got straight to it. "I am afraid she has fallen pregnant with another man's child."

"Oh dear God! What a mess! Poor Harry! But Mrs Gordon, if you cannot convince Zendaya to marry Harry, surely you can stop her from marrying a man she does not love!"

"But how Mr Goldstone?"

"There is so much more to family than just mum and dad. In the park you mentioned that Zendaya knew nothing about your father, dear, but what about her own father? Why did he not come with you to England?"

"Well I told her that he abandoned me when he learnt that I was pregnant."

"That is what you told her, but is that the truth?"

His question stunned me. Mr Goldstone had just implied that I was a liar, a heartless, betraying, cold blooded, devious liar and it suddenly felt as if the room was closing in on me. If only he had not pushed me off the path of the bus I would be free, with wings to fly. Even if I were now a minion to Lucifer, I would be in a better place. But as he repeated his question, the room stopped closing in on me because I stood up to leave, answering Mr Goldstone only at the door.

"No, it is not the truth," I knew exactly what I had to do.

Although the rain had stopped, the air was still chilly and I quickly re-entered my own abode.

Once inside, I sought out Beatrice, only to find her seated upon her bed in a trance-like state. Seeing me at the door, she immediately turned her back to me and curled up under the sheet. I sat myself down on the edge of the bed and placed my hand upon her shoulder, but she immediately threw it off. Our roles reversed.

"Why didn't you ever tell me that Zendaya had moved in with Harry?"

"Why didn't you ever ask about her new home?"

I sat in guilt, besides myself, as to how I could ever have failed to do so.

"Well she didn't move in with Harry," said Beatrice after a while. "She moved into an apartment Mark bought, but one she chose, all the way across town from Harry's. Her plan was to spend her nights when Mark was in America, with Harry and when he visited, she would stay with Mark."

"Oh my Goodness! What a twisted love story this is? How could she ever try to juggle the love of two men's hearts in such a cruel fashion? Ruthless!"

"You dare to frown upon my sweet child? When it was because of you that she was trapped. It was you and all your lies that made her a liar." Beatrice grabbed her pillow and covering her face, she screamed before she burst into tears. "And I have been a liar too. This is just as much my fault as it is yours. How could I ever have agreed to your plan?"

"I'm so sorry I dragged you into all this," was all I managed to say. Beatrice was right. I had lied and about so much more than just my name, and I was ashamed that until the events of the day, I had never before realized just how much she had sacrificed for the sake of my happiness.

I attempted to console her once more but she only rejected me with a greater fury. I waited for her heavy breathing to calm before I spoke once more.

"And what was her plan once the baby was born?" I asked, not expecting an answer, but an answer I did receive.

"Well maybe she was planning on telling both men they had become a father. She never told me."

"Babies grow up. Did she think the child would not one day tell daddy in America about their daddy in England? Imagine the psychological damage to the child?"

"Yes, she would have had to tell the truth at some point."

I felt a shiver.

"Beatrice, you have to make her come back here tomorrow."

"I will do no such thing. If she had not suffered enough from your lies, she would never have become such a liar herself. Let her come back, only when she feels ready to speak to you."

"But you are right. At some point in time one has to tell the truth, and there is so much more to the truth than just my name. I am ready to tell Zendaya my story. I am ready to tell her everything."

Beatrice sprung up like a slice of bread popping out of a toaster.

"Do you really mean it?"

"Yes. I have told her about my own father, now it is time to tell her about hers!"

Beatrice looked both horrified and delighted, a mixture of emotions all at the same time, "Oh my child," she hugged me tightly and began to cry, until finally, wiping her face on my still slightly damp clothing. "What if she does not understand? After everything you have done.

'Your Plan'."

I waited for her to seat herself beside me on the bed, thinking carefully about how best to answer, "The 'Plan' was a mistake and now that I see the consequences of my selfishness I don't think I will ever forgive myself. So if I cannot forgive myself, how can I ever expect Zendaya to? If it means one of us gets our one true love, it is a price I am willing to pay. I just hope someday you will be able to forgive me, B."

"Oh child! Of course I forgive you! I was never in agreement with your idea, even on the night we fled the Estate, but I knew then, as I know now, that it was an act of love. If I believed anything else, I would not be here," she smiled and kissed my forehead. "I love you!"

"Not just because you loved my father."

"I would have loved you either way. You are my daughter, 'our' daughter to me," she answered, squeezing my hand.

"Beatrice, I know I have never said this to you, but I love you. I love you more than I ever loved my mother."

"Don't speak that way child. The heart can love a million people in a million different ways and Mary Anne will always be your mother. That, I cannot take away from her. There is no reason to try to start comparing anyone's love."

"Do you think my mother really loved me?"

"In her own way, she must have. No more talk of this now," she squeezed my hand once more. "What's important right now, is helping Zendaya understand why you ran away and it is now your story to tell. Let her rest the night. I think we all need to. Tomorrow is your day!"

"Do you think Zendaya will return, B? How will you convince her to?" I asked.

"Just leave that up to me. I will go and see her at the crack of dawn. Is there anything that I can do for you before I leave in the morning?"

"I don't think so…actually, Beatrice do you think you could get the fireplace going, I mean light it before you leave."

She jumped up and hugged me, lifting me off the bed. "Oh my sweet Leiyah! The fire! Really?" She smiled, "Now I know that you really are ready and you can do this. Go and sleep now but before you do, please have something to eat. You need it."

I nodded.

A simple supper of bread and ham had been left on the table and I ate it ravenously. However, before I had fully satisfied my tummy, a discolored envelop on the floor caught my attention.

Realizing it must have slipped out of the diary, I rushed to pick it up. Making myself cozy on the couch, I took a better look at it. On the top were written the words *The Pram*. As tired as I was, I could not resist the temptation of reading the letter it contained and so I did.

Dear Henry

Thank you so much for purchasing the pram and the matching doll which I feel so guilty, I could not do myself. I need to stop making excuses for finding the time and do these things myself. You, as a father, would know how much happier I would have felt if I had been the one to choose it. It is exactly what Leiyah needed. I know she is so lonely and so badly wants a brother or a sister but you know I cannot possibly even speak about having a second child with Mary Anne. To put her through childbirth again? She could never bear it.

Oh but the pram! What a perfect solution! I must say you have a strange taste in toys, my friend. It is not quite what I had in mind it is so large. From a distance it almost looks like a real pram. Thank heavens! A million times lighter. When I first saw it, I was horrified it would never make my Leiyah happy but who would have guessed that its size would make her even happier! My seven year old was delighted and could not stop jumping up and down and she has been pretending she has a new sister. But my sweet Mary Anne, oh my beautiful wife, looked like she had seen a ghost. Before Leiyah had outgrown her pram, Mary Anne had ordered it to be dumped in the shed wanting no reminder of a crying child. Thank goodness you did not choose a doll that made noises, my dear Henry! Mary Anne already looks at the doll with such fear in her eyes.

I wish Mary Anne could just try to play with Leiyah, but ever since I returned to the Estate with the pram, Mary Anne has made me spend every spare moment, sitting with her next to the water's edge. That's Mary Anne for you, sprawled across one of her blue picnic blanket's, she has quite a collection mind you, her upper body resting upon my legs (Trust me Henry, she has me pinned down for hours until I cannot feel my legs), she giggles as if we were teenagers having only just met. Oh Henry, believe me, when I say I love her, but her conversations are starting to bore me.

Every time I mention Leiyah, Mary Anne doesn't even respond. I would honestly be happier if she freaked out but she damn well just stays silent. Her disregard for our daughter is starting to make me so mad. I never lost my cool before but I just cannot help it now days. Thank goodness for Beatrice. Every time we go out, I ask her to bring Leiyah out too. And so she does watching over her as she pushes the pram up and down the hill. As long as Leiyah is in the presence of her mother, my poor daughter couldn't be happier. She must never find out it is I who insists upon her presence and not her mother.

Yesterday I was just so fed up with Mary Anne's childish chatter that I just had to close my ears and turn away to admire my daughter. But instead of gazing upon my daughter, my eyes fell straight upon Beatrice.

One was the mother of my child and one mothered my child. Could it ever be possible to love both of them?

Oh Henry! What would you say if you knew how my heart really felt? I cannot possibly send this to you. You always told me writing things down helps. At least I feel better. I shall go downstairs and try to make peace with my women once more.

I wondered whether his reference to women included Beatrice and for the first time, I felt for my father. Had he lived his entire life starving himself of his one true love, at the same time punishing himself with the temptation? Had I really spent my entire life idolizing a woman who barely acknowledged my existence? An idea of a mother, an image in my mind, a desire in my heart.

After so many broken hearts I just had to heal Zendaya's. The letter written to Henry was only another sign that my sacrifice was being made for all the right reasons. So many emotions swirled through my mind. There was one thing I could now be certain of. Zendaya and the men in her life were not the only ones who had got themselves trapped in a love triangle. I pondered over Beatrice's tale, the side of her I had not known and as I tossed about on the couch believing my mind would never become still, it finally did just as the sun was about to rise.

FIFTEEN

He sat across from me, removing his shirt before throwing a handful of water from a deep metal bowl against his face. The sweat on his upper body made his skin shine in the light of the fire. He reached for the long pipe that lay beside him and with it his muscular arms, poked at the fire, raising its flames. He did not seem to notice me. I was glad. I did not want him to. I watched his every move. He stood up and shifted the firewood once more. The fire crackled. He dropped the pipe and began to walk away. 'Come back' I called, but the words I uttered failed to escape my lips. His name, of course! If I called out his name, he would turn. But I didn't know what it was. 'Don't leave me!' I called, but once more, I remained muted. I tried to raise my body and go after him but like a rock, I could not move. The fire crackled louder. I could feel its heat.

"Come Back!" this time my voice echoed through the room and I awoke in a state of shock, short of breath and panting, I tumbled off the sofa. The fire crackled loudly, followed by a strange popping sound against the grate.

Alerted to how ridiculous a sight I must have made, I jumped off, relieved to find that I was alone. I walked towards the fire and reminisced over my dream. It felt so real. There had been so many nights when I had silently watched 'him' start a fire. Days when I had watched 'him' bathe. As I raised my hands to the fire, I realized that I had fallen asleep the previous night reading the letter which still lay squashed within my left hand. I straightened it out, and, returning to replace it within the envelop, to which it belonged, I wondered whether I ought to ask Beatrice to read it.

"Goodness! Beatrice?" I said aloud.

Had Beatrice already set out to fetch Zendaya? If the fire had been lit, then she clearly must have. But how on earth she had not stirred me from my sleep whilst she had reignited life to our dormant fireplace, I was at quite a loss.

I looked at the clock, 9:15AM. She surely must have left, but before I could even call out her name, the door opened and there she was. My heart-beat escalated. There stood Beatrice, without Zendaya.

"Oh dear God! You couldn't get her to come, could you? She is not coming, is she? Oh B, but you said she would come. If she does not hear my story…getting her to unite with Harry will be simply impossible. You very well know that!" Flabbergasted as to how Beatrice had not succeeded in convincing Zendaya to accompany her, I landed myself upon the coffee table, with a heavy thud.

"Oh, Get Up Child!" shouted Beatrice, pulling me off the table and dragging me to a more suitable station. "With all the broken hearts I have had to look at in this room in the last few days, the last thing I need to be staring me in the face is a broken coffee table. Now stop being so negative. If there is anything you need to have in your heart right now, its faith. Zendaya is on her way. Actually, I'm sure she will be here any moment."

"Really? Swear to me she is. Oh, what a relief. You are not playing games with me, are you?"

"Oh child, I want Zendaya here as much as you do. Calm down. Please! Did you just wake up? Why don't you go upstairs and freshen up?"

"Oh B, how could I ever leave the room now?" My anxiety was so heightened that the thought of leaving the room and missing Zendaya's entrance was beyond alarming, something I simply could not allow.

"Alright then, I need to fix myself some breakfast. But since we both know you would perform a dramatic refusal, I shan't bother to even offer any to you."

Beatrice was right of course, I would never have joined her at the table. I was so overwhelmed I could barely keep still, and so I made my way to the window, pacing about as my eyes remained fixed on the street.

As Beatrice had promised Zendaya did return not long afterwards.

"I see her Beatrice, here she comes," I exclaimed. "Oh my word! She has brought flowers." In her hands, Zendaya clung to an enormous bunch of the brightest red roses I had ever set eyes on.

"And that my sweet child, is why she didn't arrive here earlier with me."

"B, whatever did you tell her? I simply don't deserve such a gift."

"I told her only what she needed to know. The rest of the story is yours to tell."

"B, more details please! You are not being fair. Oh what shall I say now? I do not have the strength to tell her the rest. Not after she presents me with flowers."

"You do have the strength. Admitting that there is a past you have hidden, a story you wish to tell was more than enough strength for me. Just go ahead and tell her exactly what you were going to."

Before I could think of a response to her motivating sentiments, the door opened and Zendaya ran through the door with as much steam as she had had when she last ran out, embracing me with the tightest of hugs, not letting go of me for so long that one would have imagined us to be two women who shared an unbreakable bond, being united after years of a forced separation.

"Oh mother! How could I ever have been so heartless? Of course you had a reason to change your name. I understand everything now. Kidnapped! Dear God! Of course you would be afraid they would try to take me from you too. No wonder! To have survived through such an ordeal, oh you are truly the bravest mother in the world. But look what I have gone and done to these flowers. I held them so carefully all the way here and now, silly me, I almost spoiled them. I know I so seldom say this and gosh I have been such a difficult, unappreciative child, but, I love you Mother. So very, very much! The perfect red roses for the perfect mother," she smiled lovingly, kissing both my cheeks before handing the bouquet over to me. "Sit Mother, please sit. I need to stop rambling now but when Beatrice told me that you were kidnapped, well the reason you had fled South Africa and changed your name and well everything just made perfect sense. Sit with me," she pulled me snug beside her to where I had only the previous day been seated with Beatrice.

Tears streamed down my cheeks for so many reasons. The last thing I deserved to be called was the 'Perfect Mother'. I was everything but the perfect mother and I so badly wanted to instantly correct her, but I reminded myself that once I had revealed to her my story and my so called 'Plan', Zendaya's would realize her sentiments were the furthest thing from the truth.

"Oh Mother, please don't cry," continued Zendaya. "Don't you like the flowers?"

I nodded and managed half a smile as a response, fostering all my energy into preventing further tears. Fortunately Zendaya was satisfied.

"Why did you not just tell me you had been kidnapped and held for ransom, yesterday? I never would have stormed off in such a manner, had I known about such an ordeal. And here I was making the dilemmas of my life such a death sentence. My actions were my own choice Mother, and my actions were undertaken with nothing but stupidity. But you Mother, your dilemma, I mean being held Captive, Oh my God! Well of course that was not your own choice. You were a Victim, you poor soul. Oh my courageous mother. All hail the mighty conqueror!" she said encouraging Beatrice to copy her actions in lifting an imaginary sword.

Beatrice did so without hesitation and together they both repeated the salute, "*All hail the mighty conqueror!*"

"Beatrice had said you wanted to tell me what exactly happened. How you were kidnapped? How it is that you managed to escape? How you met my father? Oh you have never spoken about Father? Did you tell him about the kidnapping? Is that why he rejected you?"

I felt goose bumps on my skin as an image of the forest came to mind but the momentary recollection disappeared with Beatrice's shrill voice.

"Zendaya!" she scolded, giving her a reprimanding stare. "Hush now! Calm down child! Can you please be patient? I have the greatest admiration for your mother for even deciding to speak about such a traumatic event, so can you please just allow her to tell you about it in her own way."

"Oh I'm sorry B, Mother. Just, oh I cannot wait to hear your story. This is just all so exciting!"

"Exciting is the last word I would choose to use. This has all been extremely overwhelming for your mother," scolded Beatrice, once more.

I listened without interruption, grateful that I was able to recollect my thoughts and better correlate the events I was about to reveal but while I listened, one thing baffled me. Zendaya appeared so content that I could almost believe that Beatrice had used some sort of time machine to erase the very existence of the love triangle. Perhaps my being blind to Zendaya's love for Harry had not been entirely my fault.

"Mother, Mother, earth to Mother are you listening? Are you ok? B, could you please take these flowers and put them in some water."

"Yes, I am alright, just a bit of a headache. A lack of sleep, that's all. Nothing to worry yourself about," I answered, savouring the scent of the roses before allowing Beatrice to remove them from my hands.

The last time I had been able to savour the scent of such a gift had been the day I had given birth. It had only been on the day that I had given birth that a man had presented me with flowers. The very same flowers I had told him I liked as we had walked along the stream at the foothills of the mountain, only a few days earlier. As much as I had tried to smile when my eyes met his, only tears had streamed down my cheeks. As I looked from Zendaya to the flowers, I could almost feel his presence. I wished to be with him once more. I wished I could be holding the flowers he had given me.

"Zendaya, I think you need to give your Mother a chance to freshen up. She was worried sick about you and refused to go upstairs. She actually slept on the couch and only woke up just before I arrived back from seeing you," said Beatrice.

"I won't be long," I answered. It was my chance to drag Beatrice away and find out exactly how much of my story Zendaya had been told. "Beatrice can you just come here a moment," I called as I reached the bottom of the staircase.

"Yes Madam?" she asked, flowers still in hand.

"Can you start calling me Leiyah, please B. We aren't pretending anymore are we? It would really make me feel a lot better." Beatrice simply smiled. "But what on earth did you tell her B? Why hasn't she said anything about either Harry or Mark?"

"Would it make things easier for you if she did?"

"Well of course not," I answered.

"Well then just be grateful and use the opportunity well. And about what exactly I said to her. It was simply that you were kidnapped and that you wanted to tell her all about what you experienced when you were kidnapped and about her father too. That's it."

"Thank you B, I won't be long."

"By the way, I saw little Peyton this morning by the way. I am sorry you missed her." Hearing her words, I froze, wishing she had not spoken. "Perhaps I should have woken you."

"I no longer care what happens to a stranger's child."

"Do not say such a thing. Every child matters, Leiyah!" she replied angrily.

"Yes you are right B. But how could I have ever had such a fixation on her when I had Zendaya."

"We both know the answer to that. Forgive yourself dear. Well we will be waiting for you. Don't be too long.

I won't," I replied, running all the way to my room.

All my time in my bedroom seemed to drag on forever, I could not possibly have been more than five minutes and upon my return, the overly boisterous Zendaya was still rambling away.

"Do you like where I have placed the flowers, Mother?" she asked.

"I love it!" I answered, which was the furthest thing from the truth.

Zendaya had placed it plum in the middle of the room, on the coffee table, right beside the contents of the forbidden delivery.

"So it can be a constant reminder of what an amazing mother you have been and how much I love you. I am sure it will be what you need, while you tell me your story. All that trauma! Oh, my brave mother!" She blew me several kisses and I blew her one back.

"Zen child, I think the mantelpiece above the fire will be better. It might fall."

I heaved a sigh of relief. 'Still my faithful B,' I thought, immediately tempted to blow several kisses her way.

"Mother you have finally lit the fireplace. I didn't even notice it when I first entered. Wow!"

"Yes, a fire always tended to remind me of things that happened when I was kidnapped. Things I did not want to remember and that's the real reason why I refused to have it lit. I am so sorry I allowed you to believe that it was because it was for your protection. That whole, 'you had almost burnt yourself story'…but you will understand soon enough."

"Oh please don't apologise. I understand so much already. You lost your mother. You believed your father had murdered her and you had every reason to. A step-mother and on top of that a step-brother so soon after your mother's death and if things couldn't get any worse, you were kidnapped. Beatrice says, because of your father's wealth. I know Beatrice says your father genuinely loved you, and maybe he did love you more than your mother might have, but you really did have too many reasons to be rebellious against him. Oh love really can be far too confusing when…" the abrupt halt in what she had wished to say, more than enough proof that her distress over her crazy love triangle still existed. Hiding her emotions truly was a talent she had mastered. That, I could conclude. "Well now, Mother," she continued. "Go on then, tell me your story. I really have been waiting far too long. It is almost noon."

"Are you ready Madam," asked Beatrice, who had still been seeing to the flowers.

I nodded. She smiled at me reassuringly before seating herself beside Zendaya, giving her a kiss on the forehead. I desperately wished I could get up and do the same but as much as I wanted to, I reminded myself of what I had finally only hours earlier accepted, the 'Plan' had failed and it was time to say goodbye. Staring into the fire, I took a deep breath in and closed my eyes, remembering the joyous cries of my baby on exiting my womb, the earth now graced with my very own flesh and blood. I looked towards Zendaya and once again silently said goodbye.

"Well Zendaya, I never thought this day would ever come but it has. I am ready to tell you my story. You have now already heard Beatrice's tale of her life, hers and mine both, until I turned eighteen, and I am not going to bore you by repeating the story of what happened before I left to live with Aunt Viola but I have to just point out a few things. To Beatrice, understandably, my mother was wicked from the very beginning, but in my eyes my mother was nothing but perfection."

"Understandably, as are you," replied Zendaya.

I bit my lips, ever so relieved that Beatrice had moved the flowers, "Yes, well my mother was my idol. She was the most beautiful woman I had ever seen and she would glide through the rooms of the Estate like a princess in a castle and when I was a little girl I had even believed she was a daughter of the Queen, being made to secretly live in another country for her own safety and mine. I was a secret princess too of course. I was my mother's princess. She was smitten with the British royal family and so was I. Well I suppose any child might have made this mistake but when she used to tell the ladies about all her visits to the many castles, I had genuinely believed she had entered them, because of a birthday invitation or a Cinderella type ball. Well, with age comes wisdom and how silly I felt when I did discover that just about every prestigious castle could be visited by a tourist and my mother had been just that, a tourist."

Zendaya laughed and I would have smiled, had not the flames of the fire reminded me of the fury the end of my tale was about to ignite.

"My mother was everything I wished to be, someday." I continued, "and when Aunt Viola passed away and left her house and money to me, it was as if God was granting me my wish to be just that, my mother. I could fulfil her dreams and return to England as she should have. If she had, had my father allowed her to, perhaps she might still be alive or at least not have had her life snapped away from her when she was so young. And so I used the money to buy us three tickets on the first flight out of South Africa. It was quite obvious that we couldn't live in Aunt Viola's house. My father finding us, would be like stealing candy from a baby, so as much as I had loved that part of England, I sold Aunty Viola's house to buy this one."

"But why all this talk about your mother being '*holier than thou*'? From everything Beatrice has said and this diary," moaned Zendaya, picking it up, "she clearly could not have been labelled as even the lowest form of 'good'." The thud of the diary against the coffee table clearly speaking the indignity Zendaya felt was applicable to my mother's persona.

"Shush child! Just let your mother speak," scolded Beatrice.

"Well my mother is in heaven and whatever the truth may be, there is no point in us trying to jury that now. But Zendaya, you are not going to understand the rest of what I have to say until you understand the woman my mother was to me. She was a loving mother who would constantly talk about motherhood. What she spoke about most is about the day she had given birth and I could not have been more proud. I was, after all, the daughter who had made her a mother. Until the day she died, I never believed she faulted and I admit, yes, I question her actions now, but I ask that you listen to my story with an open mind and remember that I shall be telling you a story based on a very different Mary Anne. The Mary Anne I believed her to be. Can you do that for me Zendaya?"

"Do what?" she responded with a look of confusion.

"Listen to the rest of my story with an open mind?"

"That's not too much to ask now, is it Zendaya," encouraged Beatrice.

"Oh alright then, but can you please speed it up and get to kidnapping," said Zendaya giving me a sulky glare, her bubbliness already withering.

"Yes of course. But allow me to start from the morning I buried the treasure box. There is one thing Beatrice has never failed at and that is keeping a promise and until the box was opened, I had not the faintest idea that my father and Beatrice had been watching me. In a way I am glad Beatrice didn't tell me. The treasure box was our secret. Something only my mother and I would ever share."

"But if it was such a special secret between you and your mother, why did you share it with Beatrice in the kitchen," asked Zendaya.

"Well I told Beatrice about everything," I replied, the realization that I had included Beatrice in secrets only between my mother and I had never struck me before.

Zendaya frowned.

"Zendaya, have you decided to interview me now, or are you going to let me tell my story?"

"Oh I'm sorry Mother, please go on. My lips are sealed." Zendaya pretended to zip her lips closed, locked it and threw away the key, giving me a mischievous smile.

As much as I tried not to, I could not prevent myself from smiling back, wishing I could be frozen in the moment forever, but like it or not, that was not one of my options. The day had indeed come, the moment had arrived. I was finally going to tell my story and reveal the life changing secrets I had worked so hard to conceal.

• • •

After ranting my feelings in the kitchen I stormed out the house, determined to spend as much time at my mother's grave as was possible. With a teary eyed vision of the lake, I was marching straight towards my mother's grave when I realised I lacked a tool to bury what I so tightly grasped. Some distance away, not spoiling the beauty of the house and almost hidden by the trees, stood the stables and a shed. Suddenly changing my flight plan, I made my way straight towards the shed.

Almost at the shed, I gazed towards the mountains. Cattle and horses lay grazing in the foreground. I wished my life could be as simple as theirs. How serene they looked, I thought as I reached the door of the shed. I had never stepped inside the musty shed before, never having had a reason to. I struggled to even find the light switch and although the rays of the morning sun had begun to enter the dirty window, it still took me a great deal of time before I found what I was looking for. But once I had spotted the spade, I tossed it over my shoulder before making a hasty exit out the door, making my way straight to my mother's headstone. The weight of the spade on my shoulder, goodness, it felt like I was hauling a bag of bricks and it certainly made my walk down the hill, a long one.

The rocks near the dam would easily have obscured the very existence of the headstone to a stranger but even from so great a distance, I had it in sight.

Upon reaching my mother's grave, I dropped the spade and flung my body on the ground beneath which my mother lay, staring up into the deep blue sky. Ordinarily, I would watch the sun rise, challenging my majestic God as to what new heights could be reached by the time I had to make my way back to the house. The sun was the only GOD I still believed in, the only glorifying power that beseeched the earth, that bothered to comfort me each day at my mother's grave site. It was the only magnanimous power that gave me its loyalty, how could there be any other GOD.

The high-pitched echoes of the Hadeda Ibis that suddenly took flight from the nearby forest, suddenly reminded me of my purpose in carrying the spade and I jumped to my feet almost as if I had done so from fear of the birds with which I was all too familiar.

After carefully placing the jewelry box beside my mother's headstone, I picked up the spade, striking it fiercely into the ground, releasing all the pain and anger I felt as I did so. Digging a small square, approximately half a meter in depth, I finally dropped the spade, and sat down, dripping with sweat.

I tried to think of the perfect words, I had been thinking all week but I just could not seem to find the perfect words. I was angry, so angry that I had not realized how tightly I had been holding the spade. Suddenly I felt my fingers burning and finally looking at them, I saw the blood. Blood! Of course! Susannah will never be my mother. I will never be her flesh and blood. Exactly! I finally knew what I needed to write and so I did.

Blood is thicker than water

Mary Anne was my mother. We were flesh and blood and nothing and no one could ever change that. Folding the page small enough to comfortably fit within the box, I realized it needed one other thing. I pulled the pen out of my pocket once more and across the top wrote out the words...

XXX
Love Leiyah

"Goodbye mummy, flesh and blood...forever!" I shouted. Although my fingers were already slightly bleeding, I slit my left index finger against the spade before letting the blood drip onto the words. Removing my mother's necklace from my pocket, I kissed it as well as its twin, which I wore around my neck. "I will always be with you Mother. When I go to England, I will be everything you ever wanted. Someday I will be exactly like you, I promise." I placed the necklace on top of the letter, closing the case, finally satisfied. Kissing the closed treasure box, I placed it gently into the hole I had dug. Finally burying it as fast as my burning finger could allow me to.

Just before I walked away, I looked at the words on the headstone once more, before reading it out aloud, "Beloved wife of Karl Johan Kleinhans. Damn him! Karl! Karl! Karl! Why does everyone worship Karl? Why won't anyone see the real Karl? This is all his fault!" I shouted, slamming the spade against his name. My body shook. "He does not deserve us, I'm going to be ok, mummy," I said out aloud, hugging the headstone, before using it as a support to lift up my body. I began to feel dizzy.

Despite that, I picked up the spade and began slashing at my Father's name several times before falling down fatigued.

"Our love for you will never die!" I read out the words that had been carved on the headstone as a tribute from my father. Shaking my head I shouted out, "Our love…how dare he say OUR and replace you within a year. Oh Mother, we are both finally free of him," I said.

Without bothering to cart back the spade, I returned to the house. Beatrice was horrified when she saw my hands, treating my fingers intensively as if she was performing an operation. I knew she was dragging the process. To be honest, I was as reluctant to say goodbye as she was.

"B, could you come with to the airport? I couldn't bear to hear Susannah's blabbering without you."

"Don't worry. I have already spoken to your father. It will just be the three of us."

"As it always should have been, I replied."

Beatrice instantly burst into tears. I was not entirely sure why.

SIXTEEN

I wonder now if I would ever have had a reason to leave had it remained just the three of us. But had it remained just the three of us, I might never have had an opportunity to be your mother, although, at this point pondering over what might have been, will really not succeed in changing anything, so I guess the point is, what did happen and so I shall tell you the rest.

The drive to the airport did in fact turn out to be the very last time the car would be occupied by just the three of us, my father driving silently whilst Beatrice cradled me in the back seat, unable to silence herself all the way to the airport. I often reminisced over the sight of them at the airport, the two of them side by side, my father with his arm around her, consoling Beatrice who cried profusely as I walked away. They both waved vigorously and I had to shove my hand into my pocket to prevent myself from waving back. Although it was only to Beatrice, to whom I wished to wave.

It pained me to be leaving her behind with my father, to suffer daily with that narcissist. *Someday you too will be free, my beloved B.* It was my silent promise to her as I turned away for the last time, or so I thought.

The white woman ahead of me in the line into the departure lounge had been cursing an unsightly couple.

"Calm down *Mevrou*. It's just his maid," replied another.

I unintentionally turned to follow their glare, all too amused to find that the couple they so vilely condemned was none other than my B who was now being embraced in a hug from my father. Them a couple? The absurdity of it. I laughed. Karl Kleinhans did not know how to love, least of all a soul as pure as that of my B.

It was but a matter of hours before I set foot on the land of my mother's birth and it was everything I could have ever imagined it to be. It was FREEDOM. I had been re-born, No boundaries! No rules! Every day was a dream come true, the only thing it was missing was my Beatrice.

Upon arrival, I could not comprehend what fascinated me the most. There was the majestic river, Thames, the sophisticated public transport and the aristocratic architecture. Well, that was certainly beyond my expectation. It was abuzz with life, even the population of all the towns I had visited in South Africa, combined, could not compete with the number of people I could have counted on the day of my arrival. It was on that very day, straight from the airport, that I dragged my aunt along with me to the Tower of London and then Windsor, one of the many castles my mother had constantly bragged about all her life. In all my wildest dreams, I could not fathom how my mother could possibly have been tricked into leaving such a country.

One of the first things that did leave me quite dumbfounded was the diversity of people.

From all the Jane Austen movies, my mother loved watching and from the way she always spoke about the land of her birth, I had only ever expected white people. The biggest surprise was that in a land that had first only been walked upon by skin as white as snow, there were even white people working for blacks. However, no one except me seemed to find it strange.

It was a week after moving in with my late mother's sister that I had my very first encounter with my teenage fantasy. It was on a morning that had begun as a complete disaster.

The remainder of my belongings finally arrived in England, I was completely denied an opportunity to feel any sense of delight, when the obnoxious driver refused to assist me with the carrying of my boxes from the vehicle into the house. After my attempts to convince him otherwise only resulted in flaring his temper further, he thereafter simply refused to even unpack them onto the pavement.

"Look here Missy," he said as he placed the first few boxes onto the pavement. "Driving is my job and I am no elephant," he said.

"Well you certainly look like one," I snarled.

"You rich snob!" he retorted.

"Excuse me! I am no snob but I certainly am richer than the stars."

"The ones in the sky or them ones I see on the TV," he asked wittily.

"Oh you are so very clever, aren't you? But I am not the one driving a van for a living now, am I?"

I pulled out a stack of money from my pocket "What if I had to pay you this?"

The driver burst out laughing and when I looked into my hands, I realized that the money I had been offering was in the currency of the South African Rand.

"Oh, I have real money too but…I mean this is real money…ooh you are just so damn annoying. I wish you had been a black driver. At least then you might have listened."

"Take your fake money and stuff it."

"And you think your British money is so great. You do not know where I come from. I come from a land where the sand has Gold…" I began, before realizing how ironic my statement was. I was actually defending the land I had just run away from. Who would have ever imagined?

"You cheeky brat you!" the driver responded. "You know what, these boxes are all yours Miss, Queen of the '*City of Gold*', because right now I am going to go and take myself a seat and read my newspaper and you had better make it quick, because when I am done reading, it is going to be *Adios* from me. Whether your boxes are out the van or not!"

"*Adios*? Goodness that's not even British. I am not yet British and I can speak better English than you can. OOH, you will be in such trouble, Mister!"

"Sure thing, oh mighty one," he laughed.

Fearing that the arrogant driver might keep to his word and speed off with my things still in his charge, I began almost tossing the boxes out the van, in a complete frenzy. If only Aunt Viola had not gone out that morning. She would surely have known what to do with one of her kind.

Stacking as many boxes as was possible, unconcerned that I was obscuring my vision in my haste, I was startled by an unfamiliar voice that I almost believed I had contrived. "My my…someone certainly is in a mood this morning," came the manly words, in a mocking tone.

"Who's there? Show yourself!" I shouted, turning around to find myself crashing head first into the very voice that had spoken, both of us falling to the ground, one of boxes breaking open and spilling its contents onto the road.

The young gentleman moaned, his head having bumped the ground. I expected the unleashing of a venomous tongue but instead he laughed. "Maybe if you weren't a fan of covering your face you wouldn't have to go around asking people to show themselves."

"I'm so, so sorry. I truly am. I promise to make it up to you." Meeting his gaze for the first time I suddenly felt butterflies in my tummy. The man was young. He was handsome, extremely handsome. Realizing the position in which my body rested upon his, I felt my heart pulsating.

I had fallen head over heels in love, literally and figuratively. He surely had to be the love of my life. The blonde hair, the blue eyes. He looked exactly like my mother and even better, was the image of our yet to be born children, they would look exactly like us, like Mary Anne and not like Karl. I could not possibly risk my child having dark hair like that of my father. The image made me squirm. It would have been a constant reminder of him.

"Your things," he said, looking at the items that had scattered onto the road, "We better get it before a car comes," he said as he stood.

As he gathered my possessions from the road, I remained sitting on the pavement, mesmerized. In a trance like state I watched his every move.

"Here, let me help you," he said, lifting me off the ground. He was my Trojan hero, '*my Achilles*' and as he pulled me to my feet, my heels immediately felt weak.

"I may have been the one who hit the ground but you certainly seem more dazed than I am," he smiled. "My name is Alex."

"I am Leiyah. Leiyah Kleinhans."

"Is that German?"

"No actually it's…" I stopped in my track and smiled foolishly at him. Alex knew nothing about the great *Meneer* Kleinhans. He knew nothing about my father's business. I really had left it all behind me. "…well that does not really matter. I have just moved to England to live with my aunt. Her name is Viola Jones," I continued, making sure to emphasize Jones.

"Are you two love birds done?" yelled the driver. "I won't be waiting for any babies to be born."

I was stiff with embarrassment

"Gosh you look like a rose," he smiled flirtatiously. Although I could not see myself, I was certain his description of me was more than befitting.

"I'm sorry about that. I was just trying to speed things up. Can you believe the driver did not even bring anyone to assist him and he has been refusing to help me."

"Allow me," he answered charmingly.

As he turned to carry the first stack of boxes into the house, I noticed a small amount of blood on his hair.

"Ouch, your head, its bleeding, please come inside. Let me get some ice. "

"I will live. Let's sort out your boxes first. Then you will have all the time in the world to nurse your wounded soldier," I was thrilled. He was surely as attracted to me as I was to him.

It was not long before the job was done and I was able to say a happy *adios* to the miserable driver and once inside, I nursed Alex's wound, doing so as slowly as Beatrice had nursed my bleeding fingers, the morning I had left South Africa. As I savoured the feeling of getting to touch his skin, I got the impression that Alex felt likewise about his accidental caresses.

Finally done, I followed Alex outside, trying to think of an excuse to make him visit once more. Looking towards the midday sun for an answer, my prayer was un-expectedly answered.

"So exactly how are you going to keep your promise?" he asked.

"What promise?" I answered flushed.

"You promised to make it up to me. The fall, all this," his hand swaying back and forth between the street and the door to the house, he did a comical action, pretending that he was collapsing from trying to lift an object as heavy as an ox.

"You are such a character," I answered, laughing. "How exactly would you like me to keep my promise?"

"How about a date?"

I was thrilled, although I tried desperately not to let it on, "It's a deal."

He stretched out his hand. "How about we spit on it," he said.

I instantly obeyed without realizing what I was doing. He did the same and we squeezed together our slimy hands. The deal was sealed. We had shared our first kiss and from that very moment we were a couple.

The next few years are quite a blur to me now, but they were the happiest years of my life. Alex and I spent almost every day together and we did almost everything a young couple would have done, partying, hiking, picnics in the park, you name it. Intimate with each other, we certainly were, but the one thing I absolutely refused to agree on, was losing my virginity before marriage. In a way, I suppose that would explain why just before my twenty first birthday, he popped a ring on my finger. I was truly living a fairytale, but a mere three days later, I came crashing back to earth.

On an afternoon when Aunt Viola was out, I had been relaxing on the couch, flipping through a magazine, when I was annoyed to have my attention swayed towards the ringing of the telephone. Ignoring it, had become a natural tendency, but strangely, I felt the need to yield to the ringing that beckoned me. When I finally did answer, how I wished, more than ever, I had not done so.

"Hello, Jones residence,"

"Leiyah?" '*Karl no, could it be*' I thought.

"Yes," I answered.

"It's your father, well of course you know that. I need you to come home."

I was stunned. It had been more than a year since I had heard his voice.

"But why?" I asked horrified at his request.

"It has to do with the paperwork you signed for your inheritance."

"What! I don't remember signing anything."

"You signed it in the kitchen, the morning you left."

"Yes. Oh, yes, I remember now. What about it?" I asked.

I remembered that morning all too well. Susannah had begun trailing me around the house like a puppy and just when I thought it couldn't get any worse, she burst into tears as if she were about to lose her own flesh and blood. My father who had been lingering nearby suddenly saw his opportunity, I suppose, and so whilst I was at the height of my frustration, he shoved a document in my face. I was already fatigued enough from my morning venture. Without even reading the heading, I had signed my name across it and rushed into the car.

"I'm glad you don't pretend to have signed it. You need to fulfill the stipulated conditions."

"Conditions? What conditions?"

"You just need to spend one week with me at the mine Leiyah. I don't want to go and have to leave everything to Willem. You are my daughter."

"It's funny how you never treated me like one. You can do anything you want with your money. Give it to Susannah. Give it to William. I don't care. I have a life of my own now and I am happy."

"I have bought the ticket. Your flight leaves next Saturday. I will see you at the airport. Your Aunt has all the details," he answered, completely ignoring everything I had just said.

"Well you have just wasted your money, because nothing you say is going to make me board that plane. I guess that's nothing to cry about because you have all the money in the world. But you know what, all the money in the world isn't going to buy me back." I slammed the phone bursting into tears, more out of rage rather than sorrow.

I needed Alex to hold me and assure me that I had escaped my father forever! Drying my tears, I grabbed my coat and ran out the door to relay the conversation to my beloved Alex. He would know exactly what to do, or so I thought. When I arrived at his apartment however, the Alex who awaited me was not the Alex I so dearly loved and his reaction was the furthest thing from what I had anticipated. When he heard of my intentions to decline my father's request, he was absolutely infuriated.

"Have you completely lost your mind!" he yelled. "Your father owns a Gold Mine. Wow! You said he had been rich but you never said he owned a '*Gold Mine*'. This is an opportunity of a lifetime for us. You WILL go and that is final!"

I stared at him in shock before responding, "My God Alex, I must be hearing things?"

"Leiyah, think of how this will change our lives. We will have all the money we could ever dream of."

"I don't want that man's money. We don't need that man's money. Alex…have you ever listened to me? I hate him, you know that I do. Don't make me go back there."

"Come on, for us baby!"

"But Alex, I came here with no intention of being obliging to my father's request. I have never cared about the success of the business and that is why I never told you about it. I am not about to start caring now. Alex, he is trying to trick me into leaving Britain, the same way he tricked my mother. He thinks the pain he subjected me to when my mother died, will be repaired by my getting more involved in the business, by my getting his money. He is so wrong. Alex, you don't know him like I do. I will never accept something from a man who does not love me. I know true love when I see it and you are the only man who truly loves me!"

"I do love you, from the very day you knocked me to the ground, I fell head first in love with you too," he smiled at me before looking at me sternly, "but people who truly love each other, are also prepared to make sacrifices for each other.

"But Alex, to go there for a whole week? I have never even visited the Gold Mine. I never really knew anything about Johannesburg. My mother had hated the fact that my father had left her all alone and gone there so much that she had forbidden him from ever speaking about it. I hated the fact that Johannesburg upset my mother so much, that I refused to ever listen to his stories and learn anything about it. My father never forced the issue. This is unchartered territory, Alex. Please don't make me do this. Even when Susannah came along, she never wanted to hear my father speak about the mine either, but her reasoning was the complete opposite. She yearned to return there. Johannesburg had been her home."

"Enough. It's just a week," shouted Alex. Leaving me aghast, he grabbed my hand and pulled the ring off my finger. "So if you truly love me you will go," he continued.

"Alex! Give it back!" I jumped around him, trying to twist it out of his grasp but of course, he was too strong. "Alex, you can't be serious. Stop this right now!" I shouted, my hands on my hips.

"On the day you arrive back, I will be waiting at the airport to bend down in front of a public audience and put it back on your finger. Imagine that! So you will go?'

"Yes I will go, but to please you, not my father." I could hardly believe the words that had just come out of my own mouth.

"Do exactly as he says, and when you come back, our lives will be everything you ever dreamt it would be."

A week later, there I was, sitting in the departure lounge of Heathrow airport. The game had changed and I was no longer in control of the cards. Still yearning to be the deceiver, I was now the one being deceived. The cards had been re – dealt and this time I had been outplayed. This time my father had won.

Picking up a magazine, as a means to allowing my thoughts to stray from the dreaded circumstance that awaited me, I cursed under my breath to astoundingly find myself turn to an article on the life of my father, the great Karl Johan Kleinhans.

From the article, I learnt that the previous year had been an extremely prosperous one for Kleinhans Gold Mines, leading my father to presently be one of the richest men in South Africa. Irrespective of how far I physically was from him, I could just never escape him. I felt like a piece of metal trying to release itself from a magnet. The world really was his playground and I was caught in his trap. It seemed that with every attempt I made to break away, I was simply only pulled closer towards him.

'From all the articles I could have turned to, why did it just have to be one centered on you?' I wondered. 'Your dream of becoming the richest businessman in the country, has finally been accomplished, so why do you need me? Wait, I know, I'm just your next conquest. Of course! How ignorant of me? You just want to portray yourself as not only a businessman, but a loving Father as well, isn't that so? Well you are not! Don't you ever think you are going to get away with it? I will make sure the newspapers learn the whole truth about THE GREAT Meneer Kleinhans. The best at digging so they claim you to be, well they sure got that right. Which other man out there could allow his wife to dig her own grave. It's a pity they did not specify exactly what it is you are good at digging.' I flung the magazine onto the seat beside me and took a walk to look at the planes preparing for departure.

The tar on the runway was completely wet, the light rain having not ceased, since I had arrived at the terminal. I watched the path of the Air India aeroplane as it made its way onto the runway preparing for takeoff to poverty stricken India, but the mere thought of accidentally landing there, rather than in South Africa, seemed like heaven. As I watched the plane climb higher towards the darkened clouds, I damned it for preventing my GOD from showing itself, my magnanimous sun.

"Here you go, cheer up dear," said a young gentleman who had been walking by, his French accent alluring my senses and instantly my teary eyes dried. I accepted his tissue tentatively, dabbing my eyes gently, fearful that I might ruin my eye makeup.

"What's the matter, Madam."

"Nothing really. Just the grey sky always tends to depress me. Quite silly, really."

"Well look over there," He pointed towards where the flight I had been watching, was now almost vanishing from sight.

"What about it?' I asked.

"Well do you not see that rainbow?"

I wondered how I had not seen it before. "I see it now," I answered.

"Well they say you will find a 'Pot of Gold' at the end of every rainbow. Have you ever heard that before?" he asked with a broad smile.

His French charm instantly disappeared. 'Pot of Gold', I could have screamed. If I didn't already know I was about to cross the skies to land straight into my father's 'Pot of Gold'.

"Damn you Karl Kleinhans! Money won't buy you out of this one," Several passengers gave me a peculiar stare and the Frenchman quickly walked away

Did that Monster think he could just swallow me up into his mine? His 'Pot of Gold! I promised myself, at that moment, that he wasn't going to win. I was not a piece of gold he could find and polish up and I would find a way out of his lair, once more.

The speaker made a sharp piercing sound, before a woman's voice rang through the corridor. It was time for my flight to board. Reluctantly, I made my way to the gate.

SEVENTEEN

I awoke with a shock, instantly alert to my surroundings.

"Are you alright dear," asked the woman along the aisle, looking towards me with genuine concern as she continued to comfort her young son who was seated between us. "You hit your head against the window quite hard there."

My head had been throbbing so much since the moment I had boarded the plane, I had not the slightest idea as to where it was that I had hit my head. I looked at my watch. We were surely already flying over South Africa, and the sky looked as gloomy as it had over England. It certainly was as angry as I was too. That was for sure, for we seemed to be in the middle of a lightning storm, the sky flashing erratically between night and day.

The little boy, who could not have been older than six, leaned over me to try to gain a better view out the window, whilst his mother stopped an air steward to enquire as to how long more it would be before we landed.

"Do you know why the sky keeps flashing like that," I asked him.

"No," he answered.

"Well that's because there is a dragon trying to catch us and those aren't really clouds. That's the smoke when he breathes out his fire. There's so many of them. Can you see them? There's one there," I said, pointing as if I could really see one. "And there, there's another," I said, pointing in the opposite direction.

I made a spooky face and glared at him, wide eyed, quickly turning when I spotted that his mother was done with the steward.

"Mummy, the dragons are going to eat us," he screamed, bursting into tears.

'*Did every dragon breathe fire*', I wondered. Whilst the child beside me began to howl louder, I wondered as to how my mind had strayed to muse itself over mythical creatures.

I always felt a little guilty for what I had said to him, but then again I convinced myself that it had really been nothing more than a playful joke rather than a malicious act I had contrived, simply because I did not wish to be the only person on the flight that was filled with fear, even if my fear did stem from an entirely different reason.

The lady scolded her son harshly, looking around with embarrassment as people stared.

"But she told me that," said the boy, pointing towards me.

"You are such a wicked young lady," responded the mother, pulling her son closer to her. "I'm glad you hit your head. It's a pity it didn't knock some sense into you."

No longer a look of concern in her eyes, she pulled her son as close to her as was possible, unable to put him on her lap as the seat belt signs were on.

I looked out the window and smiled, my misery fading in my temporary amusement.

"We thank you for flying British Airways and look forward to having you fly with us again. I must apologize for the turbulence but we will be out of the clouds within the next few minutes. We are expecting a smooth descent towards Louis Botha International Airport on this lovely summer morning. The weather in Durban is presently cloudy with a north easterly wind. The time on the ground is ten minutes past six and the temperature is 24 degrees Celsius. Cabin crew prepare for landing."

The pilot was still speaking, when the ground below came into view. The very same sight I had only just said goodbye to. Nothing appeared altered. My anxiety heightened, the misery returning.

"See, no dragons," I heard the lady reassuring her son, as we landed.

I didn't turn around to gather the child's response but as I looked towards the airport terminal, I visualized my father and it was I who now saw the vision of a 'fire-breathing dragon'. I was back in his lair.

My head hurt and I closed my eyes, resting my head against the window pane, opening them only to find that the cabin was now empty.

"Ma'am, are you feeling ill? Would you like me to fetch someone to assist you?" asked the air steward.

"Just a little ill but I think I will manage," I answered.

"I will get you someone, just in case," he answered, disappearing quickly.

Reaching to play with my engagement ring and finding my finger bare, I suddenly remembered why I had agreed to be there. I was doing it for myself and not for my father. I was doing it for Alex and I. Visualizing Alex proposing to me on my arrival at Heathrow airport, I found the courage to stand up.

Just as I attempted to bring down my luggage, I was startled by the appearance of a muscular paramedic, kit in hand, all togged up. "Let me help you with that," he said, reaching towards it and retrieving it effortlessly. "A very gothic look I must say. Is that why the steward said you looked ill?" he laughed.

"Perhaps," I smiled shyly. My mascara had clearly smudged, but the mishap of my makeup hardly seemed to concern the man, my skimpy outfit had clearly won his attention.

"Well I am glad to see you are on your feet," he continued as he began to open his kit. "Can I do a check of your vitals?"

"No, no, it's quite alright. I can manage now," I answered.

"Is someone fetching you?"

"Yes, my father is," I answered regretfully.

"Perfect, I will accompany you to him," replied the young white man who looked to be in his early thirties.

On exiting the plane, he signalled for an old black man to bring along a wheelchair. The man himself looked so old and tired that the wheelchair appeared to be a support for himself, rather than an aid for others, but, nevertheless, he made his way towards us. I was reluctant to be wheeled through the airport like an invalid but I was so emotionally drained that it did not take me too long to agree.

I truly wish I hadn't agreed, for I found myself being pushed out the door of arrivals straight into my father's clasp. I suppose anyone in a wheelchair would gain attention and my father spotted me all too quickly.

Had I been on my feet, I may have perhaps been able to camouflage myself in the crowd, perhaps hide away in a place unbeknown to my father for the duration I was meant to stay there and return to England to claim my ring. After all, Alex had no communication with my father and how could he possibly know whether I had fulfilled my father's request or not. I regretted why I had not thought of such a scheme earlier.

"Is this your father?" asked the paramedic. My father had gestured to the man who wheeled me, to push me no further.

Confusion was surely the order of the day, neither my father nor I showing any emotion.

"Yes," was all I answered.

"I will take her from here," said my father to the porter, you can go now. "I am sure she can walk just fine."

I was stunned. It was not as if I had been expecting a vastly altered and loving father, but he didn't even bother to enquire as to why I was being assisted.

The paramedic was clearly astonished as to my father's lack of concern, "Well you are correct. She has not injured her legs, but she is very weak, Sir. I must insist on accompanying you to your vehicle. Please let Joseph push the wheelchair, Sir. It is his job after all. Certainly not something a man such as yourself should be seen doing."

My father stepped aside and objected no further and led the way to his silver Land Rover, which was not parked a great distance away. The airport was after all a very small one, probably not even a third the size of Heathrow. Arriving at my final drop-off, the handsome young man helped me to my feet, whilst my father tipped the porter, who lingered no longer, carting the wheelchair away with a new-found energy.

I had been expecting the doors of the vehicle to be flung open as we approached, but to my bewilderment it housed no occupants. I was ever so grateful that Susannah had not been camping in the car, but I found it strange that Beatrice wasn't. *'Oh no, just you and I, all the way to Johannesburg. Please stop at the estate,'* I prayed, surveying the man who had already jumped into the front and started the engine. *'Calm down Leiyah. We surely must be stopping at The Estate. Why else would he have bought me a ticket to Durban?'*

I had purposely chosen to arrive in the most seductive dress I possessed, one that almost resembled lingerie, a deliberate attempt to antagonize my father. I was no longer a girl, I was a woman and I wanted such a fact to be staring him in the face from the moment he laid eyes on me. But as to what I wore, he said absolutely nothing. Flaring his temper had clearly been a failure. I was now the infuriated one rather than the businessman in his fancy suit.

I had no attraction to the paramedic but his behavior simply thrilled me, it seemed my last resort to pushing my father's buttons and earn some form of attention and so I encouraged him, deliberately dropping my purse and allowing him an opportunity to savor my silky legs. Returning it to me and doing an unnecessary check that I had everything I needed, he still hovered around scanning me from head to toe. He was so reluctant to part that he even packed my luggage into the vehicle. I smiled. At least my outfit had not been a complete waste.

"Will you be joining us too?" my father asked him, sarcastically.

The young man didn't reply. Smiling at me, before taking another look at my legs, he finally walked away.

My father climbed behind the steering wheel and not waiting for any instruction, I climbed into the vehicle too. The sooner the nightmare was over, the better. Alex and I would be re-united.

Calm and relaxed as we began our journey, my father almost seemed to smirk in victory. As yet, he had still not uttered a word to me. We had been driving for a little under an hour when, unable to restrain myself for a second longer, I lashed out at him, finally breaking the silence between us. The sound of only the radio too much to bare, I turned it off.

"The Silent Treatment," is that how you expect me to learn about the mine?" I asked.

The "Silent Treatment" continued, leading my exasperation to new heights in what now seemed like a never-ending journey. A droplet of sweat, large enough to be felt, dripped down my temples and onto my forearm and I pressed my palms to my forehead. The throbbing was becoming more unbearable. My head was beginning to feel like a volcano spewing out ash, higher and higher with every minute.

"Why do you even pretend to care?" I asked my father. "Did you not fear I was paralyzed when you saw me in the wheelchair?"

"In clothing like that, who wouldn't want to assist you?" he answered, his lips finally parting.

"What a miracle, you still possess a voice," I said sarcastically. "You know what? You are just as cruel now as you were when I left."

My father didn't seem phased by my comment.

"Alex would have been so happy, had he been there to watch all your flirtation at the airport, don't you think. The helpless maiden," my father glanced my way with an unreadable expression. I felt relief. My performance had been noticed after all.

"We love each other and that's all that matters," I answered.

"Does he really now," he said skeptically.

"Of course he does," I shouted.

"Viola says he has proposed. Can I see the ring?"

I had not the foggiest idea what to say but it seemed my father already knew too much. More than I would ever have guessed.

"Makes so much sense, why he would take back his proposal now, doesn't it," he smiled.

"What! How could you speak such nonsense," I exclaimed, stunned that my aunt had shared such information. "We are still engaged. The ring is just with Alex. He never once said he no longer wanted to marry me."

"You are still engaged. Alright then, keep telling yourself that."

I couldn't believe my father's accusation. To dare imply Alex's love was untrue.

"Why didn't you bring Beatrice with you?" I asked. If only she had been in the car she would surely have been able to put my father in his place.

"She really wanted to come but there is something you and I need to do first before we meet her at the Estate," answered my father. "Just the two of us."

"We need to go to the mine, yes I know, but surely she could have come too. Besides we would have to pass by Dargle before we get to the mine"

'Kleinhans Estate' was of course situated in Dargle, if you have forgotten.

"We are not going to the mine, or Dargle. At least not yet," he replied.

"What? Then where are you taking me?" I asked, puzzled.

"You will find out soon enough. I must admit that Beatrice desperately wishes to see you again, and I give you my word, you will get to see her once we are done" he answered.

"Your word! Humph. As if your word has value?"

Turning my attention towards the picturesque scenery, I had almost calmed, before an enormous splatter of bird's dropping made landfall on our windscreen and re-ignited my fury.

"Just Great!" I shouted out, hitting the dashboard with my right fist, "As if I didn't need a reminder of how this week is going to feel," was my response as I swayed my hands unconsciously.

Karl offered no reaction, appearing completely oblivious of my dramatic little outburst.

"Stop the car! Will you just stop the car this minute!"

My father pulled over. "Look here Leiyah. I didn't trick you. I was not the one there in London to make you get onto that plane. But from what I have heard, a man name Alex certainly was. If you really were such an independent woman, you would have been able to think for yourself and you really wouldn't be here now, would you. What you should really be asking yourself is, what does Alex want? So enough! Calm down and try and get some sleep. Why don't you climb into the back?"

Realizing I had already consumed too much energy in a battle I could never have won, I opened my door and climbed into the back. The drive to Johannesburg from the coastal city of Durban was one of the most scenic in South Africa, one I had, once upon a time, treasured and it was certainly a pity I could not enjoy it, but I was glad to rest my head. I certainly needed to. Natal was abundantly green with the most breath taking forests, hills and valleys and winding roadways that climbed and plummeted in a rhythmic motion. At some point in time I must have dozed off because when I next opened my eyes, it was to the grinding halt of the tyres being brought to a halt on a gravel path.

I sat up to find I was truly in hell.

"No, no, no! Why Father? How could you?"

The tears streamed down my cheeks. We were at The Knoll.

• • •

EIGHTEEN

My story had barely begun but my attention suddenly returned to the women in the room. One looked as startled as I did, whilst the other rushed towards her coat. In the midst of my agony, Billie Joel had decided to join us.

"*…and when she knows what she wants from her time…and when she wakes up and makes up her mind…she'll see I'm not so tough,*"

"Oh God! I'm so sorry Mother." said Zendaya, desperately trying to locate her phone.

I thought it a strange choice of song to be played as a ringtone by a woman so young. "*…Uptown girl…you know I can't afford to buy her pearls…but maybe someday when my ship comes in…she'll understand what kind of guy I've been…and then I'll win,*" Zendaya was so desperate to end the call that she knocked over the umbrella stand, tripping over Beatrice's gumboots as she tried to catch it.

"Shoo, at last," exclaimed Zendaya, cutting the call and bringing the song to an end.

"It was just the phone. Come sit now, dear," said Beatrice.

"I will, in a moment. I just have to call back. Is that alright? I will be right back," said Zendaya, rushing out the room before either Beatrice or I had had a chance to answer.

"Harry chose the song," said Beatrice, as the door shut with Zendaya stepping outside. "

"How typical. He could never buy her pearls," I replied.

"You sound as nasty as your mother. Have you forgotten the reason why you have decided to confess?"

"No I have not forgotten," I said firmly. "I was simply stating the obvious. Do you think that was Harry?"

"How would I know, sometimes you really do expect too much of me," answered Beatrice. "My guess is as good as yours."

"It surely must be Harry. Why else would she have run out like that? She looked excited."

"Well I truly hope it is Harry. But if it isn't, he will surely be calling her soon enough. He just needs a little time. But you should not have told her that you had always wished for your child to have blonde hair, Leiyah. Zendaya's hair is not blonde now, is it? Oooh, let's just pray she has forgotten such ideas passed through your mind."

Beatrice calling me, Leiyah, almost seemed to express disappointment. I immediately realized I needed to be more careful about how I planned on wording the rest of my story.

Zendaya returned, looking a great deal less tense and although I could not ask, I was convinced that it was indeed with Harry to whom she had spoken.

"How times have changed! I wonder who it was that had thought of such an idea. For a song to start playing, when someone calls, amazing isn't it. I am forever being asked why I didn't choose the 'Westlife' version but 'we' prefer the 'Billie Joel' version. Do you remember 'Westlife' Mother? They are the boys I had stuck at the back of my door, their poster, that is."

I nodded. Zendaya had not seemed to notice she had slipped up with the 'we'.

"You know, it was rather cruel of you to antagonise a poor child like that. You do realise that, Mother?"

"I was desperate to smile. It amused me. I was, after all, only twenty," I answered.

"Oh well, when you put it that way, anyway, what were you telling me? Oh yes Mother, he took you back to the Knoll. I might have killed myself, had my father done such a thing to me."

"It was indeed a thought that had crossed my mind," I answered.

"And you thought about Beatrice every single day."

"Yes, I did. I missed her. If ever I thought about South Africa, it was only because of Beatrice."

"You missed Beatrice but not your mother?" asked Zendaya

"Well my mother was dead." I answered, taken aback.

"What happened to flesh and blood forever?"

I couldn't find the words to answer her. Beatrice too, remained silent.

"I truly find it so hard to believe that you and Beatrice were that close," continued Zendaya. "Wow. I do not understand what went wrong between you, all the animosity and jealousy now days."

'You will know soon enough Zendaya,' I thought.

"But Mother, you said you wanted to tell me about my father and the kidnapping. Alex was white so he cannot possibly be my father and you have not said a word about the kidnapping."

"You are correct. Alex isn't your father."

"So, who is my father and how were you kidnapped?"

"Well allow me to continue with my story and take you back to The Knoll. All will be revealed.

• • •

"Start the car! Turn around! Take me home! Take me to B! This instant!" I shouted.

"Would that make 'The Estate' your home?" he asked, smiling.

"How dare you. You sick monster! This is not a joke. Are you so determined to torture me?"

In the midst of my tantrum, someone had opened the gate. My father started the engine again and my words having fallen on deaf ears, he drove into the Guest Farm.

"Stop the car!" I yelled, punching his left shoulder repetitively and as forcefully as I was able to from the back seat, until he grabbed a hold of my wrist, putting me at bay.

I couldn't believe how strong my father was, such an encounter between us, having never taken place before.

"Stop the car?" asked my father, sarcastically. "But you just asked me to start it. I'm only following your instructions, Leiyah, my love."

"I am not 'your' love. You can call Susannah and William that as much as you like, but I certainly am not 'your' love. Why did you bring me here?"

"Because we need closure, Leiyah, both of us do. When your mother died, we did not handle the devastation as we should have. Instead of being there for each other and voicing our feelings, we shut ourselves off, from each other, from the world. Please forgive me, Leiyah. I have failed as a father, I should have been there for you, to comfort you, to speak to you, but it's just that I could not get myself to say the words 'she is dead'," he answered, still driving towards the main house.

"And that is the only reason you have failed as a father, you think?" I replied, furiously "I know my mother took her life because of you. Susannah was always in the picture, wasn't she? Oh the mega rich boss and his skanky secretary! How could you have done that to her? How could you have done that to me?"

"Leiyah! Don't! Maybe I did marry too soon and I have already admitted that I have failed you but don't you ever make such an accusation. Spending your energy, blaming me for your mother's actions will not bring her back to us. Spend your energy on the present. The present is what matters and together we are going to bring closure to the tragedy that happened here."

"You are right," I answered. "It is about the present and right now, and at this present moment in time, I want to be anywhere but here. You tricked me. This had nothing to do with the inheritance."

"I didn't trick you. This is also about your inheritance and we will talk about that at the Estate. So I can speak to Willem and you both."

"Why do you need to speak to both of us? Oh you truly are a fearsome dragon. You intended to scorch me by forcing me to relive my mother's death and then tell me you are leaving your inheritance to William and stop calling him Willem when you are speaking to me. You know I despise that Afrikaner name. Call him William, it's the least you could do. Do you not yet understand? I don't want your money! Give it to William. I simply do not care. All I want is to get out of here. "

My father had now brought the vehicle to a stop. His head resting against his elbow, he looked deep in thought and I assume, he must have been pondering about whether to respond to my statements or not. At last, he did.

"I have bought off Henry's mine. He has chosen to start a new life with his family in Australia and I was the first to whom he offered it."

"And so what? I already read all about it. You are richer than ever. I don't care!" I screamed.

"Leiyah, you need to listen to me. There were many people who desperately wanted control of this mine, especially a man named Frederik Botha. I know it would have been ideal for his son, Frank, but when Henry offered it to me, I simply couldn't refuse. I have raised Willem, I mean William as my own, whether you like it or not and I bought Henry's mine with the intention of leaving it for William to run. But everything that carries the name Kleinhans belongs to you. I need the two of us to come to terms with your mother's death and when we return to The Estate, I want you and William to sign a new agreement. William will inherit Henry's mine and you will inherit everything else that carries the Kleinhans name, and Henry's mine is a drop in the ocean compared to everything else I already own. I will never deny you your inheritance, Leiyah. You are my daughter. But I cannot hand ownership of Henry's mine to William without you coming here and signing a new agreement. The document you signed the day you left entitled you to ownership of everything I own, if ever something happened to me." He stopped talking and laughed. "Poor Alex! Would he have forced you to come here if he had ever known you would return to England owning less? Now Leiyah, please don't be selfish and refuse to sign. Your brother deserves something too."

"My brother! My, brother? I have no brother. This is worse than I expected. You are setting up a future for him. Oh my God!"

"I am setting up a future for both my children."

"Two children? Are you finally admitting it? So you really are William's father. Oh, I knew it. My poor mother. Murderer!" I yelled.

"Leiyah! I have already told you to stop with the accusations. He is my stepson and I love you both equally and ensuring both of you have a prosperous future, is my responsibility," he said, as he opened his door and climbed out.

Tears immediately streamed down my cheeks. His declaration of an equal love for William and I truly was the last straw and on hearing that, I dived into the driver's seat and attempted to start the car. Unfortunately for me, my father had left his window open and I had a second taste of his firm grasp as he grabbed both my hands, snapping the key into his possession, before I could even fight back.

My gaze still fixed upon him, as he marched towards the main house, I was startled when he suddenly turned back towards me, marching at an even faster pace.

"I forgot to tell you. George and Cathy had to take Charlotte to the university, but George promised to send Tom to check up on us. I booked out the entire guest farm. I see the look on your face. Calm down. We are not entirely alone. The staff are here. You and I really need this alone time. I admit, having Charlotte here to talk to would have really done you a world of good, but you and I also need this time to bond. So when you see Tom, can you please just stop with all the tantrums and try to behave."

Without waiting for an answer, he walked away once more.

I was quite baffled as to how Charlotte's company could possibly have done me any good. We had not exchanged a word with each other since the day my mother's body had been recovered.

To this day, I cannot fathom what could have possessed my father into believing that our return to The Knoll, was the solution to repairing our relationship. Quite frankly, my father and I never possessed one in the first place. If I could only erase from my memory, the knowledge that his blood would forever be running through my veins.

'Oh mummy! Does he think he can torture me until I am so frail, I will just give in to his manipulations? Dear God, does he think that he can make

me feel so empty without you, that my insides will cave in like spineless jelly. I bet he thinks that he can sweep back into my life, a pillar of strength, like a hero returning from war. Well Think Again, Dad! I am never going to welcome you back into my life with open arms. Not now, not ever! Sneaky manipulative monster.'

"Who are you kidding, Leiyah!" I shouted, done with my silent sermon. I had to get away, and before my father returned.

Just as I was about to run out the gate, through which we had just entered, I suddenly made a dash in the opposite direction, the most bizarre idea coming to mind, when a horse, grazing on the embankment alongside the barn, came into view. Why did I need my father's keys when I could ride all the way to Dargle. I was, after all, an expert horse rider and if I could not escape South Africa, re-uniting with my beloved Beatrice would suffice, as more than an escape from my father.

As the leaves, having already said farewell to the trees, that had nurtured them in their youth, scuttled across the grass, almost as if racing to discover the unknown land, I too raced with them, towards the horses that pushed against their wooden fence. In total, I counted seven horses, two of which pushed even harder against the fence upon my arrival, appearing as desperate to get away as I was.

I felt guilty that I would have to leave one of them behind. I could not ride two horses, after all. But just when it seemed like I had found an ideal escape, the most ridiculous hindrance left me progressing no further. To my absolute bewilderment, I could not fathom where the gate to the fenced area was concealed. There had to surely be one. It was simply impossible to conceive that a way out, did not exist. How I wished, I had pursued show jumping.

In absolute fury, I began kicking the fence in the hope that it would break.

"Wow Girl, take it easy there," were the words called out by a distant male voice.

I turned and froze, the blurry younger version of my father becoming clearer with every step, as he approached. I felt terrified. I was surely hallucinating!

I turned back towards the horses, assuring myself that when I turned around, the image of my young father would surely have vanished.

My heartbeat escalated, I could feel it intensifying with each breath I took, but when I turned around, he was right behind me. A divinely attractive man, he most certainly was. He had spiky hair as jet black as my father's, tanned white skin, a diamond stud earring on his left ear and a tiny loop had been pierced into the end of his right eyebrow. He was muscular, very muscular and his right arm was tattooed right down, all the way to his wrist with the image of a snake. Dressed in his heavy black boots, blue jeans and a black vest he looked dangerous, very dangerous, yet oddly exciting.

This was not at all, how I would have imagined Tom to someday turn out.

"…please just stop with all the tantrums and try to behave," my father had said.

Maybe there had been more than one reason my father had asked me to behave and I knew exactly what I was going to do. **The complete opposite!** The man in front of me, was my escape from everything that was real, I immediately believed so. Alex was temporarily forgotten.

If only I had known then that the man who had left me awestruck was actually as dangerous as he appeared! If only I had known that in actual fact, he was not Tom Evans, son of George and Cathy, beloved brother to Charlotte. Perhaps, had I not taken the liberty of Christening him myself, the truth would not have been prolonged.

When I think back now, the signs were all there, staring me in the face. Fortunately it would not be too long before my folly would be realized. Unfortunately, it was still too late to protect me from the woman I would become.

My father would surely be making his way to find me soon enough. I had to encourage Tom to help me get away. I had to seduce him. That was surely the only way.

'*Time to behave,*' I thought as I leaned against the fence. Trying my best to ignore the presence of the horse that had begun to lick my hand, I struck a pose in my seductive boob tube dress. A dress, which I could at best describe, as one which covered a fraction more skin then a suit of lingerie.

"My, my….Talk about luck, sugar and spice. What have we here?" asked the man, in a voice that more than perfectly suited his appearance.

"Sorry, but I am not interested. I am afraid, it is going to take you a lot more than calling me sugar and spice before you win me over," I answered, hoping I could quickly earn more than a flirtatious compliment. Time was of the essence.

"Whoever said anything about calling you sugar or spice? I think you really need to get your head out of the clouds. This is Sugar," he said pointing to the white horse, "and this is Spice," he continued rubbing the neck of the brown horse.

"What!" I answered, gutted with embarrassment. "Oh you horrible man!" I instantaneously snapped. "Has every man suddenly turned vile? How dare you mock me? Just go and speak with my father. He must be waiting for you at the main house," I answered, wondering whether my plan to escape had just failed.

"How was I being horrible, if I was telling you the names of the horses? And whoever said you weren't a real cherry, because that you certainly are." He winked. "You seemed to be making quite a connection with 'Sugar' here before I disturbed you, absolute sugars, the both of you."

I grinned shyly. Slightly puzzled as to how he had acquired a hint of an Afrikaner accent.

"I'm so sorry I lost my temper," I said, quickly striking another pose hoping my sumptuous figure would aid him to forget my outburst.

"It's ok, there is no need to explain Leiyah Kleinhans."

"How did you know my name? Silly question! How obvious! You were after all expecting me, well probably my father, for all I know he probably didn't even mention me." I answered, still under the assumption that he was Tom. "You look so different from the last time we met."

"What, when did you see me?" he asked, looking horrified.

"Why are you looking at me like that? I was talking about when we were kids…and we played up on the hill. You were ten years old then, I think. It was my birthday and I lost my mother."

"Lost her where, on the hill?"

He looked puzzled and I could not fathom why he spoke such nonsense, but I did not wish to speak further about my mother's death and so I simply dismissed his response and got back to trying to allure him.

"I'm so sorry about earlier," I said, bending to pluck a wildflower. Although there was only one flower within sight, I took my time to do so as if I had a dozen to choose from.

"Not a problem. In fact, it was all rather entertaining," he said with a wink that made me smile. He took the flower from my hand and gently placed it behind my ear. The touch of his fingers against my ear made me shiver. I could not help but hold my breath until I could no longer feel his touch. "Don't' stress sugar. It's forgotten, all in the past. Come with me," he said.

"I really am not ready to go back to my father right now. Go see to him on your own if you must Tom."

"Why would I take you to your Father? It does not take a genius to figure out that you aren't quite seeing eye to eye right now. Forget about daddy, he won't have to know a thing," he said taking a firm grasp of my hand.

We had barely taken a few steps, before we reached the cleverly concealed gate. I didn't have to become a show jumper after all.

"Oh no, please. I'm wearing a dress." I could hardly imagine why I now said such a thing when, only minutes earlier, I had been desperately trying to kick down the fence and steal myself a horse.

"I won't be looking up your dress, not yet at least," he said smirking.

"And my heels, I cannot possibly ride in heels."

"Just kick them off," he said, and so I did.

He held out his palm, allowing me to rest my foot on it, whilst he effortlessly lifted me up and placing his other hand against the firm cheeks of my bottom, he aided me in swinging myself into the saddle. My head, still in a fog from his touch, everything began happening so fast. Still recovering from what I was certain was a purposeful squeeze, trying to control my fluttering heartbeat, I was amazed to find Tom already on his horse trotting beside me.

"Just follow my lead," he said as we began to trot faster. My balancing skills were a little shaky, but I soon felt as free as the wind.

"See what a natural rider you are. Race you to that tree."

I got there first but perhaps he had let me win. Upon reaching the tree, I saw that there was a back gate to the guest farm. Tom swung off his horse and sent it through the gate after opening it.

"Hold tight," he said.

The back exit, clearly seemed to be one that was not often used. The embankment was steep and the gravel path was clearly visible and before getting back onto his horse, he aided me down the embankment.

As I followed Tom across the valley, I could only think of his touch again and again. My father was forgotten. The sound of the birds, suddenly became soothing.

'Where are you taking me?" I asked. We had been riding for almost an hour now, entering into rural lands.

"You will see. I am glad to know, you trust a man whom you know so little about," he said, touching my face.

"You brought an end to my sorrow." I smiled shyly.

"Not everything you see, is as it appears to be," he said, smiling to himself as he stroked his horse.

"Relax, I was only teasing. So how about we gallop down to the river."

I nodded. He led the way and I followed.

"So which would you say was more painful? The piercing," I asked, pointing to my own eyebrow, "or the tattoo?" as our horses slowed to but a walk, the river now within view.

"Nothing could ever be painful for me, dear and if ever anything came close to being painful, you can rest assured, I will fix it soon enough," he answered, surprising me that his response was not more romantic.

"We have company." I said to him, disappointed that taking our intimacy any further now seemed unlikely.

Now at the banks of the river, which seemed neither too deep nor forceful, a campsite came into view, across from where our horses now stood.

Leading his horse into the river, mine following, we had almost crossed it, when Tom jumped into the water creating a huge splash. Releasing his horse's reins, he came to assist me off mine. I slid into his arms and, quite at a loss for words, he carried me onto the bank where the tent was pitched.

"Company yes, but only that of the horses," he answered.

"What!" I responded, in confusion.

"It is I, who has been camping here. Sometimes, even I need a getaway, you know," he said, with a naughty wink.

I could not prevent myself from smiling. "Well you truly chose a beautiful spot. It is so peaceful," I said, as he tied the horses.

As I watched him, I realized that my efforts to seduce him had been more than successful. But what if he intended to more than just kiss me? I had not even given my body away to Alex.

The sun was setting quickly. An owl made its presence known, not far away, the awakened crickets chirped melodiously to the sound of the water against the rocks. A bat flew low and I unconsciously grabbed his top. He tapped my chin playfully and I smiled. A blanket lay between the tent and the fire.

"It's getting dark, I said," nervously.

"Is daddy's little princess afraid of being alone with me in the dark?" he asked sarcastically, the words 'daddy's little princess' only provoking me to prove myself not to be timid.

"Of course not!" I answered, firmly. My father's request that I make an effort to 'behave' suddenly coming to mind.

'*Of Course*,' I thought. What better way to exact revenge. If Tom wished to devour my body, I would in no way object.

"That's good," he said with a smug look.

"I want to be alone with you. Alone in the dark," I grinned. Night had by now fallen.

"Well, I can tell you this much, it is going to be a night you will never forget, princess."

"I could feel the pulsation in my throat. I probably should have waited, but I didn't. I couldn't, I tilted my head towards his, allowing him to brush his lips against mine but it was a mere second before he pulled away.

The slowness of his actions produced the pleasure I desired and along with it a touch of fear. I knew that I was venturing into unchartered territory. Alex had never ventured below the belt, but I wanted Tom to. I did not care, what it was he expected of me.

"I am not here to hurt you," he said. "Tell me if you are not ok."

"Of course, Yes of course," I almost shouted out, desperate not to be torn from such a catch.

"Let's go into the tent."

I did not answer him. I merely followed where a bed had already been laid out, and a lantern burned brightly. Uncertain of what to expect, I lay down and waited. A frog croaked nearby and I bolted up stiffly.

"Relax," he whispered, reassuringly pressing my neck and shoulders. "You are safe!"

He blew out the light and the touch of his fingers running up my leg instantaneously brushed aside every hesitation I may have had.

It was the most incredible hour of my life, at least it felt like an hour, and when he finally removed his hands from my body, he lit the lantern and exited the tent for a smoke.

The air feeling a tad chill, I spotted his coat and wrapped it over me, my hand coming across a little notebook. I opened it to read that the name inscribed within was Frank, below it, Frederik Botha

"Who is Frank?" I asked as 'Tom' re-entered the tent.

"I am," he answered, before I could even meet his gaze, he had grabbed a hold of me from behind, pressing a damp cloth against my face

Nineteen

The next time that I was able to feel the African sun against my skin, it was no longer glorifying. I was no longer at the campsite. I was no longer at 'The Knoll'. No longer trapped by my father, but I was still undeniably trapped!

A storm had just passed, but the droplets of water falling off the leaves still felt like a steady drizzle to me, as I awakened to find myself lying drenched upon the mud.

The howling wind and creaking branches were all that could be heard, as I slowly drifted back to my senses. Even if the rain was still pelting against my fragile body, it would probably not have hurt me as much, compared to the pain I felt from the cold damp soil upon which I had been lying. For how long, I had no idea. I gritted my teeth as I scraped my almost numb legs against a rock. Wishing to apply pressure to my throbbing head, I tried to raise my hand towards it, only to have it violently yanked back. The cold metal hand cuff pinched my skin.

My heart beat escalating; my eyes flung open, panicked with the realization that my situation was not accidental. My eyes now open, I began gasping frantically to fill my lungs with oxygen, believing I had been completely devoid of it. My surroundings slowly became more visible as my eyes adjusted to the light.

Had it not been for the noise of the trees that towered above me, I might have misconstrued that I was in some sort of cave, but I was not. I seemed to be within the forestry that glorified the Midlands of Natal, and instead of wearing nothing but a coat, I was dressed, with a T-shirt, jeans and pumps. I desperately tried to recollect the events prior to my awakening on the wet soil, but I could not. As I tried to figure out why I no longer wore a coat, I suddenly remembered Tom's soft kisses all over my body.

"Tom! Tom, are you there? Where are you?" I called. I was still so weak and drugged that I could barely hear my own words, but I soon found out that my plea was loud enough not to go unheard.

"Awake at last. Who the heck is Tom?" I was about to answer the distant male voice when I realized that he did not speak to me.

"Beats me! Who cares anyway," replied the man who was really being questioned. "I told you to tie her mouth shut, Michael."

I could not see them, but from their accents it was clear that English was not their first language. They spoke with the same accent as my beloved B. The men were black.

"What have you done to Tom?" I yelled.

"That's a relief, Benny, I was beginning to think the concoction she was given might just have been too lethal. Sometimes with that Frank, you never can say."

On hearing Frank's name, I suddenly awakened enough to recall that the name of the man, whom I had allowed to deflower me at the campsite, was actually Frank and not Tom. But apart from remembering that he had left me to have a smoke, before answering my question, when my hand fell upon the little notebook, I could remember nothing further.

"Frank? What have you done to him?" I shouted.

"Benjamin, just listen to this chick, now she remembers Frank!" exclaimed Michael's almost teenage voice, bursting into laughter.

"Seems like her memory is a little all over the place if you ask me. What time did Bradley say the 'Big Boy' would get here?" asked Benjamin.

The fear suddenly gripped me once more, Michael, Benjamin, Bradley…how many men were there? Would Frank have been able to outsmart so many men?

Whilst Michael and Benjamin continued to make a mockery of me, I lay still, in the hope that I would learn what they had done to Frank, praying that he was still alive, that they had not hurt him. My own situation suddenly feeling completely trivial, I wondered whether the forest I was now trapped within, could be the very same forest beside the campsite that Frank had led me to.

I closed my eyes tightly before pushing my lids so widely apart that they hurt. Why I could not awaken myself from this nightmare, I could not understand. It was all surely a nightmare. It had to be. I had mastered the art of forcing a dream, I did not fancy to end, when I was as young as seven. If I could just do it again, I would wake up to see Frank beside me and the tent overhead. Becoming more desperate, I bit my lip! The pain was excruciating. It was not a dream.

The droplets of water no longer falling from the leaves, I felt a sudden desire to link the voices to their faces and so I pushed my body up. The palms of my hands were being pushed deeper into the wet soil than my body was being pushed up.

"Hey look, she is doing press ups," came the voice that I had now linked to being Michael's. Both men burst into laughter.

"Are you doing press ups?" It was the voice of Benjamin

The men, who were huddled under a cloth tied to sticks, were seated on a tree stump and seemed to have been playing cards, but they both now stared at me.

Michael's hair was twisted into triangular-like cones resembling pyramids and he was cleanly shaven, with a look of mischief permanently painted on his face. Benjamin's hair on the other hand was short and coarse and he had a long beard typical of Santa Clause, except of course, that it was black. Michael looked but a teenager, whilst Benjamin looked to be in his forties.

They suddenly began speaking in isiZulu, and I shivered more than I had from the cold. What did the black men wish to do to me that had made them suddenly switch over to their mother tongue. Scenes played out before me, my mind now on overdrive.

For the first time in my life, I wished I had paid closer attention to my Beatrice's language lessons rather than only being able to translate her lullabies. My mother had always classified them, the natives, sinners and Beatrice had always tried to prove to me that they were wrong. The Apartheid regime had just been abolished, but these men, they really were sinners. Was Apartheid justified after all? They had kidnapped me and who knew what they had done to Frank? Had my mother been right all this time?

"Frank…Frank…FRANK!" I called out his name once more.

Michael stood up and made his way towards me.

"I'm afraid you are not going to find him like that sweetie," came his response, now standing before me.

I fixed my gaze on his shoes, terrified to look up, but my doing so, failed to help. He ran his fingers down my cheeks and all the way down my neck. I shivered.

The other man burst into laughter.

"Tell me where Frank is right now? If you have hurt a hair on his body…"

"And I guess you are in the seat to order me around," answered Michael, cutting me off.

"Bring her inside and get her cleaned up, she will catch a cold. We need her alive!" called out a voice from a distance. He gave his instruction in isiZulu but I was able to pick out enough words to understand what he had said. He sounded like the devil himself.

"Yes Boss!" replied Michael, his tone of voice instantly becoming submissive.

Michael removed the cuffs that had me chained to the tree. I attempted to flee but instantly I realized it would be a futile task, as I did not have the strength to fight them for I could barely maintain my balance. In fact, I was relieved when Michael lifted me up, and carried me up the embankment in the direction of the man with an aggressive voice.

We walked through, well of course I was being carried, through what I would only describe to be a passage way, one such passageway, for there were many, since we were surrounded by rows and rows of mountainously tall trees.

It was indeed a forest or a plantation, trees as far as could be seen and although the clouds were now parting, the thickness of the leaves blocked out so much of the light, it still remained dull.

The men were now once more conversing in English. It seemed they were switching languages tactfully, their words being uttered in English, when they desired that I clearly understand their intentions.

"Oh Damn you Bradley, for seeing her naked body. I want my turn now," said Michael as he dropped me into the arms of Bradley. "Why did you dress her Brad? I want my turn."

"Touch her and I will break you," snapped Bradley.

Terrified of Michael, I clung tightly to Bradley who now held me. Strange, as he was my captor too. He was an extremely muscular man, with broad shoulders and braided hair. He could not have been older than thirty and despite my situation, I could not help but notice how good looking he was.

As we reached the top of the embankment, the trees parted and we came upon a large metal construction. It seemed to be some kind of storage facility or perhaps even an extremely old factory.

As Bradley carried me inside, I expected to see a large empty space, but instead, it began with a passageway with several rooms and a metal stair case that led to only a second floor, an area I could not see. Beyond the rooms, which seemed like offices, there were beds. There was even a room with a shower and a toilet. We surely could not be too deep within the forest, I thought. The moment I was strong enough, I would contrive a way to escape.

Bradley dropped me onto a mattress and whispered something to Michael before walking upstairs.

Alone with the man, who had just run his fingers down my cheek, I felt terrified. I almost expected the man before me to order me to take off my clothes and rape me before ripping my body apart like a bear. My mother had always said such things were expected of them, but it was not what Michael did. After being ordered by Bradley to leave me alone, he did exactly that.

"There is a towel over there and you will find some clothes in that packet," said Michael, pointing first to the towel and then to the packet, "I will be waiting outside. Shower quickly and I mean quickly. The bathroom is over there."

Picking up the towel and the packet, I took my time to lift myself off the mattress, but once I was standing, I followed his instructions. My clothes were already wet and covered in mud so I thought it best to stand under the shower in them, but standing under the spout I saw only one knob on the wall. I turned it to find that my expectation was correct, as it released only cold water.

Shivering even more than I had outside, I covered my body with the towel and opened the door.

"You have forgotten to show me how to get the hot water." I said to Michael.

Michael laughed hysterically and I immediately realized that there wasn't any.

"Gosh you really do deserve the name princess, don't you?"

'Princess', that word astounded me. He had been there. The men had been at the river. It was more than clear. They had been listening when Frank had called me a 'princess'.

Whilst I retreated to complete cleaning myself off, I pondered over how we had not discovered their presence at the river. My mind being a million miles away, I took my time, but it was not what I should have done, because in that time, I seemed to have somehow forgotten that I was being held hostage and the man whom they had addressed as boss, swung the door open, dragging me out with only a towel draped around me.

"Do you think I am going to be playing your stupid games? You are no one special here, do you hear me? " he yelled, before giving me a tight slap.

My cheek stung!

I raised my hand up to my face, my towel falling down.

"Yummy, yummy. Damn you Brad! I just have to touch that now." Michael began walking towards me and I quickly picked up my towel but before he had gotten close enough to attempt to yank off my towel again, Bradley intervened, pushing him against the steel sheeting I could call a wall.

"Get out! Dare you try to ever touch her body again and I will break your legs," yelled Bradley.

Michael rushed out, without responding.

Bradley marched towards me and I prepared myself for another blow but instead he did not strike me again, but pushed me roughly into one of the neighboring doors.

"Get dressed!" he yelled, locking it quickly thereafter.

Perhaps I might have obeyed him but I had forgotten the packet of clothing in the bathroom.

Terrified of what I may turn around to find, I stood staring at the darkness of the locked door, until the stinging of my cheek had ceased. When I was finally brave enough to turn around, I was still too afraid to move, for fear that I may find myself falling onto a floor of spindles and so with only the certainty that the area upon which I stood would not lead me to my death, I sat, eventually allowing myself to sleep with only the towel around me.

When I awoke, the light was on. The spindles I had imagined did not exist. I surveyed the room to discover it to be far bigger than I would have imagined. There was a bed, a table, shelves and even a toilet. Two doors led to it. At some point in time, the packet with the clothes had been placed within the room. Removing the clothing from the packet I dropped it in sheer horror. Was the top that it contained actually my own or was it a sheer coincidence? How close were we to the The Knoll? Did I pack that particular shirt for the trip? For the life of me, I could not remember. It felt like a lifetime ago, since I had packed my bag and I had not opened it since I had mustered the courage to finally drag it down Aunt Viola's staircase, back in England. Nonetheless, such a shirt, I definitely had once owned.

Was I right below my father's nose, exactly as my mother had once been? Was he simply sitting at the resort, leaving it all up to the officials as he had done with my mother? Surely he had learnt his lesson! Did one of the kidnappers have access to my cabin? A hundred more questions swirled through my mind, before I convinced myself that it was mere coincidence.

Time would tell if I was wrong. I dressed myself and lay on the bed, waiting. Wondering if I would be found, wondering if I would die.

Michael was the one to open the door. He entered silently. He did not say anything. Had I been asleep, I would not have known of his presence. I knew it must have been him, who had brought in the packet.

He handed me a meal. It was soup in a tin bowl, that looked like a bowl that had been used for the animals, but I was so hungry that I did not care. I did not so much as hesitate before putting my lips to it. Michael watched silently. He took the bowl back and was gone. The same meal was brought for supper.

The room did not have any windows but it did have vents. I could hear the voices of the men, but it was useless for they spoke only in isiZulu. It was as if they knew I would be able to hear them, that I was trying to listen in on them, make out whatever words I could, string them together, desperate to uncover what fate awaited me.

My mind swirled with assumptions of what Michael and Benjamin had been saying to each other in their African language. Did they intend to use my flesh to prepare their *muti*. It was often spoken of, that human flesh was at times used to prepare the most powerful forms of traditional African medicine known as *muti*, in South Africa. Beatrice had often spoken of it and to my knowledge, used it herself, although she assured me, that what she used, was only made of animal meat and no more. I began to wonder whether one of them was a *Sangoma*, which was what an African witch doctor was referred to. Perhaps the man who carried me? Why else would he protect my body?

Beatrice had once shared with me, her opinion of why such tribal medication was so much more effective than anything purchased in a pharmacy, leaving me absolutely mortified that she would succumb to such *voodoo* (black magic). I had always been of the belief that such Zulu witch doctors were female but who knew what my purpose was for being there? I could picture a haggard witch with long blond hair, holding a magic wand and a broom stick, dancing around a *potjie pot* on top of a fire, somewhere outside. At that very moment, I almost smiled in my moment of terror, since the witch I had invented, had skin that was white, a scene I had recently watched in a Halloween movie.

I had been locked within the abandoned building for three days before Benjamin finally dragged me outside. It was a blistering hot day and the rays of the sun pelted through the thickness of the leaves, making my surroundings ten times brighter than it had been on the day I had last been outside. The day I had awoken, still partially drugged on the wet ground. The ground looked almost carpeted with the dry spindles of pine. I ran it between my fingers as if I had fallen upon a treasure of gold coins. For some strange reason I thought of the story of 'Rumpelstiltskin', the classic tale by The Brothers Grimm. Was I only to be set free once I spun it all into gold? The idea of bribing them with Gold was clearly impossible. Ironic, some might say. Especially since my father owned the greatest amount of Gold in the country.

As we walked up the incline, I slipped.

"Oh thank you, thank you, thank you," I cried out to Benjamin as I grabbed a hold of his leg.

"Get off me, you damn snake," he cried, kicking me off.

I fell hard against the tree, astounded.

"It's been three days and I don't give a damn what 'Boss Man' says, Michael, but if the 'Big Boy' does not come and get her today, I will not be taking her body back into that building." His words were spoken purposefully in English. That was more than clear to me, a threat on my life, he intended for me to hear.

"If you kill her now, it would all have been for nothing, Benny. Brad will never let us down," said Michael.

"Us! I have been in this game eighteen years. I was only thirteen, the first time. Don't you even dare try to tell me what would be best." He continued to yell at Michael, switching to isiZulu.

Whilst they argued, their attention was temporarily diverted from me and I had managed to slip away a considerable distance before landing myself straight into the arms of Bradley, the so called 'Boss

Man'

Instinctively, I covered my face, awaiting my slap. But after seconds of not receiving any impact, I looked up to find Bradley looking at me, but now with a gun in hand. The moment had come. I saw my life flash before me. The faces of everyone I had loved. My mother stood at heaven's gate, Beatrice, Frank, even my father, William and Susannah were saying farewell. He grabbed a tight hold of me and pulled the trigger but the only thing it hit was the leaves above.

Although still terrified, I sighed in relief. If Bradley wanted to shoot me, surely he would have already done so.

"So, Oh mighty Benjamin, is it me or you who just lost us our hostage?"

Benjamin's hand had been on the gun, that rested on his belt but he moved it away slowly.

"You know what, I'm out! I will not be baby-sitter to any fairy princess a second longer. The 'Big Boy' is not coming. It was not a part of the plan. Riots at the mines will surely take more than a year to calm down. The plan was to kidnap her and that was it. Hand me my money. I'm leaving!"

"I have no money to hand you now."

"How much did you ask for? My father will pay you. I assure you." I answered. Thinking that it was my father, rather than Frank whom they called the 'Big Boy'. My father will come get me and stop calling him the 'Big Boy', he is a man and a very important one at that," I shouted out.

Benjamin laughed, "Whatever you say princess." Turning towards Bradley, he continued rather sarcastically, "I see she has got your plan all figured out there, 'Boss Man'. I would watch out, if I were you."

Before either Benjamin or Michael could respond, an extremely loud noise, sent Michael hurling in my direction. Baffled at first, I soon realized that the noise that continued to grow louder was the sound of choppers. Though the helicopter was not in sight, I began jumping up and down, desperately hoping that I would be seen.

"I'm here! Don't go! I'm right here!" I shouted

Michael grabbed me and covering my mouth, he tossed me over his shoulder, rushing towards the doors of the abandoned building.

"Put me down. Take your money and let me go!" I screamed as he let me onto my feet. As Michael dragged me further into the shelter, he tied a cloth over my mouth. Still I managed to sink my teeth into his palm, but only for me to receive a kick against my tummy.

From the noise that passed, it seemed that several helicopters were flying overhead. They had to have come in search of me. Why else would the men have taken cover? Whether I had a good sixth sense or not, I never quite knew why, but at that very moment, I could not be more convinced that I was still in Hilton. The Knoll resort, probably within sight, if I could only find a gap within the trees. No wonder Nelson Mandela had managed to dodge his captors in this very area for such a long time. There had been so many places to hide. On my ninth birthday, my father had stopped to show my mother and I, Mandela's capture sight, but as a little girl, it had earned barely a glance from me. The history of it, I cared nothing of. If only I had known the full story, perhaps I might use it to the contrary and be found.

As the noise passed, Bradley untied the cloth that had prevented me from screaming. As the tears streamed down my cheeks, heartbroken that I might have been found, Bradley approached me once more. I raised my arms in defense, but I opened my eyes to hear words I almost believed I imagined.

"I'm sorry I raised the gun to you. Don't be afraid. I'm not going to kill you."

Before I could digest what he had said, he disappeared, like a mirage.

A furious Michael, who was still yelling aloud from my bite, pushed me back into my room. I wondered whether Bradley had even been there or I had imagined it. He had sounded so kind.

Benjamin left that day and having parted in violence, I hoped that he would betray his comrades and tell of my whereabouts. Little did I know that the men would remain in communication, and it would not be the last time I would see him.

TWENTY

ow that I think back upon it, I completely understand Benjamin's abrupt departure. If it was not based entirely upon his confrontation with Bradley, he was surely beyond peeved that there was no communication from the so called 'Big Boy'. He must have anticipated the entire saga to be resolved in a matter of day, at most a week, as did I. But it was not to be. Although it was many months until I was next confronted by him, Benjamin surely had some means of keeping an eye on us, because when it finally did become beneficial to him, he knew exactly where to find us.

The same routine played out each day. I remained their prisoner, locked in the room by night, outside during the day, a long metal chain clipped around the ankle of one leg, my hands cuffed together, I was kept like a yard dog, given a bucket for a toilet.

It was not as if I did not try to escape. I tried several times until I had learnt, what became to me a very important lesson, '*Thou ought not to fight if thou will not win*'.

It was the first day since Benjamin had left, and now that it was just the two of them, I foolishly acted on the belief that I now had a chance to escape. The cuffs around my hands just unlocked, I instantly began clawing at the face of Michael, only to receive a punch as hard as a brick against the bottom of my jaw. The bunch of keys he had been holding, ripping a deep cut into the dry skin of my lips. The inside of my mouth bled from the impact of biting my own gum. I truly do not know what

I had been thinking. My foot had, after all, still been chained to the tree the whole time.

On my second attempt, Michael had yet to chain me, when I managed to fling a stone at him in an attempt to escape, only to feel the same stone being flung back at me so hard that I immediately fell flat onto the ground before having moved more than a meter away. I had been wearing a dress and when Michael reached me, he bent down and slowly began running his fingers up my still silky smooth legs. Frozen, keeping my body almost statue-like, I feared the worst from Michael's mischievous sniggers.

"Michael! What the hell are you doing?" screamed Bradley, his voice suddenly now right upon us.

"Lucky girl you! Don't you worry, I am going to have my turn," whispered Michael into my ear as he handed over the chain to Bradley.

Michael's intentions being more than clear, I realized that trying to escape from him was too great a risk. I wondered whether his behavior towards me would alter when the effects of my having waxed, were no longer evident.

Perhaps the 'Boss man' was my next bet, despite him looking physically more dangerous. I always wondered whether he had kindly apologized for pulling out his gun.

As the days passed, the cold water no longer seemed so cold each time I showered or maybe it was just that my thoughts were now elsewhere.

Although Michael was generally passive, I soon began to fear him more than I had feared Bradley. He looked at me as if I was bare and when he stood outside the shower, I could not take my eyes off the door, fearing he would enter and force himself upon me.

I felt more a slave than a hostage and in the time that I lay idle, I was drawn to study each of the men in more detail. Whilst I would have described Bradley's skin as being brown, Michael's skin tone was even lighter, only a few shades darker than my own tanned skin, to be precise. It seemed completely absurd to me that the South African whites could consider themselves so superior to others like Michael when they, especially the white woman, would spend hours wasting the daylight hours in the pursuit of resembling skin such as his. Michael was always cleanly shaven and I wondered where he kept his shaving blades. He would probably share them with me soon enough as he clearly could not take his eyes off my silky skin. Michael's skin still looked soft and boyish, only adding to his look of mischief. Bradley's hair, although braided did not hang long, and he always seemed to have a degree of stubble.

Whilst Michael could not seem to keep his mouth shut, humming and whistling, making a mockery of me at every opportunity he saw possible, Bradley on the other hand was silent, unless something resolved him to be otherwise.

The 'Big Boy' as they still chose to call him, had yet to come. I could not understand what was taking my father so long. Benjamin had expected him almost immediately, so they must have left him a map or some co–ordinates. Was the ransom they demanded, a sum he was not prepared to pay? My father and I had never really gelled, but surely my life was worth more than any sum of money. After all, if he had entirely no interest in me, why on earth would he have so much as bothered to contrive a reason for me to even return to South Africa. I tried to put together the pieces of the puzzle, but there was something about the kidnapping that was not quite adding up. I just could not seem to place my finger on it.

As I would lie under the trees, trying to figure out how it was that I had been kidnapped, I could only guess that it had been when Frank had gone for his smoke. He surely must have hidden, when the men approached, followed me and then gone in search of my father. It was the logical explanation for the delay.

I constantly tried to learn about Frank's whereabouts, but those questions would soon cease, not because I no longer cared but because I was petrified as to what had become of him. But after a week of pestering them as to what had become of him at every opportune moment, Bradley completely lost his temper, reminding me of my place, that I was his hostage and that my mouth should remain shut. Clearly unable to tolerate my questions any longer, he grabbed me by the neck and held me up against the tree, his grip around my neck so tight, I could not even scream for Michael's aid.

"You shut your damn mouth this instant because if you don't, I will strip you off your clothing and let Michael enjoy your body. Is that what you want," he yelled.

As he dropped me to the ground, leaving me gasping for breath, he banged his head against a tree and pulled at his braids.

"How did I get myself into this?" He cried. "See what you are making me do. I don't want to hurt you! Beautiful Leiyah, what is wrong with you? Dammit!"

He walked away, leaving me in shock. Although I was thoroughly confused as to whether the overwhelming shock was due to the fact that he had almost killed me, or to his having referred to me as 'Beautiful Leiyah'. It had never crossed my mind that he even knew my name.

I promised myself that I would do as they said. Each time I recalled the way Michael had run his fingers against my skin, I shivered, and Bradley's threat terrified me.

A little more than three months had now passed. The chain they used for my leg slowly became longer. I had not had an encounter with Bradley for a long time. But just as Michael was about to attach the handcuffs, he suddenly called out in isiZulu. He had spoken too fast and I was not able to make out what he said. As Bradley approached, I expected the worst but instead he merely took the handcuffs away. I was stunned.

They fed me well, the meals now varied. At times, tinned beans, even fish over the fire. The clothes that the men wore each day changed. I knew that civilization could not be very far off, but the helicopters I still searched the sky for, did not return. They had come so close to rescuing me. Why had they given up? I simply did not understand.

I was now able to venture far, at times away from their sight, able to study the birds, try to chase squirrels, search ladybugs, for anything that moved, actually, and collect sticks. At times, I almost had fun, forgetting where I was.

I was grateful for the freedom to wander in-between the trees, intertwine my chains and then try to retrace my path, not hurrying to untangle myself. I had something to do. I had a game to play, unlike the men. But on a night that Michael had arrived to see the entanglement I had created, he began yelling furiously in isiZulu. He pulled off his belt and began lashing me against my back. I had already received five strikes and I probably would have received more, had Bradley not run forth. Bradley pulled the belt from Michael's hand and while I expected him to strike me too, he struck Michael instead.

This was the last straw for Michael. It was now his turn to leave.

"And you are so good. Imagine what your mother would say?" Michael asked Bradley.

"My mother or your mother? Do we not share the same blood?" replied Bradley.

As the tears streamed down my cheeks from the pain of my lashings, I was astounded to realise that Michael and Bradley were in fact brothers.

"My mother never had time in her life to spend with me. She only sucks up to the white people. She dumped us on the farm. Have you forgotten the reason you agreed to do this," said Michael.

"I do not hate our mother for what she did. She did what she had to. What she does not know will not hurt her. I am a grown man and I may do as I please," answered Bradley.

"Aah, now I understand why you protect the pretty lass. I don't need to listen to you just because you are older than me, especially not if you are going to strike me because of her. I am leaving," he replied. "You will never get what you want, you know. She will never, ever be yours. You are a fool! She will never love you."

I was completely baffled. Was the 'she' me or their mother? Surely Michael spoke of their mother. How could Bradley possibly love me? I assured myself that the pain on my back was surely making me delusional.

As Bradley and Michael returned to the abandoned structure upon the hill, I heard a loud and startling noise. As it slowly approached, the dry pine leaves crackled under each step. I was once more overwhelmed with fear. Was it a lion, maybe an elephant? I feared the worst, before my logic reminded me that such animals did not roam freely, even if I was in Africa. I had lived in South Africa until I was eighteen and I was not oblivious to the knowledge that the wild were confined within reserves. But again I panicked, for I did not know for certain, where it was, that my captives had brought me.

I heard the sound once more and was about to insanely yell for the help of my captors, when the image of a man came into view.

"Dad…you have come for me!" I said, not loud enough to be heard.

My father had finally deciphered the map! I would be free! But, as the figure approached, I realized the man was not my father, but the younger version of him who had lifted me onto a horse. Instead of being disheartened as he approached, I only felt more joy. It was Frank.

"Frank, Oh Frank you are alive, thank God! I never doubted that you would be. I knew you would find me. I knew it would be you." I shouted out my delight, wanting to run into his arms but as he signaled me to be quiet, I hastened to remain still, suddenly remembering my situation.

"Poor little princess," he said as I grabbed a hold of him.

I had expected him to kiss me. To hold me tighter, but he didn't. Perhaps, I was too dirty.

"What did they do to you? How did you manage to get away? Oh dear God, Frank, thank goodness, you look unharmed. What took you so long? Can you open the lock? Quickly! before they come," I said, following him, until I could no longer walk towards him. "Why are you walking away from me? We do not have time Frank. Can you not see what they have done to me," I said pointing to my healing lip and the bruises on my arm.

"You should be happy you are alive," he responded coldly.

"What…" I was baffled.

Frank stood motionless, and as I stared at him, it struck me that he had a packet in his hands. "Has my father sent you with the ransom money, Frank? You have the money with you, don't you? How much was my ransom? How much did they want? Frank! Are you listening to me?" I asked, beginning to raise my voice, "Are there police nearby?

How far are we from the road? Do you have some sort of device on you? What on earth is going on, Frank?"

He looked towards the dilapidated building behind me, and I turned to see we had an

audience.

"Run, Frank, run, save yourself," I screamed, but to my dismay, he stood.

"What is the matter, is the 'Big Boy' not listening to poor little princess?" asked Michael, bursting into a rapture of laughter. Across his shoulders, was a large bag.

"The 'Big Boy'," I said, looking towards Frank, stunned, "You…No it cannot be…it was you all this time! You are the 'Big Boy'?"

His answer was a smile of satisfaction.

"But why Frank?" I pleaded for an answer.

"She talks too much, doesn't she 'Big Boy'" said Michael.

"Why would you do this? Even if my father no longer loves me, you love me. I know that you do." I was completely bewildered.

"Love! How can you love someone after a few hours? Leiyah Kleinhans, you really deserve to be called a dumb blond," answered Frank.

"But you felt something for me…in the tent. Frank, I know you did."

"Yes, I sure did feel something. The taste of sweet revenge," he answered.

"Revenge? Why? What about me could possibly make you vengeful?" I asked, still utterly baffled.

Frank kicked at a loose stone, amused at my disillusionment.

"Cheer up princess, you should be saying, "thank you, Frank", he decided to keep you alive," said Michael.

"Stop calling me princess. Is my father not paying you a ransom." I asked, not expecting him to answer.

"He did."

"Then what am I still doing here. Let me go!" I screamed.

"Daddy's little princess better still behave. You are alive, aren't you?

So just live in the moment. I promise, I will keep you very entertained," answered Frank, slyly running his fingers down my arm and kissing my neck. I cringed!

"Well, I will see you in town, Frank. I'm on my way. We will talk in Johannesburg," said Michael. "At least, I got to see your naked body once," he said, before winking. Raising his hat to both Frank and Bradley, he set off.

"Where is Benjamin and why is Michael leaving?" asked Frank.

"I will explain when we are inside," answered Bradley.

"Frank, please tell me, why you did this? Why am I still here, if you got the money." I pleaded one last time.

"It isn't about the money. It is about control. And the only person who should be in control here, is me. Your father robbed me of what should have been mine, and dammit! I will not rest until it is, until he pays."

"I will speak to my father. Whatever it is you want, he will give it to you."

"Why would he give back what he took away? My father has been trying to buy off Henry's mine for more than ten years now. But your father could not care," said Frank kicking hard at a loose stone.

"Oh my God! Your father is Frederik Botha?" I answered aghast.

"Yes he is. Finally you comprehend, Kleinhans. I was beginning to think you never would. I had to bear the brunt of being his illusive illegitimate son, but at least I knew that he would someday hand it all to me. I was not going to remain his hidden son forever. When my mother was dead and his reputation was no longer at stake, he was going to buy that mine and I would be the millionaire, I deserved to be. But Henry sells to your father."

"My father isn't to blame for that, Frank."

"I don't care. The protests have already begun, but the great Karl Kleinhans isn't there, because he is desperately trying to find his daughter. So I will keep you as long as I have to, until his mine goes bankrupt and he is forced to sell it to me. Oh isn't victory sweet."

I could not believe what I was hearing. A funny feeling passed through my body and I suddenly began throwing up. It had become quite common in recent weeks, and I assumed that the fish, I was given to eat, didn't quite agree with me.

Bradley opened the packet of goods Frank had brought.

"Oh my God, Tampons!" his tone of voice sounded different. He sounded shocked.

"Yes, what's wrong? What have you been using?"

"How could you be so stupid, Frank? That explains it."

"Explains what, Brad?"

"You have made her pregnant."

I couldn't believe what I was hearing! Could it possibly be true? Was I having my kidnapper's baby?

"Oh dammit! Hell! But I thought about that. It cannot be! I took the precautions. Well, I certainly can't deal with her and a baby. Besides, her father will never know if she is dead or alive."

Frank raised a gun to me and from the expression on his face he was not playing, but to my absolute astonishment the gun was kicked out of his hand.

"Wait! Forget the baby if there is one. I will deal with that. Her father may ask for pictures."

"You are right," replied Frank. "Clever thinking! I brought some beer too. Let's go talk."

Even with no one to talk to, I was speechless. Did Bradley just save my life or was it really just a scheme? For some strange reason my heart told me that it was the former.

TWENTY ONE

Frank, my supposed savior, whose safety I had spent the last three months praying over, was actually the mastermind behind my kidnapping and not Bradley. I could hardly begin to comprehend it. Frank was the 'Big Boy' and after months of obsessing over him and believing he was the love of my life, he had almost pulled the trigger on me, and he surely would have, had Bradley not intervened.

In a way, I was surprised that Bradley kicking the gun out of Frank's hand, had not resulted in an altercation, but I guess Bradley's reasoning was sensible enough. After retrieving his gun, Frank spent the rest of the day in the abandoned structure with Bradley, leaving only at sunset, and when he left, he didn't even bother to check if I was still chained to the tree. I watched in dismay as he disappeared up the hill.

After Frank left, I waited earnestly for Bradley to come and fetch me. It felt like forever until he did. I was desperate to voice my pain to anyone, even if he were my captor.

"Am I really pregnant?" I asked, as he walked towards me.

"I don't know. I think you might be. You have been throwing up quite a lot. I have heard that women throw up a lot when they are pregnant."

"How could I not have noticed that I was not menstruating?"

"I guess there were crazier things going on," he answered.

Although my ankle was still chained to the tree, it almost felt like we were having a normal conversation.

He bent down and turned the key, making no comment about the chains being in a tangle. Before he had even attempted to wrap his fingers around my wrist, I was already marching up the hill ahead of him. I could have by now walked to my destination with my eyes closed, but I stopped to relieve myself in the bucket toilet that would have been easily accessible to me, had my chains not been all in a tangle.

When only hours ago, I would have rather remained constipated than even dared to make use of it, if I feared either of the men were near, instead, I uncaringly dropped my pants, exposing the entire lower half of my body to Bradley. He immediately turned away, seating himself a considerable distance away.

"Tell me when you are done," was all he said before lighting a cigarette.

I cried, as I relieved myself, it being some minutes before I was done. Bradley, I knew, could hear me, and I waited for him to summon me to silence, but he did not. I cried louder, wanting him to say something, I yearned Bradley's aggression for it would once more help me feel like the priceless hostage, whose life had a purpose, but he continued to sit silently pulling on his cigarette.

After cleaning myself with several jugs of water in a bucket within reach, I continued to my destination without alerting Bradley, again deliberately attempting to trigger his temper.

"Stop!" he shouted.

I smiled, his command making me feel alive once more.

"Turn around. Come here," he said.

I had almost reached him when I slipped on the dry pine leaves.

"Be careful now," he said as he caught me. "You now have a baby you need to think about." He put his hand momentarily against my tummy and smiled.

I was stunned. I couldn't understand the love in his voice. I was surely imagining it. Something about the way he smiled, reminded me of Beatrice. He put his hands against my back to guide me down the embankment but the instant I felt his touch, I screamed.

"What's the matter," he asked.

"The belt," I answered.

"It won't happen again. I promise. I know exactly what will help when we get to the water."

"What water?"

"You will see. Close your eyes."

I obeyed.

Bradley hooked his elbow firmly under mine and guided me to my unknown destination. We walked in silence but after the incident with Frank and the gun, my heart told me that I could now completely trust Bradley.

After what felt like half an hour of walking, perhaps it was less, after all, my eyes were closed and we walked slowly, I began to hear the water.

"Just a little bit further," he said.

"No problem," I answered, as if walking with my eyes closed under the command of my kidnapper was pleasurable. I guess in a way it was the happiest I had felt in months. From the way in which Bradley had spoken to Frank, he seemed to understand that although I could always be rescued, nothing could ever undo a pregnancy. I will probably never be able to explain why, but I knew that whatever it was that Bradley wished for me to see, it was intended to make me smile.

"Slow down," he said. I smiled. We were after all walking so slowly.

Bradley brought me to a stop and I could now hear the lapping of the water.

"Open your eyes," he said.

Opening them, I grabbed a hold of his arm to convince myself that I was not dreaming. I trembled in disbelief.

"Am I dreaming Bradley? Is it really…" I could not bring myself to complete the sentence but I didn't have to because Bradley did so for me.

"Kleinhans Estate. Yes it is."

I suppose I should have jumped into the water and immediately swam all the way across the lake to the bank on which the brightly lit house stood, to the bank where my mother's grave lay, but instead I just stood there in disbelief.

"You mean all this time, I have been so close to home. Oh my God! That explains my clothes. Oh my word! But how did you get into the house. Are there workers from the house who have been involved in kidnapping me?"

"The answer would be yes, but they have had no idea that they were being used for information. Believe me, they would never want to see you hurt. They are completely innocent."

"Thank goodness," I replied.

"Now about your back. Take off your top," I froze once more and under the moonlight my expression must have been readable because he instantly reassured me.

"I promise not to hurt you. I just want to put some wet reeds against your back and use my shirt to tie it in place. Is that ok?"

I nodded, feeling much more relaxed. Instead of feeling glad I wore a T-shirt and jeans, I strangely felt disappointed I was not wearing a dress. My skin still remained smooth. As predicted, Michael had supplied me with shaving blades before choosing to leave.

Still transfixed by the image of my house that had been within walking distance, the whole time, I was about to undress when I turned around to see Bradley already without his shirt.

"Oh my God…you look…how did…I mean…the shape of your… it's…I…" I couldn't find the words to express how in awe of his body I was.

He laughed, as I smiled back shyly. He did something ridiculous that made the muscles of his breasts move, first the left side, than the right and I laughed, forgetting that I had ever complained of any pain on my back or worse still, the pain of learning I would soon give birth.

As I admired his semi-clad body, I felt my heart beat escalate. Under the starry night sky, he looked like a photo of a model out of a magazine, except with slightly darker skin. His upper body looked simply superb. He even had a six pack. I never knew black men could have such abs. I was tempted to touch them or perhaps ask if I could, but before I could act, his words broke the spell that had entranced me.

"Let me find the right reeds. It's one of the few things my mother showed me."

"What happened to your mother? My mother died when I was nine. Did your mother die too?" I asked, taking off my T-shirt and dropping it onto the ground. My hands automatically crossed over my breasts. I had not been wearing a bra.

"No. She is alive but I hardly see her. Michael and I were brought up by my grandparents, by the elders of our village. If you had to ask Michael that question he would probably say she died in his heart when he was still a child."

"Why?"

"She left us to start working for a white family and I guess Michael always felt abandoned. You can't blame him. She loved their child as her own."

"And what do you feel."

"Sometimes you don't have many choices. She did what she thought was best, I guess."

He said no more and I watched with the greatest admiration as he bent down and dragged the reeds through the water. When he stood up, I automatically turned around and as he gently dabbed my bruises, I felt the greatest pleasure, but more from his actions than the cooling sensation against my bruises.

"I need you to hold the reeds against your back for me, so that I can tie it in place," he said. I put my hand against the wet reeds, surprised when he adjusted the placement of my hand. "That's better."

I nodded, deliberately dropping my other hand, the hand that had still been covering my breast.

He tied his shirt effortlessly. But I was disappointed he did not study my upper body further. In fact he did not even glance at it.

He sat down and I followed suit and for several minutes we just sat in silence. Although Kleinhans Estate stood right in front of me, I was now more interested in the man who sat beside me.

"Don't you want to put your top back on?" he asked.

"It won't fit over me. With your shirt tied like this."

"Maybe I should put it on then," he said, with a silly smile.

"No, no, I like it, without," my words stunned me. He smiled and looked back across the water, but I couldn't take my eyes off him.

"What's your real name?" I suddenly asked.

"What?" he asked, looking towards me puzzled. As our gaze locked for the first time since he had led me down the embankment, a desire to kiss him suddenly overwhelmed me, and I might have, had he not spoken again. "Why would you ask that?"

"Well you see I have a maid. Beatrice is her name. But that was not her real name. She had an isiZulu one too. It was just easier for my grandparents to pronounce, I guess. Can you imagine I made it even shorter for her? I call her B, pronounced like the insect Bee, I guess, but well, I always wrote just the first letter of her name in all our secret letters."

"Secret letters? Is that part of the job of a maid," he asked.

"Well she was more of a Nanny to me than a maid. Actually she was more of a friend to me then a Nanny."

"I see," he said his gaze meeting mine once more, this time however, his expression was solemn and he quickly turned away.

I honestly don't know what came over me, but I attempted to make him smile with Mrs Swart's racial opinion of why blacks were given two names.

"You know I once went to a party where my father's friend's wife, her name was Mrs Swart, said that blacks always gave their babies two names, so that they could try to be more like the whites, but their choice of names, such as, Gift, Precious and Lucky, well it always made her laugh. She said that when women named their daughters Beauty, she always thought they turned out ugly!" I laughed awkwardly.

"My name is not Lucky and I certainly have not been lucky. What are you trying to say?'

"I don't know really. I just wanted to make you smile. I'm sorry."

He laughed. "Doesn't Swart mean black in Afrikaans? Isn't that funny?"

"You understand Afrikaans?"

"Of course! Silly, beautiful Leiyah," he smiled. "I speak three languages when you only speak two."

"How do you know so much about me?"

"You would be surprised," he said, throwing a stone skillfully against the surface of the water, it skipping several times until it finally sank.

"I speak a little isiZulu you know," I said in defense.

"Oh yeah? Alright then, tell me you love me in isiZulu," he said, smiling shyly.

"What?"

"Tell me you love me in isiZulu Leiyah Kleinhans," he repeated, running his fingers through my hair, he smiled.

Beatrice had said 'I love you' to me in isiZulu a million times over, but mesmerized by his gaze, the words simply would not come to mind.

Instead of saying anything, I leaned towards him and ran my fingers over his braided hair. Perhaps the whole Stockholm Syndrome really did exist. I could hardly understand how, but I knew without a shadow of a doubt that I was falling in love with him, if I was not already in love with him.

"Leiyah Kleinhans," he said, leaning closer towards me. "I love you."

Before I knew how, his lips met mine in the longest, most passionate kiss a teenage girl could possibly fantasize about. Well I wasn't quite a teenager, but it felt like my very first kiss, not Alex's kiss, not Frank's kiss but a real kiss. It was true loves kiss.

But when our lips finally parted and he gazed towards me, the response he received was certainly one that caught him off guard.

"Then why did you kidnap me?" I asked.

How I wish it was a question I had not asked, because it brought us both to reality and all the intimacy and romance catapulted to an abrupt halt.

"Because I was angry, I guess," he answered, turning away. "Michael wanted his revenge and I was just being an older brother and I wanted to protect you too."

"Revenge for what? And how can you protect me, if you kidnapped me?"

"I simply couldn't allow Michael or Benjamin to sleep with you. It is very complicated, Leiyah."

He stood up, pulling me to my feet with him.

"It's time to go."

I started walking towards the forest.

"NO, we are not going that way. Follow me."

Bradley led the way along the edge of the water and I followed until I realized we were going closer towards the house.

"Where are you going? You are going to get caught," I said.

"I'm taking you home."

"What? No! You can't! What about Frank? He will kill you. If you let me go, you will never be safe. I cannot just walk away and leave you in danger."

Bradley tuned around and kissed my cheek.

"You really are sweet, you know that. But you are forgetting that I am 'Boss Man'. I will be able to take care of myself. I will just tell him that you managed to escape. I promise not to tell him that I let you go, if you don't." He smiled. "Now go hun! Before I have to kiss you again." He squeezed my hand. "And here is your T-shirt if you want to change when you are closer to the house."

"Keep it, and promise never to forget me," I answered.

"Believe me when I say, I will never forget you. Now go!" he ordered.

"Thank you Brad, for everything," I said.

My bare chested kidnapper simply waved, before putting both hands into his pockets.

Reluctantly, I finally turned away and continued on my 'long walk to freedom'.

Just as I was approaching the curve close to the stable, I heard voices. One of the voices was that of my father's, the other was too soft to be heard. My father was holding tightly onto a woman as she sobbed into his arms. I instantly remembered that my father was a cheat. All the reasons I hated him, came flooding back to me. From the figure of the woman, I knew it was not Susannah. I couldn't believe it. My father had cheated on my mother with Susannah and now he was cheating on Susannah with God knows who. In my heart, that was proof enough that my father was a murderer. On top of that, I suddenly remembered everything Frank had said to me. Had it not been for my father, I never would have been kidnapped in the first place and instead of searching for me, he was here at the estate with another of his lovers in his arms. Did I really want to go back to the man I had been trying to escape from at 'The Knoll'.

As I watched in disgust, my hand brushed against my tummy and for the first time I felt the slight bump. Unable to save myself from the indignities of my father, I was determined not to allow the same fate to befall my child.

I turned around. Bradley was still standing there. I looked towards the scene with my father and then back towards Bradley. I knew exactly what I needed to do. I ran, but it was not into my father's arms that I ran.

Bradley picked me up and swirled me around before kissing me even more passionately than he had before.

"Are you sure, Leiyah?"

"Yes, I'm sure."

"Then we have to get out of here. We will leave in the morning. I won't let Frank find you, my darling. I promise."

"Thank you, Brad," I answered, kissing him on the cheek.

"You are free, you know. You can leave whenever you want to."

"I know."

I felt as if Bradley had just asked me to start a new life with him. As if he had proposed. I felt free of being a Kleinhans.

Crazy really, as only a few months earlier, he had struck me so violently. But he had shown me mercy. He was a different man. I saw the real Bradley. A man who never showed me aggression again, a man I loved.

The next morning, we left the abandoned factory. Fleeing in a van, stolen from my very own Estate, he took me to his village at the foothills of the Drakensberg Mountain range and there I stayed until I finally did make my 'Grand Entrance' back into the world I had become accustomed to at Kleinhans Estate.

• • • •

TWENTY TWO

“Oh Zendaya, I so wish I could go on talking about the years I had spent in hiding. After the night we had stood across from The Estate, I was no longer a hostage, but I would always believe myself to be a victim, because by choosing to live a life with Bradley, I fell victim to another heart-breaking fate that would not have taken place, had I returned that night to my father. If only I could give you a daily account of what came to be, tell you all about the majestic beauties that lay at the foothills of the Drakensberg, in the almost three years I lived there, oh what a world I did discover! The Apartheid regime had truly created different worlds within one country. That was for sure! But in the rural village, I found happiness, a feeling I had last felt, before my mother had died, happiness greater than any emotion that Alex had stirred within me. You know, I will never forget the image of what held me, when I first arrived in the village of Bradley’s birth. Who came to greet us first, but Michael himself, running around and playing soccer with a little boy on his shoulders, he looked no more dangerous than a young spirited man playing babysitter to the kids of the village. The villagers stared at me as though I were an alien. Ironically, an old man crinkled his nose at me, the way Mrs Swart might have done with one of her African workers. I was not welcome, but Bradley soon brought their loud banter to a halt. After months of pure bliss to my greatest shock, Bradley left me, as I assumed all penny-less men do. I had nothing and no one and so I returned to Kleinhans

Estate. I needed to bring closure to my loss. I needed my B even if it meant returning to my father. But enough about that, the person whose fate I wished to alter, was yours and not my own, and I believe you now know enough to understand why I did, what I did. Why I came up with my crazy 'Plan' and dragged Beatrice here with me. You will hate me, but I believed I was doing what was best, for everyone."

"Oh my God, Mother! You stayed away three whole years when you had a chance to go home and what is this 'Plan' you are going on about. Here I was, feeling all sorry for you. It was all your own choice."

"Goodness Zendaya, do you not hear yourself? Are you forgetting that I had already been made pregnant, that I had been chained for months and repeatedly abused?"

"No, I have not forgotten. You gave a very vivid account of it, some of which I would rather not have heard. I cannot deny that I truly feel for you, but goodness! Mother, you were right there, in front of your house. There it stood, across the water. Instead of dashing towards it, you just stood there, admiring its grandeur from afar. "

"Zendaya, I stood beside Bradley, frozen in shock, of the sight that I beheld."

"Then why did you not act upon it, once unfrozen? A woman with any sense, would have acted completely otherwise. I mean you had a chance to go back, but you didn't. You kiss a man once and you base your future on it. You proclaim to be in love."

"Well how long have you known Mark for?"

"That is not the point, Mother. You chose to stay with one of the very men who abused you. I simply cannot fathom your thinking."

"I felt something for him that night, and in the months to come. I simply cannot explain. I fell completely in love with him."

Beatrice who had been sitting very deep in thought, now suddenly intervened.

"You do realise, it was your father and I, you saw that night. I have already described to you how we so often met at the water's edge. We would pray for your safety and I would cry in worry."

"I realise that now, but how was I to know that then, B?" I answered.

"So when did you start thinking with your brain and not your heart and make Bradley take you back to The Estate. Wait, you said he left you. When? Why? And when did you return?"

"He left me within the first year. I spent almost another two years, living like a hunter and gatherer, when I realised I needed to cry. To tell someone what happened. I needed my B."

"You speak as if both of you were truly in love. He saved your life and then he just left you. I don't understand and you stayed in his village for two more years. Oh God!" Zendaya looked truly puzzled. To be honest, so did Beatrice.

"We did truly love each other. You know, Bradley just leaving without even a goodbye, is something I myself still struggle to understand. With everyday, our love just grew stronger. He took me to the caves in the mountains, showed me the painting of the San, taught me to milk a cow, oh the list would never end. We would sit by the fire each night and I would fall asleep watching him tend to it. But the day I gave birth, he wasn't there. He just disappeared!"

"The day I was born. Oh Mother, please tell me more, why all the suspense. I understand now that you never told me about my father because he was your kidnapper, but I thought the great revelation of my father would have something to do with you wanting me to marry Harry but you have hardly said anything about Frank. The revelation of your past in South Arica, has thus far, not made me change my mind about the wedding in any way. Surely you have something more mind-blowing to reveal."

"In fact, Zendaya I do. Just promise you will not bolt out the house until you have heard everything."

"Oh yippee! I knew it! I promise," responded Zendaya, looking like a child about to open a Christmas present.

How I wished I would not be the one to permanently erase her expression. But I knew the time had come for me to reveal the truth. 'Goodbye Child', I thought. Taking in a deep breath, I attempted to steady my heartbeat before finding the courage to speak once more.

"It began as a really beautiful day. In the rising sun, the dry grass looked golden, like the very precious metal, the trekkers had come to South Africa in search of. In the distance, summits that pierced through the clouds, boasted the blessings of the first bouts of snow. It was deemed an act of magic by the people of the village. I did not like the snow. I felt such an anger for this sight but it was not the cold it brought, but its colour that angered me. It just had to be white, didn't it? Why was everything white, almost magical. In my eyes, the black peaks against a bright blue sky, looked far more splendid without the hindrance of frozen ice. Bradley had gone to town and I was alone, but who should return, but Benjamin and Frank. Perhaps it was my shock upon seeing them, that I went into labour. Whilst giving birth in the *rondavel*, Frank ordered a sheet to be held in such a way that I could not see the lower half of my body. The baby was born. I was overjoyed to hear it's cry. One of the ladies told me that it was a girl. I asked to hold her, but before I knew what was going on, Frank ordered Benjamin to remove the child from the room and kill it. I desperately tried to get up and go after him, but Frank held me down. I never even got to lay my eyes on my precious little girl."

"They killed your baby? I had a sister? Oh my God! But that means my father was not one of your kidnappers. I am finding this extremely difficult to understand, Mother. Then who was my father? None of this is making any sense."

"The business losses my father incurred when he had sought to find me, were never forgotten. Although no longer the wealthiest man in the mining industry, he still remained in the top one hundred wealthiest in the country," I continued, avoiding her question. "I could never forgive him for that! You know, Zendaya, had that wretched man not been so wealthy, none of this would ever have happened. I had no choice but to leave South Africa, so I came up with the 'Plan' and though it took Beatrice a long time before she agreed, here we are. If I continued to live with my father, it might have all happened again. I was terrified my kidnappers would return for me. I was terrified the kidnappers would return and take you. My only child being taken away from me, was painful enough." I shook my head.

"Only child!" said Zendaya her face flabbergasted." Her normally unreadable face expressed that she was clearly struggling to put together the many pieces of the story she had just heard.

I looked towards Beatrice, but her eyes were focused upon Zendaya.

"Only child!" she repeated.

"The child that was born, when I was kidnapped, I never even got to touch her. All I ever heard was her cries, the priceless wails of my newborn infant. The cry of my child, I would never hear again."

Zendaya sat silent, looking aghast.

"When I returned to Kleinhans Estate, walking all the way, like a tired foot soldier, there you were, laughing uncontrollably as your granny tossed you up into the air. The moment I laid eyes on you, I knew you were the answer, the solution to losing my own! You were, after all, about the same age as my own would have been. I may never again have heard the crying of my own flesh and blood, but I had you and with you, I would start a new life."

"No, no, no," Zendaya shook her head in rage, with shock. In disbelief!

She looked towards Beatrice, pleading for some assurance that my words had been a lie.

"You separated me from my real family."

"Beatrice is your real family. I never separated you" I answered.

"My real father. You robbed me of my real father," cried out Zendaya.

"Your real father had tasked his mother with the duty of raising you. Just like Beatrice had to make the decision to separate herself from her sons, her real children, for their own benefit, I merely did the same. I did this to give you a better life, Zendaya. Do you not understand?"

Jumping to her feet, Zendaya marched straight over to the red roses she had bestowed upon me with such joy. Her face, now a complete contrast.

"You did not do this for me. Oh my God, you did this for yourself! What Beatrice did was a selfless sacrifice. You have made me live a lie, all for your own selfish benefit. All you ever wanted was to be able to say that you were a mother. I feel so sick!" she said, grabbing a hold of the flowers. "It is so strange, you know. One colour can mean so many things. Red communicating love, red representing blood." She plucked off one rose and silently pulled apart each petal. "Blood is thicker than water. Blood is thicker than water. Blood is thicker than water." Zendaya kept repeating the words as she paced across the room. "Perfect mother, indeed! How could I have been so gullible all these years?"

"I did adopt you, Zendaya," I replied, well aware that such a statement was meaningless, I knew not how else to reply.

"But that was not enough, Mother was it, because in your heart, I never was your child. 'MOTHER'. Oh God, I will never ever call you that name again. You will start appreciating a time I once did. But me… my skin was too dark. My hair was too black. Every time you looked at me, you wished I was another child, your own flesh and blood. You wanted a white child, with blond hair. You wanted a child like 'Peyton'."

"I tried Zendaya. I really did," I said, not denying my attraction to Peyton.

"The truth has finally been revealed," she answered, still slowly plucking and destroying each red rose.

"I would have lost my will to live, but there you were. I knew you were there for a reason. Upon seeing me, Beatrice screamed so much with delight that you began to cry and when I took you into my arms, I knew instantly, that we belonged together. God had given me a second chance to be a mother and I grabbed it. I could make you my own, but the plan was, I had to get away. Beatrice was against it but she understood, when I explained. I simply could not stay in South Africa because everyone knew the truth. That you were Beatrice's granddaughter and not my flesh and blood."

"Oh my God! Make me your own!" The tears streamed down her cheeks.

"You see, you can marry Harry, even if he is not your child's biological father. You were not my flesh and blood, but still I have been a mother to you. Our lives, yours, mine and Beatrice's, it is all the proof you need, that you don't need to go ahead with this wedding. That is the reason, I have told you the truth. I want to fix my mistakes. So I beg you, don't marry Mark! God gave me *you*, and I accepted you. Harry will accept your child too," I said.

"You accepted me! You accepted me! Oh God! It all makes sense. All my life I have been begging for your attention! All my life, I have just never been good enough!"

Beatrice just sat and listened. Clearly torn between her love for both of us."

"You have never loved me, mother. You have never loved me as a daughter and you will never be able to love me as your daughter. You know what, you wanted me to be exactly like your mother and you are, cold and heartless, just like Mary Anne."

"That's not true. I do love you."

"But not as your own flesh and blood. You never even tried!"

"Blood is thicker than water. Blood is thicker than water. Blood is thicker than water." Zendaya kept repeating the words as she paced across the room, still breaking apart the roses.

"Stop saying that, Zendaya," I pleaded.

"I never ever want to see you again! From this day onwards, you are nothing to me Mother!"

"I accept that, but what about the wedding?"

"If anything, your story has only confirmed one thing. I have to marry Mark. How could I expect Harry to accept a child who is not his flesh and blood? You couldn't."

With one last rose left, she tore it off its stem, throwing it onto the ground and crushing it with her foot.

"Beatrice, give me some time. I am not ready to talk to you either."

Gathering her things, she walked out silently and as I watched, I could always visualize Susannah gleefully cutting a string that tied us.

Beatrice just sat and for a long time, neither of us spoke. Finally, she got up to leave the room, but before she did, an idea suddenly sprung into my mind.

"Beatrice, wait."

"Yes," she answered, short and simple.

"Zendaya's father, if I were to buy him a ticket, would he be able to come to England? If Zendaya is still so adamant that she will marry Mark, as much as I know her heart says otherwise, then perhaps she could finally get to meet her father, her *real* 'Flesh and Blood'. He is the father, I robbed her of, and he could walk her down the aisle as a real father should."

"Yes, I am sure he would be all too happy to come."

She left the room, without saying anything further.

There are only certain moments in your life, when you experience the purest form of joy and happiness. You thereafter spend the rest of your life yearning for those very same feelings again. The feelings, when your heart sang with joy and your desires were met. The moments when the world seemed so perfect and everyone and everything seemed to be at peace. But then the happiness ends. You look at the world again and in the blink of an eye, the world is no longer as it should have been. I ask myself, was there ever any peace, now that I only see war? The laughter has turned to sorrow, the smiles have become tears.

I realize now that I had seen only what my heart wanted me to see. When my heart felt love, I saw a happy world. When my heart felt sorrow, I saw a world at war. But now it is time for me to forget what my heart feels and see the truth that I have, for so long, made myself blind to.

TWENTY THREE

The day of the wedding had finally arrived. The arrival of the package from South Africa had in every way possible, set in motion a phenomenal disaster, tearing apart lives, like the sinking of the Titanic. The Will, however, and who would claim its proclamation had not been spoken of since it was last disclosed to Zendaya, on the day she had admitted her pregnancy and run off into the rain that had battered the street and when I had run in vain after her.

There I sat, idle in the same room, as always. I had told my secrets, Beatrice had told hers and Zendaya's had in the process come to light. But instead of uniting us it had only pushed us further apart. We were just three vastly different women with very different tales.

"Oh, Leiyah, what genius!" shouted Beatrice, rushing into the room. "Zendaya and Ziphokuhle have bonded like a house on fire," said Beatrice, already dressed for the 'Big Day'. "You should see the happiness on Zendaya's face. I last saw such a look when, as a toddler, she boarded her first plane. The day my feet last stood on African soil! Buying my son a ticket to be here, has fixed all the problems"

"What! How can you think that way? It has not fixed anything. I relived my past, believing she would marry Harry. Instead my story only pushed her further into a loveless marriage and you can only gloat about her happiness. What will happen when her father is gone? Have you ever stopped to think about that? Will her face shine with happiness then?" I asked.

"She may grow to love Mark, perhaps, and to every mother, a child comes first and a lover second."

"Every mother, besides my mother and I, I suppose," uttering the truth, I truly felt ridden with guilt."

"Enough of that! You gave her a home and you tried. She will forget Harry in time."

"Did you ever forget my father? I think not, and I certainly never forgot Bradley."

"Yes, well, we still found the courage to live and Zendaya will find that same courage too. I know she will."

"I hope so," I answered in a condescending tone that Beatrice instantly frowned upon.

"Well, I hope you have changed your mind and you will now at least be attending the wedding."

"She does not want me there," I answered.

"You don't have to talk to her, but at least come and watch."

"Why? To try and keep up the lie to the rest of the world that I am her beloved *Mother*? In time they will all learn that Zendaya isn't really my daughter."

"You know, Leiyah, even if I had not fed you from my very own breasts or been in love with your father, you will always be my daughter to me. I didn't give birth to you. True, but that means nothing. I was robbed of the opportunity of getting to know my own children and I am the one who is wrong to be saying this, but I love you more than I love my own children. Just forget your mistakes and come. Keep your distance if you choose. Besides, you will finally get to meet my son."

"Hip Hip Hooray," I said, sarcastically.

"By the way, he has heard of your troubles and he has asked me to give you this letter. Oh where have I put it? I will be back."

A letter for me? I was still trying to fathom why on earth Beatrice's son would write me a letter, when she returned with the letter in her hand. I accepted it, but simply placed it upon my lap.

"He says the information it contains is urgent and you need to read it immediately."

"What could your son possibly write to me that is urgent? Did he say thank you, for stealing my daughter from me."

"Oh, stop this. Just read his letter and stuff your pride and stubbornness and just come to the wedding. In her heart, Zendaya will want you there. Oh I'm tired of that miserable look on your face. I am leaving. She will always be your daughter to me and you should feel the same." This time, it was Beatrice who stormed off, slamming the door shut behind her.

As I sat there, playing with the letter in my hand, I thought back to the first time I had laid eyes on Zendaya. An absolute angel, she was. Why had the 'Plan' not worked out as I had imagined.

For the strangest reason, I tried to picture Mark. It had been so long since I had seen him that I could barely remember what he looked like and so I decided to walk up to Zendaya's room in search of a photo of him.

It had been many years since I had entered Zendaya's bedroom. She had demanded her privacy when she was thirteen years old and I could hardly believe that I had not objected or found a reason to invite myself within. Zendaya was right. I had not even tried. As I stood in the centre and looked around me, I was astonished at how different the sight was from where I now stood as compared to the view from the door. I could hardly believe I was standing in my own house.

Searching the room for a photo of Mark, to my astonishment, I found none, but assuming it was elsewhere, I continued looking.

My eyes fell upon a chest of drawers with a panel that opened up into a mirror. It was the only item in the room, purchased when I had been present. The others, I had left up to Beatrice. I remembered her thrill at the secrecy and mystery. If only she had known then, how dangerous a secret it was, I wondered whether she might have still chosen it.

It stood closed and I tried to remember how to open it. Running my hands all along it, I finally found the well-hidden clip. As I slid the panels open, I felt like I was dreaming. Photographs of all sizes had been stuck to the edges of the mirror to create a dynamic frame. Every photograph spoke the magic of the most passionate love and joy. Every photograph was of Harry and Zendaya.

"What are you doing, Leiyah," I said aloud.

I had to stop the wedding. As I stared at all the photos of Harry, I knew that now, more than ever.

I ran out the room, almost falling as I bolted down the stairs, halting only long enough to grab my coat and throw my cell as well as the letter from Beatrice's son into my purse, but just as I flung myself out the door, I crashed, straight into Mr Goldstone.

"Oh my dear," he looked most dire, "I had to come and get you. I was on my way to the church, when I opened the card to be sure I was headed to the right one, when goodness! the groom, oh my dear, how can this be so, the groom is not Harry."

"I know Sir, I know…"

"My dear you have to do something. You have to stop the wedding."

"That is exactly what I am going to do, Sir. Oooh sorry, Flowers," I said addressing his dogs. I blew them a kiss, as I jumped over, having a very close shave, and almost crushing one of them, giving them the biggest smile, I had smiled in years. "Leave it to me, Sir, I called, as I ran down the street."

Grabbing my cell out of my purse, I dialled Beatrice, "Quick, dial Harry. Make sure he is at the wedding, whatever happens. I am on my way."

I began frantically signalling for a taxi, grateful to have one approach me almost instantly.

"Are you alright Madam?"

"Yes, I just need you to get me to this church as fast as possible," I answered, showing him the card.

"Hokey, Dokey," he replied.

I expected the journey to be a long one, but the church was one that stood pretty much in the centre of Town and it did not take us long to get there. I tossed the driver a far greater amount of money than the meter had read, in fact almost doubling his fee. But before the driver could even acknowledge the money, I had already rushed out the door.

The music had already started and everyone was standing. I wondered where Zendaya would be entering from, having not seen a procession outside.

"Oh God, Oh God!" I said aloud, the music drowning my words, I prayed, I was not too late.

As I desperately searched for Harry and Beatrice, I noticed a group of little children standing at the entrance of a corridor within the church. Just as I was about to make my way towards them, Beatrice popped up behind them. After scolding them to stand still, she rushed towards me.

"Where is Harry?" I demanded.

"Just come with me," she said, grabbing my elbow and leading me to the front of the church.

"What on earth are you doing, B? The plan is to stop the wedding. Is Harry coming?"

"I called him. We can only wait," she answered, pulling me into the row of seats reserved for the family.

"Beatrice, let go of me. I have to stop her."

"Object when the priest asks that question. Now, just at least watch her walk down the aisle with my son. Can you at least agree to that?" she said, scolding me like a disobedient child.

"Fine," I uttered, my tone still defiant.

The people around me began whispering and I turned to see the entourage approaching. The children were still up to mischief. Turning my attention away from them, I searched the hall for Harry once more. I was stunned that he had not showed. Surely he would?

"Doesn't Zendaya look simply stunning?" I turned, following Beatrice's gaze.

As I caught sight of the pregnant bride, ironically dressed in white, in the arms of her father, I suddenly felt as if I could not breathe, but it was not because of Zendaya. No, not Zendaya. Oh No! It was her father, who had left me flabbergasted. Oh dear God! Her father was…. was it really him?

"Bradley! Is this a dream? Beatrice, is Bradley your son?" frantically grabbing a hold of Beatrice, I pleaded for a response, an explanation.

But of course, Beatrice had no idea what had now led me to fall into my seat.

"I think you are too stressed, child. That's Ziphokuhle, my son. Bradley kidnapped you remember. Just stay seated."

The groom's aunt touched my shoulder, "Oh she looks exactly like you, Hannah dear."

She did look exactly like me, except with a darker skin tone. Her smile, her jaw, every facial feature, I saw myself in her for the first time. Could it really be possible? But how? My daughter had been murdered. Taken away from me.

Whilst still struggling to ascertain if I was hallucinating, the music had stopped. Zendaya had been handed over to Mark, but instead of standing beside the couple or taking a seat at the head of the hall, Bradley quietly crept out the side door.

"Where are you going?" called Beatrice, as I got up in pursuit of Bradley.

"To look for Harry," I answered. I had no time to explain.

I had to find Bradley or Ziphokuhle or whatever his name was. But after exiting the hall as fast as he had, I was astonished to find he was nowhere to be seen.

Sitting down on the staircase, I rested my head in my hands and as I did so, my elbow hit my purse. The letter? Of course! No wonder it was urgent.

The contents were thick, the letter was long. It read as follows....

To my dearest Love, Leiyah

I wish I could have told you all those many years ago, the truth. I wish I had expressed to you in words, how very much you meant to me. Said to you how much I loved you, how much I still do. But I know you could read my feelings each time you stared into my eyes, the very same way I could read yours.

In this life, that we live, we often don't realize how much we need something until we no longer have it within our grasp, until we have lost it. Although I lost you, I vowed to protect you and our darling daughter Zendaya. It means 'a gift'. She has been a gift, from God, a gift for you, a gift to us both. Ziphokhule + Leiyah = Zendaya. She was us. Even if we could not be together.

After reading only the first few lines of his letter, I burst into tears. I really had robbed myself of a life that could have been wonderful. I had blinded myself to all the opportunities I had been allowed. All the happiness that had surrounded me, I had pushed away. Just like Ziphokuhle, who now yearned for what he had already lost, so too, did I.

"I won't be blinded, not again…By blood or not. Zendaya, you will always be my daughter. Please forgive me." Words spoken out aloud from the bottom of my heart, I wished that through some insane channel of communication, Zendaya would hear me.

My sobbing subsided, but tears still streaming down my cheeks, I continued to read the letter.

Please forgive me, but I never meant to take advantage of your innocent body that first day you became a part of my life. I had been so intoxicated. I know that, that is no excuse. But until I had laid eyes on the baby, I myself remained uncertain as to whether the encounter had been a reality or whether my imagination was merely playing tricks on me.

When Frank ordered Benjamin to kill the baby, before you had even seen her, your pain was my pain. God had made me return to the village in time and I followed Benjamin. My love for you was so great, I was determined not to let anyone harm your child.

At that stage, I had not even laid eyes upon the baby, but just before Benjamin could throw the child off the cliff, I managed to grab the child. He tried to get the child back, but I was prepared to die before he did

Our struggle ended with Benjamin rolling off the cliff. I unwrapped the baby and my lustful illusions became a reality. The child was mine. The child was our daughter. I sent the baby to my Mother, happy to know she would always be near you.

I could not be a part of your lives, not while Frank was alive. But I kept a close watch over you, visiting discreetly. Thank you, for bringing our daughter into my life.

I once said to Frank "I never wish to be a Father!" I wish I could take those words back. I may be Zendaya's biological father but I was not there for her, as a father should be. I am grateful to God that you were there to be a Mother to her, as a Mother should be, my dearest LOVE "LEIYAH".

Yours forever
Ziphokuhle

Each time I read the words, Love Leiyah, I cried, more ridden with guilt. Zendaya was my daughter. She always had been. I had just been too blind to notice.

"Leiyah...I'm here," whispered Bradley from behind.

I turned and stared, as if a ghost stood before me.

"Bradley, you are Ziphokuhle ...you are...I cannot believe it..."

"Believe it," he smiled.

I wrapped my arms tightly around his waist as he wiped away my tears, afraid he might disappear, afraid he was only a figment of my imagination, inadvertently, dropping the letter in the process.

"Please forgive me!" He spoke sincerely, feelings of guilt, clearly evident in his tone, as he ran his fingers through my hair.

"Forgive me!" I replied.

'*Forgive me, my darling daughter*', I thought, a vision of Zendaya, so angelic in her bridal gown came to mind.

Releasing me slowly, he looked into my eyes and smiled, kissing me slowly. He stopped quickly, seeking my approval and I kissed him back.

"Walk with me?" I nodded, but just as we were about to reach the road, I remembered my purpose in rushing to the church. I was supposed to stop the wedding!

"Wait! I need to talk to Zendaya."

"My Mother! My Father!" the words being uttered through deep gasps of breath, I turned around to see Zendaya, right behind us, with the letter, I had dropped, in her hand.

"You are my real mother! *Blood is thicker than water*! Really! What did you do? I am your blood and still you could not love me. Beatrice did not give birth to you, but she loved you as her own child. She loved you more than her own flesh and blood. Oh God! What am I doing here? Harry! Oh Harry, wait," she called turning towards the road.

There was Harry, standing at the bottom of the gate and on seeing him, Zendaya bolted into his arms.

"What's going on?" asked Bradley, looking around in confusion.

Mark could now be heard screaming from the church door, ordering Zendaya to stop. The rest of the crowd were sprinkling out. "Don't worry, Leiyah, I will fix it. I will fetch her, wait here."

"No! There is nothing to fix. You have already fixed everything," I said, having quickly stepped in his path.

"Leiyah I don't understand?" Bradley was flabbergasted.

"I will explain everything, just kiss me. Just know that your daughter will finally be happy and so will I," I wrapped my arms around his neck and before he had an opportunity to respond our lips had locked.

"If you say so," he answered, after kissing me, as I had ordered.

When I turned around, Harry had just mounted one of the horses that had been eating a bundle of hay beside the wedding carriage, pulling Zendaya into the saddle behind him.

"Leiyah, Ziphokuhle? What is going on?" Beatrice, having just sprung up behind us, had clearly watched us kiss and she looked flabbergasted.

"B, I want you to meet Bradley?"

"What? No!

"It's not a lie, B, and guess what? Everything is finally as it should have been."

"My son is Ziphokuhle not Bradley Leiyah, enough with the lies!" cried Beatrice.

"Just as Hannah is Leiyah," I said, smiling from Beatrice to Bradley.

"I will explain in time Mother," said Bradley to a very confused Beatrice.

"You had better, son," she answered, shock written all over her face.

Bradley kissed his mother on the forehead and as he hugged me lovingly we watched the sight of Harry and Zendaya disappearing from view.

The extremely rowdy crowd having now exited the church seemed to be demanding answers from Mark. But the three of us couldn't care less. "Let's go home," I said.

"I have also wanted to visit your home in London," said Bradley.

"No, I mean our real home. South Africa!"

Beatrice looked completely stunned. Bradley overjoyed.

"Do you really mean it?" asked Beatrice, jumping up and down in ecstasy.

"I do mean it B. Maybe there was a reason my father gifted me with his Will. He has united us. Let's leave before Mark harasses us," quickly I said, spotting him approaching.

As we walked towards the townhouse I smiled. Bradley wasn't just my one true love, he was the son of my beloved B and the father of Zendaya, my child, my daughter, the daughter I thought I had lost. We were indeed three vastly different women, but our secret tales were intertwined.